UNDER HIS SPELL

As I stood outside the cottage, the clouds parted to reveal a full moon which silhouetted Castle Rhyweth standing on its promontory in the distance. A wreath of fog covered the fields surrounding the castle, blanketing even the thick woods in the valley that lay between the rise of ground where I stood and the rock upon which the castle guarded the fishing harbor.

Then a wolf howled on the moor above the cottage. The hairs on the back of my neck prickled at the sound. I fastened my eyes on Castle Rhyweth, feeling strangely drawn to it, remembering that last night when I had been in Lord Rhyweth's arms. The memory still warmed my blood and I felt an answering cry within my heart as if I too were as lonely as a wolf on the moor.

As if in a trance, I moved toward the castle. I walked far enough so that the fog began to swirl about my feet. I stood some moments there, looking over the strange country I had come to. And much later, when I finally went to bed and closed my eyes, I still saw the castle in my mind. It seemed as if I floated out of my body and went upon the moors where the wolf howled. And there, in my dreams, Lord Rhyweth waited for me.

THE SWIRLING MISTS OF CORNWALL

PATRICIA WERNER

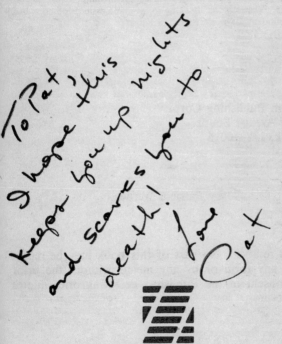

To Pat,
I hope this
keeps you up nights
and scares you to
death!
Love
Pat

ZEBRA BOOKS
KENSINGTON PUBLISHING CORP.

ZEBRA BOOKS

are published by

Kensington Publishing Corp.
475 Park Avenue South
New York, NY 10016

First printing: March, 1990

Printed in the United States of America

For Tina and Carolyn

Acknowledgments

Thanks to Mary Jo Putney for her clarification on the British peerage; and to John Ferguson, Professor of Organ and Church Music at St. Olaf College, for his technical advice.

Chapter 1

January 1887, New York City

A matronly woman in black approached me, dabbing her eyes with a handkerchief.

"I'm sorry about your father," she said. "My Delbert always said he was a good man to work for. A decent man."

"Thank you." I shook hands with the last mourner who had attended my father's memorial service. Her husband guided her out, and I was left standing alone. I noticed finally that the organ music had stopped.

After a moment there was a slight cough behind me and I turned and nodded to the tall slim man in a black coat who had appeared from somewhere in the chapel.

"If you'll just step this way, Miss Fowley," he said, gesturing for me to follow him, "I can show you to the withdrawing room."

It would be some time before the funeral director would present me with the urn containing my father's ashes, so I let him lead me to a small sitting room closed off from the front parlor by heavy green velvet drapes. I took a seat on a well-padded armchair and stared ahead of me. There was a Bible on the small round table to my left. A portrait of winged angels adorned the flocked wall opposite. No doubt the room had been furnished with articles intended to console the bereaved and to help one contemplate the afterlife.

The corner of my mouth came down in grim irony at the somewhat different view my father held about his own afterlife. For Leslie Fowley did not plan to go to either of the conventional places reserved for the dead.

I rose and went to the curtained window, pulling the lace aside to glance at the hurly-burly street below. Clerks and messengers wove around top-hatted businessmen, while private broughams squeezed between commercial wagons and drays carrying crates and kegs. Industry had marched north on the heels of the householder in Chelsea, so this part of New York was a tumble of factories, breweries, shops, residences, and more somber establishments like the one in which I found myself.

I dropped the curtains to wipe my eyes with the back of my glove. It seemed macabre to sit here and wait for my father's bones to turn to ashes. I pulled the thick velvet cord that hung in the corner.

The tall, somber funeral director who seemed to have no footsteps appeared immediately, and I told him I had decided not to wait.

"You can deliver the urn to our . . . , that is, my house, can you not?"

He bowed slowly and with much reserve, his expression appropriate. "Of course, Miss Fowley. This afternoon."

I took my leave of him. He helped me into my coat, and then held the front door for me. Upon stepping over the threshold, I nearly collided with a man in a gray top coat and bowler hat. He hastily excused himself; then hurried into the funeral parlor as I proceeded on my way.

The cold air helped revive me, though its dampness foretold of rain. I fell in with the noise and clamor about me, sidestepping a small boy chasing his barking dog along the sidewalk. It was only half a mile to West 18th Street. I would walk, which was much less trouble than looking for a hansom cab in this neighborhood.

I hurried my steps, the walk helping me order my thoughts, although I could now feel the first few drops of rain on my bare head, having removed my beaver bonnet, and shaking out my auburn curls before I reached the steps leading to our brownstone on a tree-lined residential street. The noise of Eighth Avenue was left behind here. There was only one vehicle on the block, and that had pulled up opposite our house. As I turned on our front steps, I glanced up the street behind me. The man in the gray top coat and bowler hat I had nearly run over had turned onto my street, and I wondered if he lived nearby.

But I gave it no more thought and climbed the steps. The door opened.

"Hello, Elsa," I said to the familiar plump figure in black crepe who greeted me. "Have you been waiting for me?"

The housekeeper stepped back to let me enter. "My dear Rhionna, you're home, thank the Lord. But it couldn't be all over so soon, I mean . . ." She waved her black-edged handkerchief then brought it up to red-rimmed eyes.

I stepped into the hall and removed my coat, placing it on the coat tree.

"Oh, Elsa, you mustn't cry any more." I laid a hand on her arm, wanting to comfort her, but she shooed me ahead of her into the parlor.

"Would you be wanting tea?" she asked, still sniffing

into her handkerchief.

"I could do with some tea. And bring yourself a cup as well."

The poor woman had been devoted to my father, but she had refused to accompany me to the crematorium.

"T'aint fittin'," she had told me. She didn't hold with my father's wish to be burned up. But I had pointed out that his will had been explicit on the matter.

"Burial's a waste of good land," I could still hear him say. "Burning's much neater."

And the unconventional beliefs he had taught me said that the spirit dwelled outside the body once one's days on earth were done. After getting one's bearings, the spirit picked up a new body and went on.

I tried to remind myself that he was right. Indeed, when I had last gazed at his limp figure in the hospital, it was only an empty shell. His spirit had certainly moved on.

I stepped to the window of our parlor and glanced out at the brownstone houses opposite. The carriage across the street pulled away and I followed it with my eyes. Glancing down the street, I saw that the gray-coated man with the bowler hat was nowhere to be seen.

Elsa's sniffles announced her return, and she set down the tea set with a rattle. Easing myself into a chair, I bent over to loosen my high-tops, for I did not intend to go out again today. Nor did I expect callers, my father's colleagues having paid their respects earlier.

"Here, let me pour," I said, afraid that Elsa's shaky limbs would cause a disaster on our carpet.

We settled back with our cups, and I waited until Elsa had gotten control over herself. I supposed my concern with Elsa kept my attention off my own problems. We sipped in silence, then I returned to unlacing my boots. I was just getting them off when I heard a whine. Rufus, my black Labrador retriever stood at the arched double doorway, cocking his head pensively.

"Oh, I'm sorry, Miss," Elsa said in confusion, seeing the dog. "He was scratching and scratching at the back door."

"It's all right," I said. "Come here, Rufus." He bounded over the carpet to me, stopping by my feet and placing his nose in my lap, his eyes turning upward endearingly.

I bent down so he could lick my cheek then I petted his head. Father had never allowed Rufus in the front of the house, the dog being consigned to his bed in the kitchen. A tightness tugged at the back of my throat and tears threatened as I scratched the dog's ears. I imagined I'd let Rufus have the run of the house now that Father was gone.

As if following my thoughts, Elsa sighed, setting her cup down and resettling her spectacles on her nose.

"What will you do now, my dear?" she asked, staring at the floor.

I lifted my chin, the way I did when I had made up my mind about something. For I had already dealt with the very question.

"I will go to Pendeen," I said, speaking of the village where my father had grown up in West Cornwall. "Aunt Winifred is there, you know."

"Cornwall!" Elsa's blue eyes widened, and her mouth dropped open as she stared at me. "You mustn't go there."

"Why not? I've never seen it, and I want to know my aunt before it's too late. She's my only living relative."

I stood up and paced to the mantel in my stocking feet, as if trying to persuade not only Elsa but the pictures in the oval frames that stood there. I gazed at my father and mother in sober poses that belied their youth and my grandmother, who I favored in hair color, height, and even the birthmark on the side of my throat. And there was one of my baby sister who had died. Grief tugged at my throat. I was the only Fowley left in America now.

"It's right that I should have some family, for I've none here. Only you and Rufus."

"But your father said . . ."

I turned around. "Yes? What did he say?"

She wrung her hands in her black crepe apron. "Well, I don't . . . I mean, it's just that I know he wanted you to stay here. There's his business to dispose of."

I pressed my lips together and shrugged. "His manager, Henry, can look after the business until I decide what to do with it."

I had the forbearance to refrain from reminding her that it was because of my father's import business that he was now gone.

But I went on. "I think some time with my aunt is just what I need in order to decide what to do for myself."

I wondered how Elsa knew my father, Leslie, didn't want me to return to Cornwall. I'd been alone with him in the hospital when he had reached for my hand in a last effort and pleaded with me.

"Stay in America, my girl," he begged. "Whatever you do, don't go to Pendeen," he said. "You must not go."

"Yes, Father," I had said.

Then he had died. But I had been born in America, and had never seen the land my father had been so reluctant to speak of these last years.

I would never have considered leaving my home if it hadn't been for the uneasy feeling I had about my

12

father's accident and a letter I had found in my father's desk when I was writing out the funeral announcement. It looked like one of Father's business letters, and I would not have bothered to read it except that I dropped one of the sheets. When I picked it up, the last paragraph caught my eye.

Beware Leslie, I feel you may be in danger. I am a very sick man and do not want to believe that which I suspect. I die before my time, burdened with the knowledge that I have been responsible for such evil. This is the punishment for my sin. In all I tried to do, I never meant for this to happen.

My father in danger? He had not told me. My skin prickled as I scanned the beginning of the letter. To my surprise, it was dated two years previous. It was from Cornwall, that was certain. But the last page was missing, so I could not tell who it was from.

I don't know how long I sat at the desk, rereading the letter, the mystery of its warning growing larger with every minute. I became more than convinced that my father's death was no accident, and I became obsessed with knowing the cause of it. If it was no accident, who was the perpetrator? And what was the danger spoken of in the letter?

Father had instructed me not to go to Cornwall and I had promised him I would not go. I sorely wanted to obey his wishes. But even as I sat so long in the study that day, I began to wonder if I could live with the knowledge that my father might have been deliberately put in harm's way.

I could hardly take the matter to the police. What evidence did I have to give them? An inconclusive letter with no signature. The longer I sat there, while shadows crawled across the room, the more I felt I had to satisfy myself on the matter.

I dragged my thoughts back to the present. Elsa continued to mumble something about no good possibly coming of my crossing the ocean. I said nothing, my thoughts still on the letter I had found in my father's study. The letter had started my thoughts in a certain direction.

Oh, perhaps it was my grief seeking an outlet, wanting to blame someone for what I considered a senseless death to a man of forty-eight. The more I thought about it, the more odd it seemed that my father had been standing directly under a crate that day when the cable broke.

Whether it was that thought or the letter or both, I did not know, but had many questions about my father's untimely death, and I believed the answers was across the sea, from whence the letter had come.

I sat with Elsa as long as I could before our low spirits became too oppressive. Then I took Rufus upstairs with me and considered what I would need to take to Cornwall with me. For I would leave as soon as was decent, maybe sooner. Father did not believe in long periods of mourning.

I told myself that Elsa's anxiety was misplaced. Hadn't my father known me well enough to realize that just because he had entreated me not to go to Cornwall, that that was exactly what I would do? For I could not live knowing that there was an opportunity to discover the mystery of his death and then not pursue it. I had cabled my Aunt Winifred, and she wanted me to come since now we were each other's only living relatives. It was the end of February, and my father had been gone two months.

Now here I was on a ship that had had difficulty

holding her course in a storm that had blown all day. As the rolling of the ship increased, I began to feel more and more claustrophobic in my small cabin, where I had been ordered to stay. The voyage had lasted six weeks, the weather worsening only in the last few days. Though I wasn't given to seasickness, the motion of the ship since midnight had brought my wretched stomach to my throat several times today. Now water crept under the cabin door, filling me with terror.

I threw open the door, for I didn't want to drown here. Feeling that only the air on deck would rid me of the horror I felt in the small quarters below, I sloshed through the water to the steps.

On deck I heard the cry from the front, "Breakers ahead." Then desperate commands to the helmsman. There was a wild scramble to reset the sails overhead.

Though it was not yet night, the sky was darker than it should have been at four o'clock in the afternoon. But it was the coastline ahead that struck me. Through the rain, I could see dark, jagged shapes that appeared to rise straight out of the water. The rock-bound coast stretched for miles, and from where I stood, I could see no bay or harbor where the schooner might put in. Rocks tumbled over rocks where there ought to be a beach. Yet there was a glimmer of light ahead, off to port, and I wondered if a lighthouse was directing us to some inlet as yet unseen.

Lightning flashed, and I glanced at the tangle of lines overhead, the crew climbing there like flies caught in a spider's web. It began to rain harder now. I turned, thinking to go below again, when suddenly a great wave slapped the side of the vessel, spraying me. My feet slipped out from under me and I landed on my bottom as the ship lurched with the wave.

Thunder cracked overhead, and it seemed as if the

ship were caught in the terrible grip of an unseen hand. I felt her struggle to regain deeper waters, and yet the tug of current pulled her relentlessly back.

The rain plastered strands of hair about my face. I slipped and slid, trying to regain my feet and get hold of something with which to pull myself along. Then I heard Rufus' familiar bark. Claws scrabbled across the wet deck, and a mass of wet fur and a pink tongue assaulted me.

"Rufus," I said. "How did you get up here?"

Nevertheless I was glad to see him. He was all over me, obviously joyous at having escaped his cage in the hold, where he had unhappily spent the voyage. I held him tightly, for the ship was pitching with such ferocity I feared that any moment another mighty wave might pull us over the side.

"We must get below," I shouted, as if Rufus could understand my words. There were no other passengers on deck, and the crew worked furiously fighting the vicious storm. I wondered at our predicament. Where was the harbor we were trying to make?

I got to my feet now, trying to pull myself toward the hatch that led below. It struck me that if this were my welcome to Cornwall, then perhaps my father's warning had been correct. If his spirit was watching me now, it even occurred to me that he might be expressing his displeasure in this storm. Had I put myself in peril against my father's wishes only to come to this watery end?

One of the masts cracked, and the ship foundered toward dangerous rocks that now threatened our starboard side. All was chaos as the helmsman was thrown from the ship's wheel, which spun of its own accord as if some ghost steered the ship directly toward the treacherous rocky coast. Again I was filled with the weird sensation that some unseen hand was dragging us to our doom.

"Father, where are you?" I cried involuntarily, whether from panic or in some sort of petition to his spirit.

I slid along, one hand on Rufus' collar. Wind and water clutched at the ship, and I felt the jolt that meant she was breaking up in the shallows. A sailor just ahead of me stared through the pelting rain at my pitiful figure. He shouted something and then shoved a life preserver into my hands. I had just got it around me when the deck tilted, and I slid toward a swirling wave that reached up like a giant hand to pluck me from the foundering ship and drew me toward the dark, cold water.

The icy shock stunned me, and I swallowed the ocean, certain of my own chilly death. I went under then clawed upward, gasping for air when I reached the surface. But Rufus paddled toward me, nudging me with his nose. Driven by instinct only, I clutched his collar and felt the movement as he began to pull me away from the wreck. I was half-frozen but I must have been able to kick my legs even though they were tangled in my skirts.

We paddled for what seemed hours, and I thought my strength would give out. I could go no further knowing that my weight could easily pull the dog down with me. My eyes closed of their own accord, and I felt myself weakening and then, thinking my lungs to be full of water, and my fate sealed, something solid came up to meet me.

Chapter 2

Someone dragged me up the beach, but I was only dimly aware of what was happening about me. Images appeared before my eyes, but how much was real and how much was caused by my desolate state, I could not tell. There was shouting, and it seemed our ship had become a tilting shape of tangled masts and lines, her bow stuck in the sand. Though my body was in shock, my mind began to register bits of what went on about me.

"Wreck! wreck!" seemed to come from above me in a chorus as figures ran past, down to the beach, whether to assist the crew and passengers who struggled for safety or to gather up the spoils, I did not know. For in this part of the world I knew a wreck was considered an act of God, and no one here would have any compunction about rushing to the disaster to see what nature had brought them.

There was no harbor, so we had not reached St. Ives. Where were we, then and what had lured us to these rocks?

I was soaked to the bone, unable to move my limbs. Rufus licked my face, and I became aware of a sharp pain at the base of my skull. I shut my eyes again, prepared to surrender to the darkness that threatened to seize me.

Suddenly I felt myself scooped up into strong arms. Opening my eyes, I peered into the rugged face of a man who carried me farther up the beach. He deposited me like one of the bolts of cloth that was being salvaged from the wreck. But he leaned me against a rise where I was more sheltered from the wind. A blanket was deposited over me, and then my rescuer went back toward shore to continue his work.

Sheltered somewhat and finally believing that I was not yet going to die, I could see better the scene before me. Men and women with lanterns, axes, crowbars, carts, wheelbarrows, and sacks ran past in waves, as if they had all assembled beforehand, waiting for the ship to crash. I was still dazed by the sea, shivering in my blanket, and felt as if I were floating away from my body. It was as if we had sailed to the rim of the world and the figures around me were phantoms from Hades.

There was more shouting, and two new figures came into my view, equally as macabre as my thoughts. A path seemed to clear before the tall man with a dark cloak draped about his shoulders as he strode into the midst of the chaos. A stunted figure followed him with a lantern. I wondered why the dwarfed figure bent over so until he turned in answer to the cloaked man's orders. Then I saw the hump that pushed up from his back, shortening his neck, his ears hugging his shoulders.

The hunchback scurried after the man in the dark cloak, who was now issuing orders in a comanding voice.

"You there," he said. "Take the survivors to the castle. And you," he pointed to someone else. "Pile what you can salvage over there. Jonas, take count of

19

what's brought up."

In moments the melee seemed to come somewhat under control. My mind alternated between dizziness and fascination as I watched the men and women scramble about. The survivors were now being led or carried up a path to my left, but steep cliffs blocked my view of where they might be going.

My rescuer came back to me and knelt by my side, and now I could see his squarish features and light-colored hair better.

"Can you walk?" he asked me, in a heavy Cornish accent. "If not, I'll have to carry you. Lord Rhyweth's orders. He wouldn't like me leaving you here."

My limbs ached, but I nodded, thinking it preferable to try to struggle up than be slung about by this man again, however helpful his intentions might be. But I didn't get the choice, for the man in the black cloak came up to us now and held a lantern in my face.

"Is this the girl?" he asked.

The man by my side nodded. "Found her in the water, sir."

"Well done, Elwynd. You may get back to helping the others. I'll take the lady myself."

Rufus paced at my feet and now began to bark. The man called Elwynd got up and made as if to lead Rufus away, but this lord I presumed to be Elwynd's master stayed his hand.

"Is that the girl's dog?" he asked.

"Seems like," muttered Elwynd.

There was a shout from the shore. "Lord Rhyweth, sir," called a young man with gangling arms and legs who came stumbling toward us. "The dinghy's gone out five times. Got all the passengers we could find."

"Very well, John." He looked out over the scene. "I would ask that you try to haul up as many casks and crates of goods belonging to the owners of this vessel as you can, but I can see that that is impossible." He shook his head and dropped his shoulders.

I could hear the bitter resignation in his voice and realized that this Lord Rhyweth meant to help salvage what he could of the wreck, but that he was powerless to stop the villagers from their scavenging. He dismissed the boy and turned his attention to me. I braced myself as he handed his lantern to the hunchback and knelt to lift me up, but he did not throw me over his shoulder like a sack. Instead, his eyes probed mine as he asked me how badly I was hurt.

"I don't know," I stammered, then I realized that his hands gently sought my limbs to see if anything was broken. I struggled with more words.

"I . . . I think . . . I can stand."

"Nonsense," he said. "And even if you could, you're in no shape for the climb ahead of you."

His arms were strong as they slid under me, and he swept me up, swinging me around so that I could see beyond and above the cliffs that had been sheltering me. I gasped at what I saw.

The path from the beach rose sharply to granite cliffs that towered upward. Where the path left off, steps had been cut in the rock leading upward in several switchbacks, so steep was the granite face. I followed the path easily with my eyes as the train of survivors, rescuers, and scavengers alike climbed upward.

But it was the battlemented towers that commanded the extreme height above that made me draw in my breath. Though it was still raining, I could see the outline of the castle that seemed to grow out of the rock which served as its foundation. The cliffs were indeed steep, the route tortuous from this view, and I had to agree with Lord Rhyweth that I was not quite

21

up to it on my own feet.

He hoisted me against his shoulder, and I saw Elwynd, wiping the rain off his face, watching us. I had not thanked him for pulling me out of the water.

We left the shelter of the rocks, the storm still raging. Rufus followed as we began the ascent, and I clung to the man carrying me, my hair tangling over my face in wet strands. My bruises made me cringe as we took each step, and I struggled to blink back the rain to see first the shipwreck on the rocks below us and then the silhouette of the castle rising above the granite cliffs.

Lord Rhyweth's breathing was labored, and several times he stopped to catch his breath, but he refused to put me down. Finally we reached the top, where the others had come before and crossed a stone arched bridge spanning a ditch. I clung tighter to Lord Rhyweth as I looked down. At the bottom of the cleft below, a spine of rock joined the rock peninsula on which the castle sat, to the granite wall we had climbed. The waves washed right up to this spine, sea water percolating from one side to the other of the bridge we crossed a dizzying distance above.

We passed through the arch of a gatehouse and crossed a cobbled courtyard lit by torches that blurred in the mist. Then we came to broad stone steps, about which people were scurrying. We climbed the steps then passed through an arched doorway into a large entry hall. I was more alert now, albeit cold and wet, and I wanted to get down.

"You'll be safe here," Lord Rhyweth said. His voice had a sense of command about it, and I could understand how he had managed to put at least some order into the chaos and panic that had reigned on the beach below.

"I think I can walk," I said, though I still shivered.

"Nonsense," he said again. "I'll see that you get to a warm bed. You'll need a doctor." He spoke over his shoulder. "Jonas, take the dog to the stables and feed him."

I strained to see to whom he was sending Rufus and my eyes widened when I saw the hunchback take Rufus by the collar and try to lead him away. Rufus gave a low growl, looking after me, and then I was doubly surprised to see the hunchback kneel and speak something to Rufus, whose growls turned to small whines, and then he meekly followed.

As I was carried up a curving stone staircase, the sight of filckering candles in their wall sconces gave me some comfort. But I was dizzy still, and when we reached the third landing, Lord Rhyweth carried me along to a heavy oak door that was partially open. There we entered a large, comfortable bedchamber where a fire had been lit in the stone fireplace at one end of the room.

"See to this young woman," he said to the chambermaid who was poking up the fire. Then he placed me on a loveseat at the side of the room.

For an instant I met his compelling gaze. Then he stood and turned away to issue orders to the maid.

"The doctor will look in on her as soon as he's finished with the more seriously wounded. See that she rests." And then he left.

The girl by the fire was emptying more coals from a bucket, and after wiping her hands on her white apron, she came to me.

"Half-drowned, you are, from the looks of you," she said, clicking her tongue. "Half the village must be down on the beach, though Madam Olga gave orders we was to stay here and miss all the excitement. She's the head housekeeper, so we have to do as she says."

The maid was a young girl with springy curls that

23

hung in haphazard ringlets beneath her starched cap. She had bright blue eyes and a turned-up nose. But it was her expression that put me at ease. She seemed alert and intelligent, and as her hands flew about me bringing what comfort she could to my condition, I added competence to my estimation of her qualities. I thought her age to be a few years younger than my own.

"Best get out of those things now," she continued. "I'll fetch you something dry to put on. Can you help yourself, miss?"

"Yes, thank you," I said, though as I moved to do so the pain in my head came back, and my fingers couldn't seem to move the first button I attempted through the buttonhole.

"Oh, and my name's Gwynneth. I'll just fetch those things."

"Thank you, Gwynneth."

While she was gone, I tried to undo the buttons of jacket and had some luck. By the time she came back, I had gotten the jacket undone, but the laces on my hightops were too much to attempt. I lay back with a moan.

"I seem rather helpless, Gwynneth." I said.

"Not surprisin', since you've just been dunked in the sea. What was it like? Did you have to swim or did a boat bring you to shore?"

She brought some towels and wrapped one around my head, massaging my scalp dry as she talked. I could see that the excitement of the wreck had aroused her curiosity, and that she was infected with some of the same anticipation and horror that had impelled the villagers down to the plunder. I tried to answer her questions, though my mind was still not entirely clear, and my lips were swollen, hindering me from ready speech.

24

"It was cold," I said, and started to shiver again, for now we had my traveling suit off me and were peeling away my petticoats, camisole, corset, and drawers. Then she handed me a fluffy towel with which to dry myself. She applied the shoe hook to my wet laces, and got me out of my boots and stockings.

"Hold your arms up now," she said.

My skin was chafed, and I was grateful for the soft negligee, she draped over me. Then she walked to the four-poster bed that stood in the center of the room and pulled down the covers. I crawled between linen sheets and she patted the covers around me. I hadn't fully answered her question about what I had just been through, but a more pressing concern now came to mind.

"My dog Rufus. Do you know where they've taken him?"

"You've a dog with you, now?"

I nodded. "If it weren't for him, I would have drowned. He pulled me ashore after we went overboard."

Suddenly I longed for that friendly face as my numbness began to be replaced by aches and pains and the uneasiness of strange surroundings.

"Well, I can see about your dog if you'd be wantin' to know. Best rest quiet now, until the doctor comes. Would you be wanting anything else in the meantime?"

"Could you bring Rufus to me? He's used to sleeping at the foot of my bed."

I didn't like the thought of Rufus being kept in a strange place, not knowing what had happened to me.

She frowned as she attempted to tuck some of her unruly curls under her white cap. "Madam Olga wouldn't like it. Animals upstairs, if you know what I mean."

25

"Oh my."

My lower lip started to tremble, and though I felt foolish to cry over such a thing, my ordeal finally overwhelmed me. Gwynneth's eyes rounded as she studied me, and I could tell she was forming the opinion that I must be a temperamental and spoiled miss to cry so for my dog. Nevertheless it seemed to produce the desired effect.

"I'll see what I can do," she said. "Mind you, I don't promise anything. But I can at least see if the dog's been cared for."

"He . . . he went with the hunchback," I stammered, now shivering more in spite of the covers bunched up around my neck.

At the mention of the hunchback, Gwynneth's face paled slightly and her mouth drew into a straight line. "Yes, miss. You rest now, like I said."

She picked up the glass oil lamp from the bedside table and left me. I tried to close my eyes, but when I did so, images of the wreck, of people scurrying across the beach, of the cries of victims in the sea pervaded my mind. I might have dozed a bit, but I did not rest easily.

Some time later, the door opened again and a white-moustached, stocky man with a black bag came into the room. "Hmm," he said, marching across the room. "Well, let's have a look at you."

He bent over me and then pinched my cheek, pulling down the skin to examine my eyes.

Gwynneth had reappeared with the lamp, which she placed on the other side of the bed and helped the doctor fold back the covers so he could examine all my limbs and look for any broken skin. As he did so, I was reminded of Lord Rhyweth's hands making a similar hasty inspection as I lay on the beach before he picked me up.

"Nothing broken," said the doctor. Then he examined my head where a bump was already forming.

"Does it hurt?" he asked as he felt gently about. Though he only applied the slightest pressure, the pain ripped through me and I cried out when he touched the sore spots.

"Hmm," he said again. "Contusions to the skull. Bed rest and let mother nature do the healing," he said.

Then to the maid. "I'll send something to make her sleep. See that she doesn't get up. And keep her warm."

He placed his hand on my forehead, where I was beginning to sweat and then listened to my heart. "She's taken a chill, but she looks strong. She should be all right. I'll look in again on that head."

"Anything else, doctor?" asked Gwynneth as she saw him to the door.

"No, no, just make sure she doesn't move around."

"Oh, doctor," Gwynneth stepped with him outside the door, and I could hear only snatches of their conversation, but I thought I caught the words "wants her dog . . ."

I had closed my eyes, but opened them again when Gwynneth came back. She stood beside the bed with one hand on her hip. "He isn't so fond of the idea of your havin' your dog up here. Says it might disturb you."

But I was feeling a little stronger and more determined now, so I said in as strong a voice as I could, "He won't disturb me. In fact, I'll sleep better with him beside me here on the floor. It's what I'm used to."

I was perhaps sounding silly, but here I was in a strange place in a foreign country with no one to turn to, having most likely lost all the belongings I had brought over on the ship, and it seemed to me that having the comfort of my dog was the least these people could do for me.

I could see her blue eyes waver, then she shrugged. "Well, I'll see."

She left, and I thought I would have to be content with that. I had no more visitors for some time and though I tried to relax, I could not. And I had to lay carefully so as not to hurt my head further.

After a time, the door opened, and there was a rustle. Then a bedraggled, furry nose nuzzled the covers next to me. A smile lit my face.

"Rufus," I said, reaching over to pet him. "No, stay down."

He had begun to leap up at the sound of my voice, but he obeyed my command ordering him to stay off the bed. Even at home he had not been allowed on the bed except when I was certain that Elsa or Father would not find out. So he was well schooled in this.

"Oh, thank you, Gwynneth," I said. She approached the bed and set a tray on the table beside it.

"He'll have to keep quiet. And I'll have to take him down again in the morning. The master and mistress would have a fit, to say nothing of Madam Olga."

"Yes, all right. Just so he can spend the night."

All would be well. If Rufus could spend the night here, I would trust him to their care in the morning.

"And here, take this," she said, holding a mug. I took it from her, and she let go once she saw I could hold it steady.

"Is it from the doctor?"

I glanced up in time to see her eyes change color. "No. It's from the herb woman."

I had taken a sip and looked at her curiously. "The herb woman?"

"Hannelore Treleaven. She knows as much of doctoring as anyone. Knows what to give you to make you sleep or do away with the cramps or a toothache."

Already the draught seemed to have a soothing ef-

28

fect, and seeing that Gwynneth would not be satisfied until I'd drunk it all, I swallowed more of the warm liquid. I wasn't much used to medicines, but I drank it down then lay back. Rufus had curled up on the braided rug beside me.

Gwynneth extinguished the lamp beside my bed, and then only the firelight from the still flickering coals cast a warm glow over the room. At first I could hear the sounds of footsteps scurrying past my door. Most likely other survivors from the wreck were being taken care of, and more than once I heard the scrape of something being dragged along. Rufus lifted his head at each new sound, but then evidently satisfied that all was well, replaced his nose between his paws.

I began to dose, the images from the wreck now vying with other pictures in my mind. Voices came to me and events that were absurd in their combinations. I saw Elsa waving tearfully at me and then my father standing on a ship. Then, from very far away I heard what sounded like organ music and thought at first it was the funeral music being played at my father's memorial service.

I must have turned over, for I winced in pain and came partially awake. But the music continued, the notes rolling upward and downward, making me think of the tossing of the ship. Reedy sounds, then more muted ones. It faded away, then came back stronger.

I came awake. There was no music now, only wind rattling the diamond-paned glass at the casement windows. I felt chilled and pulled the covers tighter. Something about the strangeness of the castle hovered about me, and again I thought that if Father knew, he would not wish me to be here.

The coals were almost gone, and Rufus, sensing that I was awake, came and placed his nose on the edge of my bed.

"It's all right, Rufus," I mumbled. "We should go back to sleep."

Then exhaustion claimed me, and I was as good as my word.

Chapter 3

It was as if I were in the sea again. I could not seem to wake up, and there were sounds, voices, images all around me. When I struggled to open my eyes, blurry faces hovered over me, and I heard snatches of conversation, but disjointed, overlapping other words and pictures. And my mind was unable to form answers or my lips to say them.

The doctor was there several times, always bending into my face, his white moustache muffling his words. Gwynneth's head appeared near his, and her mouth moved. I struggled to answer her, but the fuzziness overcame me and I slept again.

And at night strange music played far away. More faces peopled my world. The lord of the castle who had carried me came one time. I heard his voice distinctly, but I was unable to see him.

". . . how long has she been this way?"

Then another voice answering. ". . . was all right when I left . . ."

I opened my eyes once and saw him looking down at me, his penetrating eyes as dark as the night he brought me here. Yet there was something frightening in them.

Once a raven-haired woman came. Her beauty was

as refined as the lord's presence was commanding. She peered at me with icy blue eyes but did not speak. Instead, another voice in the background said, ". . . may be with us some time . . ."

The dreams continued, and I thought I heard someone call herself my Aunt Winifred, and I tried to speak to her. And then there was another older woman. Cool, bony hands clutched mine, and I knew this could not be my aunt, for hers were smooth and lovely as in the photograph I had seen of her from years past.

". . . evil things happening in these parts . . ."

". . . wreck's an omen of things to come . . ."

". . . land's cursed, if you ask me."

"She'll be carried off like the others . . ."

All were things I could make no sense of, and I was no longer sure who spoke the words or if I dreamed them. Since I could not wake up, I tried to sleep. I sought darkness, for it lulled the ache at the back of my neck. But even when there were no pictures there was the torturous music, some funeral dirge and then the sounds of fire and brimstone that made me long for peace as I tossed and turned, sweat breaking out over my skin.

One morning I awoke, aware that I was still in a strange place, but no longer tormented by the pictures, though my head still throbbed with a dull pain. But the room about me held fairly steady, and then I heard a whine and Rufus was halfway on the bed, licking my face.

"Rufus," I said, petting his now fluffy fur. "Am I awake?"

My mind seemed to clear and I petted and hugged my dog. I had to lay back gingerly, but as I moved my head from side to side, I could tell it was much better.

"Well, now, look at this."

Gwynneth had entered with a tray and mug, which

she set down. Rufus got to the floor and looked up with imploring eyes at Gwynneth as if asking forgiveness for trying to get onto the bed.

She gave him a pat, then stood with hands on hips, her mouth pulled back disapprovingly. But I could see the half-smile in her eyes, and when she leaned down to pet him, he licked her hand. I could see that Rufus had made a conquest and that his well-being here was assured.

"Well now," she said, turning her attention to me. "You had us worried. I'm glad to see you've come out of your fever."

"How long was I delirious?"

She cocked her head. "The last two days. Doctor's been to see you. Lord Rhyweth, too. Everyone's been concerned."

"I see."

So the faces I had seen in my dreams were real, or at least some of them were.

"Now that you're awake, I'll have cook make you some breakfast. You'll be needing some nourishment. In the meantime, best drink this."

I eyed the drink suspiciously. "From the herb woman?"

"Nay, from the doctor. He says you're to take it with your meals or just before."

I took the mug and sipped it, then held my hands around it, soaking up its warmth. "I'll drink it slowly then, while you bring the food."

She fussed about me, plumping up the pillows and smoothing the bed covers. Then she stood back to examine my appearance.

"I can brush your hair afterwards, if you like, and put it in a braid. You've got too much hair for a snood, to my way of thinking, it'd fall out against the pillows."

"A braid would be very nice. But I can brush my

33

hair myself if you bring me a brush and mirror."

"You drink that and eat first. We'll worry about your toilet later."

She grinned impishly at me as Rufus wagged his tail. "Never fear. You won't be having any visitors except for the doctor until I say so. Isn't that right, Rufus?"

And with a flounce she was off to fetch my breakfast.

"Well, Rufus. And how long have they let you stay here? It was my understanding that you were to be returned to the stables in the mornings."

He smiled his doggy smile and laid his nose against my arm.

"Ah, I see. It pays to make friends in high places."

Then he surprised me. There was a knock on the door, and he immediately went under the bed. Before I could answer, "come in," the door opened and a short slim woman with gray hair tucked under a cap entered. She wore a prim black bombazine dress and starched apron, and she held her shoulders straight and her head proudly. Dark eyes snapped at me from her determined, set expression. When she spoke, it was with a foreign accent that I could not place.

"Good morning, miss. I'm glad to hear you're better. Olga Stamenkovic, at your service. You may call me Olga."

She crossed briskly to the casement windows and cranked them open, letting in some fresh air. Then she returned to the bed.

"I've orders to make sure you have what you need. You'll want to eat a good breakfast, for we haven't gotten anything down you since you came. You're a lucky girl to be alive."

I clutched my mug tightly as she bustled about me, tucking in corners and inspecting everything efficiently. But she failed to look under the bed.

"Thank you," I said "I do feel better, though my head still feels sore."

"You must be sure and keep warm. It's damp here. You wouldn't know that, I suppose."

"Well, I do know a little of Cornwall. I am in Cornwall, aren't I?"

"Of course you are. I don't suppose you've had any time to orient yourself. Your ship wrecked on the rocks below. This is Rhyweth Castle you're in. Lord Rhyweth brought you here."

Light dawned. "Rhyweth Castle? Then I know where I am. My father grew up in the village of Pendeen."

I thought her eyes narrowed a bit as she looked at me. "We thought as much. Though your ship was bound for St. Ives, some leagues distant."

I frowned in thought. "It seemed there was a lighthouse. Is there no harbor here then?"

She busied her hands with the covers but would not meet my gaze. "Aye, there's a fishing harbor, the village is right on the edge of it. But it wouldn't be deep enough for a ship that size. And you were around the point from the village."

She brushed her hands together, looking at me. "I'd best be getting on with my inspection of the rooms. The maids have been a bit careless of late."

I assured her that I understood and watched her go. I had been struggling with my expression and then burst into a grin as I set my mug aside. "It's all right, Rufus, she's gone," I said.

Hearing his name, he came out, thumping his tail on the rug. I was beginning to wonder what else had occurred while I had been delirious. Rufus had obviously learned when and from whom to hide. He was a very smart dog, but Gwynneth must have had a way

35

with animals to have trained him so quickly.

I knew she would return momentarily, and there was a task I had to perform first. Though I was a little unsteady on my feet, I threw back the carefully smoothed covers and put my feet on the rug. Then I picked up the mug Gwynneth had brought and tottered over to the windows in the large stone bay. The light blinded me when I looked out, for I had been so many days in darkness, but I could see enough to tell that the cobbled courtyard was directly below, and no one was in sight.

I tossed out the liquid from the mug, and it splashed on the stone wall as it fell. Then I hastily returned to my bed and set the mug down. I might have been overreacting, but I had never had the need to take medicine. My father always recommended good food, rest, and fresh air over any strange concoctions to fix most things that ailed a body, so I was suspicious of herb mixtures and tonics alike. They just didn't agree with me.

I slid between the covers just in time, for Gwynneth returned and set a tray before me. She removed the lid from steaming platters, and at the sight of the food I could tell that there was nothing wrong with my stomach at least. I was starved.

I made quick work of the food, and asked Gwynneth to pour me a second cup of tea. Then we set about my toilet. I donned a quilted dressing gown, and Gwynneth took me along to show me where a modern bathroom had been installed, complete with claw-footed porcelain tub and water closet. However, it was quite drafty there, so while I was gone, she took Rufus out and got a tub of warm water delivered to my room and set it before the fire. I undressed, slipped into the soapy water and took my time washing and soaking.

While I sat in the hip bath, Gwynneth obliged me

with gossip and otherwise answered my many questions about the region I found myself in.

"I want to thank you for taking care of Rufus," I said. "I think you've made a friend."

She smiled and patted the top of Rufus' head. "I love animals. Haven't had any of my own since I've come here."

I wondered what had brought such a spritely girl as Gwynneth to this old, damp castle on the rim of the world and when I asked her, her cheeks colored, making her freckles stand out.

"Lord Rhyweth is very generous to his help, and I had my aunty to help support," she said. She poured more hot water to heat my bath then busied her hands massaging my scalp with soap.

"I was born in the North, but my parents died young, so I was raised in St. Ives. My uncle's a miner. Laid off from the mine there though and had to go to Truro to find work. Only comes home once a year."

"Then you don't get to see him very often."

She shook her head. "Nay."

"Tell me," I said "How close is the castle to Pendeen village?"

"You can see it from the high point on Cliff Road. That's just around the bend from the gatehouse, not far."

"Then I must immediately send word to my Aunt Winifred. If she's had word about the wreck, she'll be worried about me."

"Your aunt's already been to see you. When you were in that daze. Sat by you for a long time, she did. She was that worried."

That was one of the faces that had appeared in my delirium. So not all had been dreams. I wondered what Aunt Winifred would look like, for I had only seen an old photograph of her when she was very young.

After toweling dry, I donned a clean nightdress, for Gwynneth said I must stay in bed until the doctor pronounced me fit, but that today I would receive visitors. Then she arranged my red tresses in a thick braid and wound it around my head, tying the ribbons of a quilted bed jacket beneath my chin.

"Aye, the green ribbons match your eyes, miss," she said, pleased with the effect she'd created.

"Thank you," I said. "I do feel more presentable."

Gwynneth left, saying she still wanted me to drink the herb mixture that came from the herb woman for it ought to help me gain my strength sooner.

My visitors started arriving almost immediately, the first being the lord of the castle himself. He announced himself by a brief rap on the door and then strode in. He seemed taller than I remembered, yet his step was almost soundless as he crossed the room. I did not remember that he wore his hair long, and it was tied behind his neck with a black band. Unusual, considering that the fashion of the day was to wear the hair short. Neither did he wear a moustache like most men. He bowed slightly.

"Good morning, Miss Fowley. I hope you are feeling better since your unfortunate mishap."

His voice was a smooth baritone, and I remembered how it had penetrated the chaos on the beach the night of the wreck.

"Thank you, my lord. I am very much better."

His dark brown eyes were webbed with black, and a glimmer of light came into them as he said, "We have not been formally introduced yet. I am your host, Geoffrey Wycke."

I blushed in modesty at appearing before him in a bed gown, but I did not look away.

"I want to thank you for your hospitality, my lord," I

aid. "I hope I shan't be troubling you too long."

"It's no trouble, I assure you. I believe fate has brought you rather near your destination in any case."

I nodded, my curiosity aroused. "I see you already now who I am and where I am going."

His lips pulled up at the corners slightly in response to the sharpness of my tone, then he sobered his expression and said, "We took the liberty of examining your clothing to see if your identity could be found in case we found it necessary to notify the next of kin. There were certain letters in a satchel, which disclosed the information."

I glanced down at my bed jacket, realizing that I had given no thought at all to what had become of my clothes. I had even forgotten the letters I carried. Further embarrassment flooded me as Lord Rhyweth continued to look at me dressed so.

At first I thought he seemed amused at my dilemma, but then he bowed his head slightly. "No invasion of your privacy was meant, of course. The letters were brought to me after they had been dried. I will see that they are returned to you."

"Thank you."

He paced toward the windows and glanced out, hands clasped behind him. The day seemed to be sunny, though I had heard this was not often the case in this part of the world.

"Is this your first visit to Cornwall?" he asked, turning back toward me.

"Yes, though my father grew up here. I have heard of Rhyweth castle."

"What have you heard of it?"

His interrogative tone startled me, and I stumbled over my words. "Only that my aunt is one of your tenants. My grandfather was a fisherman as were the other men of the village. Little else."

39

"I see." He appraised me. "What you say is true. Winifred Fowley is a good woman and a reliable tenant. I expect she will be gratified that you are quickly regaining your health."

"Will you send word for her to come to me? If it is not far, that is."

"The distance is not great. She will come."

"Then perhaps I can return home with her. Surely I must not impose on you when my own aunt's cottage is near."

He glanced again toward the window. "I am sure your aunt will be very anxious to offer you her hospitality. But the doctor may not find that you are ready to be moved."

I began to be irritated with his solicitations and rustled the bedclothes. "Oh, surely I am over the shock of falling into the water. And the bump on my head is healing."

"You mustn't be too hasty. Here you can be waited on hand and foot until you are fully recovered, while your aunt would have to do for you as well as for herself. You would not want to make extra work for her, surely?"

His words were gentle and coaxing, still I was growing impatient each moment that I was made to stay in bed.

"I suppose you are right," I said begrudgingly. It was true, my aunt would be in her later years, and the last thing I wanted to do was to add to her burdens. If anything, I planned to be a help to her.

He came close to the bed again. "When you are well enough, I should like to invite you to dine. In the meantime, I trust you are in good hands. The mistress of the castle will look in on you this morning. You can let her know if you find fault with any of the service. Good day."

40

He turned on his heel and left, closing the door softly behind him. I stared after him. At his words, my heartbeat had risen and fallen. I didn't know why his surprising invitation to dinner should affect me so, but my reaction changed immediately at the thought of the mistress of the castle. Of course he would be married. I had not thought of that.

I felt restless after he left, and decided to try my legs. They proved steady enough, so that when Gwynneth returned with the herb mixture, she found me up and about. I sat down again in the window seat, where she brought me the potion.

"It's steeped leaves from the angelica plant, miss. Good to ward off a cold. Calms the heart and makes you sleep."

"All that?"

She nodded. Her voice took on a more conspiratorial tone. "It does something else, too."

I tilted my head expectantly.

"Wards off evil spirits."

I blinked. "I was not aware that I was in danger from them."

She thrust the mug toward me. "You can never tell. Best drink it."

I thanked her for it, and then when she left, I threw it out the window. I was feeling stronger, and no medicine or herbs were going to help me. What I needed was food and fresh air, and when I was ready, exercise.

The woman who entered shortly thereafter could be no other than the mistress of the castle. She was tall, like he was, with dark hair, snapping blue eyes and prominent cheekbones. She wore a bengaline day dress of light and dark blue stripes with plain navy apron overskirt. Her hair was done in an elegant coiffure and held in place with jet combs and pearls.

Her features were sharp but well proportioned, her skin porcelain, yet she pulled her lips into a grim line. From her apparent maturity, I guessed her to be somewhat older than myself.

She gave the effect of floating across the floor to where she stood some distance from me. I rose from the window seat where I had been sitting.

"You must be Rhionna Fowley," she said. "I am Morwenna Wycke."

Her cool eyes seemed to bore into me, and whereas I found some warmth in Lord Rhyweth's presence, there was none of it in hers. I sensed the impatience in her voice, and if Lord Rhyweth suspected I would be a burden to my aunt, it was nothing compared to the nuisance I must have become in whatever way to this lady.

"I am glad to meet you," I answered. "Lord Rhyweth told me you would look in on me."

"Yes, of course. I trust you've everything you need? The wreck put a strain on us, but that's over now. Four men lost their lives that night, and we feared for yours."

When I straightened, I found that I was as tall as she was, and I stood so, for it gave me more confidence. I did not like to be an unwanted guest, but it would be worse to propitiate. I could show my pride too.

"I plan to leave," I said. "As soon as the doctor will let me. I am most anxious to see my aunt. And I would not want to continue being a burden to your household. I can see that you must find it a strain."

I did not mean to sound so catty, but at my words, her eyes rounded and her mouth jerked. She averted her gaze and paced a few steps.

"That is not what I meant. You are welcome as long as you need be remain here."

42

She forced her hands to her side, but the confusion had not left her face as the air seemed to crackle around us. "Do not hesitate to ask for anything you wish." And then she turned and hurried out.

Her nervous manner startled me. Apparently I did not have the skill required to be a tactful castle guest. But that had always been a flaw. I often spoke before I thought. My father and Elsa had chastised me for it. I supposed my impatience often showed in word as well as deed.

Thinking to make myself useful, I went to the fireplace to see about the fire, which had burned down. I refused to act the invalid, and though I had to be careful how I moved my head, I decided that most ordinary tasks would only help strengthen me, for muscles got weak if left idle for long.

Rufus had hidden under the bed while I had visitors. Now he came out and watched me, wagging his tail.

I found my bedchamber quite comfortable, though I wondered how long I would have to remain in it, for I was anxious to leave. But little did I know that day how deeply I was already being drawn into the web at Castle Rhyweth.

Chapter 4

My dear niece,

You cannot imagine the joy in my heart that you are safe. When I had news of the shipwreck, I hastened to the castle, only to find you in a dangerous delirium. I feared for your life and would have sat by your bed day and night if Dr. Pearce had not persuaded me that there was nothing I could do, and that my own health would suffer if I should do so.

Lord Rhyweth was kind enough to offer that I remain as his guest in any case, but I hope you will understand my reluctance to do so. I am not comfortable anywhere but in my own humble cottage. There is no one here to do the milking but myself, and though I was uneasy leaving you at the castle, William (the doctor and I are old friends) promised to keep watch over you and relay your condition to me until you can be moved.

This morning, Lord Rhyweth sent me a message that you are awake and seem to be recovering your health, and I am hastily penning this while the messenger waits in the garden. If the handwriting is shaky, it is because I am hurrying and because I am not in the best of health today myself and so will come tomorow, at which time I will at long last be united wiht my dear niece. Until that time, pray keep safe.

Your Aunt Winifred

I folded the note that Gwynneth brought me and laid it on the side table. I was sitting in the upholstered lady's chair next to the fireplace with Rufus at my feet, for I had refused to return to the bed. Though Gwynneth fussed, she could see that I was no more to be treated like an invalid, and that I would enjoy the rest of the day's recuperation sitting up. Already I was chafing for something to do.

"What does it say?" Gwynneth asked after I read it.

I suppressed my smile. The note was not sealed, and I wondered if she had truly restrained from reading it. Then again, I did not know if she could read.

"It's from my aunt. She's going to visit me tomorrow."

"I'm sure she'll be glad to see you. Have you met her?"

I shook my head. "Only through letters. I've never been to Cornwall before, but she and my father were close, I believe."

"Were they now? And your father, when did he go to America?"

I screwed up my brow. "I'm twenty years of age, and I think he was in America several years before that."

"You be twenty and never married? I mean, I know it's none of my business."

I smiled ironically. "Unlike most women, I've never been in such a hurry to marry." I sighed. "I know, I don't want to grow old alone. But I had my father to take care of since my mother died, and we were good company for one another."

She looked at me curiously, and I realized with some compassion that for a girl like her, it would be difficult to understand a woman who was not anxious to marry. I found it hard to explain myself sometimes.

"I suppose it's because my father and I had such a

45

good time of it." I continued. "We used to talk about books and music. He encouraged me to learn his business too. He was very advanced in his thinking."

I shrugged, petting Rufus, who had stood up and stretched. "That is, most people called him eccentric. But he did not think that getting married and having babies was all a woman could do."

Gwynneth kneeled on the rug in front of the fireplace. "Did you know your mother then?"

"A little. She was quite beautiful as I recall."

"With hair like yours? And green eyes?"

I smiled. "Yes, with hair and eyes like mine."

Gwynneth and I were smiling in companionable silence and she reached over to pet Rufus when the door opened. Gwynneth shot up straight, and I turned to see what the interruption was, as Rufus skulked under the bed. Olga entered, carrying a garment over her arm wrapped in a linen sheet, which she laid out on the bed. Then she carefully unwrapped what appeared to be a gown of brown velvet and white lace.

"Mistress Wycke sent you this," she said turning to me. "She thought you might enjoy wearing it in the evenings, since you've not had time to replace your own belongings."

I rose and approached the bed, surprised as I gazed at the plush gown. The puffed sleeves were long with lace edging at the cuffs and at the bodice. Olga had also brought several petticoats to go under the generous skirt, made of yards and yards of the rich material and gathered up in flounces knotted with black velvet.

"Please thank your mistress for me," I said. "The gown is lovely. I am truly astounded at her generosity."

"No reason to be astounded. Something had to be done if you are to go about the castle in decent dress."

I blushed. As usual, I had blurted out words not quite appropriate to the occasion. But I could think of no adequate apology. It was only that I felt I was a nuisance to Morwenna Wycke, and therefore I was surprised she would lavish so lovely a gown on me when a plainer one would do.

"Tell her I appreciate her thoughfulness."

That seemed to satisfy the housekeeper. "It might be best if you tried it on. If you need any alterations, Gwynneth can help you."

"Oh, yes," said Gwynneth. "Do try it on."

I obliged them, the two women helping me get the gown over my head and then fastening the hooks and eyes, which I could never hope to reach. It was a perfect fit, and there were black kid slippers with rosettes of brown and black silk ribbons to match. It was only then that I remembered Lord Rhyweth's invitation to dine when I was well. I decided that I would never be any fitter to go downstairs than I was today, and besides, these four walls were beginning to close in on me. I needed something to look forward to. Therefore, I took on an authoritative tone and addressed Olga.

"Please tell your mistress that I am ready to accept his lordship's invitation to dinner. I feel the need for a change of scene."

The housekeeper accepted the request with a nod, and I couldn't help but compare her formality to dear Elsa back home. The thought brought me a wave of homesickness, but I swallowed it at least until Olga had departed. Then I turned to Gwynneth.

"Help me out of this thing, Gwynneth. It's several hours until dinner. And I suppose I must wait until I receive word if I may go downstairs in any case."

"Now don't you fret, miss," said the maid, perceiving my moodiness. "You'll be about your business in no time. I know it's hard bein' confined like you are when you're sick. But that was a nasty bump you had on your head. And when I think of that freezin' water brrrr." She shook herself. "I'd say you're lucky to be alive."

"I know. But the swelling on my head's mostly gone down," I said, touching the sore spot gingerly.

I got back into a dressing gown, and soon Dr. Pearce came to examine me. After he had performed his ministrations, he stood back looking at me, smoothing his moustache with one hand.

"I'd say you can be up and about. You've a mighty strong constitution, young lady. But don't push your luck. You still need plenty of rest. Time for the body to regain its strength. Don't over do."

"Then I can dine downstairs this evening?"

"I'd say that would be all right. But don't overtire yourself." He repacked his instruments, wished us good day and left.

I was jubilant at the thought of a formal dinner. For one thing, I was vastly curious to see more of Rhyweth castle. To me it had always been some far off place, dominating a landscape that had sounded harsh and mysterious the few times I had succeeded in getting my father to speak of it.

I wondered if the dinner would be lavish or spartan. For I knew absolutely nothing of the Wyckes' habits or circumstances. Naturally one expected the lord of a castle to live comfortably, but besides the obvious fine construction of the gown I was lent and the carvings in the heavy wood furniture of my room, I did not know.

Olga reappeared to tell me that dinner would be at seven o'clock. "Take the main staircase," she said. "The dining room is on the first floor."

The rest of the day passed slowly until it was time to get ready for the evening. Gwynneth dressed my hair in a neat coiffure with ringlets down my back. She gave me a hand mirror to see myself in, and I ap-

48

proved her work. Since I had no jewelry, I tied a wide black velvet ribbon around my throat. Dangling from it was a cameo that Gwynneth loaned me, saying it had belonged to her mother.

"Surely you do not want me to wear such an heirloom," I protested when she tied it on me.

"Nonsense," she said. "You can't go without something around your neck. And my mother would be pleased."

"Then I thank you. It is lovely."

Truly, the plunging neckline of the gown did seem to call for something at my throat to make me feel less bare. The gown's sleeves covered my arms from shoulder to wrist, but I feared my neck and bosom would be chilly. Seeing my dilemma, Gwynneth found a black fichu to go about the shoulders, and she tied it on me just before I was to descend.

I looked again in the hand mirror, and from what I could tell, Gwynneth had created a lovely effect with her handiwork. I could see the dreaminess in her eyes as she watched me prepare to go down. My heart went out to her. What joy could there be for servants whose lives were devoted to helping others, with little frivolity and no luxury of their own. I could say nothing, but I think the look I gave her conveyed much. I considered Gwynneth my friend, though our stations in life were different.

Rufus came to stand by her side, and they both watched me out the door. I was glad that at least my dog could give her some companionship in my absence.

Once outside my room, I proceeded with much interest along the corridor past several other oak doors on heavy iron hinges, coming at last to a large curving stone stairway. I held my skirts so I wouldn't trip, for I couldn't see my feet with the number of petticoats I had on.

The next landing was much like the one from which I had come, with large tapestries covering the walls, but another flight of curving stairs brought me out into a wide hall. Here, two servants dressed in black satin livery stood at attention, and when they saw me, they opened arched doors, through which I proceeded.

I did so and found myself in an anteroom around which old armor and coats of arms were hung, some of the weapons behind glass. I glimpsed a chapel through a half-open door off one side. In this setting, I could easily envision a squire preparing for knighthood in days of old, keeping vigil in the chapel the night before the ceremony.

The liveried servants went ahead of me and opened another set of doors, and I entered a large dining room, the doors shutting behind me.

The flicker of the candelabra on the long dining table and the magnificence of the room took my breath away. The decor was the same heavy woodwork I had seen in my own room, and there were tapestries on one wall, rich in material and hoary with age, the other wall being carved panels with repeated motifs including simulated columns, acanthus leaf brackets and rectangular medallions with stars in the center. Lion-head capitals were repeated at the panel tops. Two stone bays contained diamond paned windows.

Above the large stone mantel at the other end of the room was an elaborately carved oaken overmantel. The center panel was the devil's head, and the whole was divided into four sections by four lion-headed capitals on pilasters. Arching timbers intersected at the top of the cathedral ceiling.

I was so in awe of the place that it took a moment before I realized that Lord Rhyweth was approaching me from his position by the fireplace. I must have been staring and gave a little start when he came within my vision and gave a bow. He was elegantly attired in black tails, white ruffled shirt and white tie.

"Good evening. I can see that you are much better. May I inquire if you feel in as good health as you appear?"

I blushed to the roots of my red hair, but tried to maintain my composure. I was not used to being in the presence of an English lord, neither did I know how to handle his suavity. But as I had done in the presence of Morwenna Wycke, I stretched myself tall and lifted my chin.

"Thank you, I feel quite well. It is good to be up and about."

He smiled, and his appraising glance raked over me from my coif down to my shoulders, his eyes flickering as they passed over the cameo which rested above my décolleté, and then his gaze swept over the gown, coming to rest again on my face. It was as if he had peeled away not only my social veneer, but the pins of my coif and the material of my gown as well. My reaction to this strange sensation was to place my hand on my chest as I drew quick breaths.

Mistaking my discomposure for fatigue at being up, he offered his arm to lead me across the room. Seeing that I must take it or sway on my feet, I placed my hand on top of his, letting my arm rest on his black sleeve. I was again aware of the strength in the arm that led me, and could hardly believe it was my own feet that carried me. But I found myself handed into a high-backed carved chair a short distance from the head of the table. The butler, who Lord Rhyweth addresssed as Godreven, appeared from nowhere and slid the chair beneath me, and then Lord Rhyweth took his seat at the head of the table.

Godreven poured wine, of which Lord Rhyweth

approved, then left us. As my host raised his glass, I followed suit. It was only after taking a sip that I came to my senses and realized we were alone.

"You must not drink the wine too fast," he said. "Though a bit of stimulant will do you good."

The butler reappeared and served the soup, and Lord Rhyweth placed a large white linen napkin on his lap. I did the same.

I gulped down what I had taken in my mouth then set my spoon down. "Are there no others joining us?" I asked tentatively.

"The other survivors of the wreck were able to leave the castle. Only you remain."

I swallowed. I had not even given any thought to the other poor survivors, but of course I ought to be interested in the results of the wreck. "I understand that four men lost their lives," I said. "Was the damage also great?"

He frowned, twirling his wineglass. "Unfortunately, that depends on how you look at it. For the corporation that owned the ship, there was a loss assuredly. I do not know if the owners were well enough fixed to continue in business. I was not familiar with their names. As to the goods, a small amount of them were brought here where I can guard them until the agents come for them. But the majority of the wreck went to the villagers who are used to such scavenging."

I nodded remembering the greed I had seen on their faces. "Such calamities seem to excite people to an extreme state in which they are perhaps not themselves at all," I said. "Still, it is frightening to think of the looting that went on that night." I remembered something of Lord Rhyweth's efforts to stop it.

He tossed back his glass again and then said, "There is a prayer said to have been composed in the last century. 'We pray Thee, O Lord, not that wrecks should happen, but that if any wrecks should happen, Thou wilt guide them to our shore for the benefit of the inhabitants.'

"It is unfortunate, but part of life here," he continued. "You cannot ignore and despise a region to the brink of famine and then expect it to wish the fattest ships in the world a safe journey past its shores, or to show fine scruples when some of the fat is washed up at the door of this rim-of-the-world economy. However much one respects the law or even represents it, one cannot help but sympathize with some sort of equity the sea doles out upon occasion."

I was intrigued by this sort of Robin Hood philosophy. "And yet you showed some concern for the anguish of the ship owners."

He shrugged. "I do not know the ship owners, though I did what I could for them."

I knew something of what he spoke, for my father had often commented on Cornwall's poverty ever since a large number of the tin mines stopped producing some years ago. Now Cornishmen relied mostly on fishing. But my father's instruction to me of the legal rights and disputes over ownership of flotsam, jetsam, and wreckage had not left me an expert on the matter.

But Lord Rhyweth had not fully answered my question. He made no mention of Morwenna, which I considered rude since I was a guest. So I took it upon myself to inquire directly.

"I thought perhaps your wife would join us," I said.

He stared at me, lifting one dark brow. "My wife died some time ago."

I already felt a bit fuzzy-headed from the wine and from the excursion downstairs, and for a moment I felt as if I floated in a strange limbo. Still, the dark-haired lady who had loaned me the very gown I wore could be no ghost.

"Mistress Morwenna . . . " my words died on my lips.

He pulled his mouth back in an amused smirk, and then he wiped his lips as Godreven removed the soup.

"You mean my sister. Thank the fates she is only that. I hardly think I could be married to her."

"Your sister?"

"Yes. Morwenna is mistress of the castle but not my wife. She is rather temperamental and did not choose to dine in company this evening."

I wondered at the emotion that flooded me. I felt more nervous to be left alone with Lord Rhyweth, wondering how I would sustain the evening's conversation with him, yet the knowledge that he was not married validated some knowing feeling I had had when I'd first met him.

Godreven brought the main course, stuffed saddle of lamb with mushrooms and onions, and I lit into it with relish. After several bites I noticed that Lord Rhyweth had barely touched his food. I felt embarrassed by my gluttony and lowered my fork self-consciously.

"The food is very good," I said. "Are you not hungry, Lord Rhyweth?"

I thought his complexion darkened slightly at my forward comment, but he answered. "Perhaps not. My appetite leans toward other delicacies."

I wondered at this strange comment. For could not the lord of the castle have served what he himself enjoyed eating? He continued to sip his red wine slowly and watched me finish my meal.

The plates were removed and the next course served. But I had been so greedy with the earlier courses that now I slowed down a great deal. We were silent for a time, and then when coffee was served and the butler had disappeared, Lord Rhyweth spoke again, surprising me with the subject of his conversation.

"I was married," he said, reminding me of my earlier faux pas.

I lowered my eyes and smoothed my napkin. "Perhaps you do not wish to speak of it."

"On the contrary," he said. "I feel disposed to conversation this evening."

With the wine in him, and now with the liqueur he had added to his coffee, he did indeed seem more disposed to speak.

"My beloved wife, Elizabeth, had delicate health. She died two years ago."

"I'm sorry."

He nodded in acknowledgment, but seemed to sweep it away with a gesture, his fingers coming to rest again on the handle of his coffee cup. "Perhaps you would be entertained by some more of our family history," he mused.

"If your lordship would like to tell me. I always find family histories of great interest."

"Do you now? My father was Arthur Wycke, the Viscount Rhyweth. I am half Hungarian. My mother was a Hungarian lady."

"I believe my father mentioned your father. I did not know your mother was Hungarian."

Something began to excite me. At the mention of Lord Rhyweth's family I held out hopes I might pick up a clue. *Beware Leslie. I feel you may be in danger.* Who had written that message to my father from Cornwall? Could it have been one of Lord Rhyweth's family?

But he was going on. "It was a marriage of convenience, the type of match my father's father expected, for it brought my mother's fortune into the family, you see."

I did see, but I was amazed at his candor. Still, I

was fascinated, having had little social intercourse these last days, and Lord Rhyweth's refined manner and eloquence held my attention. I found in fact that the more he spoke, the more questions I had, small snatches of thought bubbling up from what I had heard of this place and this family from my father in years past, pieces of conversation that I had long buried, but that somehow must have been filed in my mind for the eventuality that I might one day see the land of my father's birth. Though I never dreamed it would be in the present circumstances. Lord Rhyweth continued about the rest of the household.

"You may have met my housekeeper, Olga Stamenkovic."

I nodded.

"She came here with my mother from Hungary. I always wondered that she did not return to her native land after my mother had died. But her situation is good here. Perhaps she would have to work much harder in her own country. I do not know."

"I've met her."

I thought of the Hungarian housekeeper and of the strange feelings I had around her. I could still not tell why she made me feel so ill at ease. I felt as if she did not quite approve of my etiquette.

"I should perhaps tell you about Jonas."

"Jonas?"

"The hunchback you saw me with the night of the storm.

"Oh yes." How could I ever forget the picture the two of them made coming out of the darkness into the tumult that night.

"You need not be afraid of Jonas. He was outcast by the villagers when he was a lad because of his deformity. I pitied him, you see, saw the goodness in him rather than any imagined evil that the village children foolishly condemned. I defended him once as a boy, and he has been loyal to me ever since."

I swallowed more wine, now knowing how to answer this.

"I tell you all this because you may remain my guest here for a while. It will be helpful if you know what to expect."

"It may surprise you to learn that I am a composer of a minor sort," he said. "I work at night. It is a habit formed when Elizabeth was ill. She developed an allergy to the sun and spent most of the day indoors, dozing. But at night she arose and would sit by the fire doing her needlework, while I composed on the harpsichord."

There was an intricately designed quilt on my bed, and I wondered if Elizabeth had done the fine handiwork. But I refrained from asking, although I found I was oddly curious about his wife.

"Later when she worsened and could not rise from bed, I had a pipe organ installed in the castle, finding in that instrument a better release of my energy."

"An organ." Realization dawned. "Then that is what I heard in my dreams. I thought I was going mad, but the music must have come from here within the castle."

"I apologize if my playing disturbed you. I would not like to think my music drove you mad."

I colored in embarrassment. "That is not what I meant."

He gave me an amused smile and again I felt as if he looked beneath the trappings of my gown to my very skin.

"I'm sure it isn't. Would you like anything else to drink?"

Since my stomach was full to bursting and I feared I would float away from the amount of liquid I had consumed, I shook my head. "No, thank you. I am quite satisfied."

"I wish I could say the same." His words were spoken softly, and not meant for me to hear, I believe.

We rose and he led me from the dining room to a formal parlor. I was not paying attention, and though we had made several turns, I had lost my bearings, and I did not know what part of the castle we were in now. But the room in which he placed me on a love seat before yet another large stone fireplace was elegantly appointed with brocade furniture, a thick oriental carpet, flocked wallpaper, and an enormous chandelier suspended from the ceiling.

Its crystals glittered from the many candles that had been lit in it, and so heavy did it look, I was glad I was not sitting directly beneath it. But I could see that a woman had had a hand in decorating this room. It was more like the finely furnished drawing rooms of the wealthy as I imagined they would live.

I turned the conversation to the present. "Now that I am well, I am most anxious to go to my aunt. I had a letter from her today. I fear she is not feeling well."

He frowned. "You are free to go, of course, if Doctor Pearce agrees. But I hope you will consider remaining my guest for a while."

I did not know what to say. "That is kind of you, but I am sure I am only a burden here."

"You must not think it."

His eyes dwelled on my face, causing my cheeks to warm. Then he adopted a more businesslike expression. "Your aunt's cottage is small, and though her natural generosity will dictate that she keep her niece there, you might not find her circumstances as comfortable as you would wish. It might be better for her and for you if you stayed on here."

His manner and his words flustered me, and I was feeling light-headed and worried that I had taken too much wine.

"I appreciate your generosity, Lord Rhyweth, but . . ."

Suddenly he was sitting next to me on the loveseat. "Perhaps it is not generosity as much as selfishness."

I swallowed. Lord Rhyweth was a very attractive man, and in my present wobbly state, I did not trust my own responses. I felt very much the young innocent, unused to such long exposure to such a man. And yet I was aware of something else as well. All evening his glances and his formality in addressing me made me feel very much a woman. I knew he appreciated the flattering lines of the gown his sister had loaned me. And the plunging neckline that had at first embarrassed me made me feel bolder as the evening went on. My fichu had slid down around my shoulders, and I did nothing to shift it to cover more of my décolleté.

His glance lingered there, causing me to nervously finger the cameo tied round my throat. I must have known what was about to happen, and while I feared the consequences, I craved this new experience at the same time, perhaps thinking that this might be my last night in the castle, and if I embarrassed myself I would not be here to see Lord Rhyweth after tomorrow.

His fingers touched mine, and I let go of the cameo, which he held. "This is a lovely thing," he said. "Where did you get it?"

It caused me further embarrassment to have to tell him I had borrowed it from a servant, but I said, "Gwynneth said it belonged to her mother. It is an heirloom."

He did not mock me. "Then it has sentimental significance as well as beauty," he said letting it drop again. And instead of removing his hand, he placed it on my bare shoulder and looked into my eyes.

"You are very beautiful, my dear. The firelight dances in your hair." He looked deeply into my eyes as if searching for some answer there. "I believe you are the loveliest young woman I have ever seen."

I could say nothing, only stare back at the depths of his dark eyes with their black webs, where I felt myself drowning. My heart was beating so loudly I was sure he could hear it. His arm had slid around my shoulders without my noticing, and his hand pressed me forward so that I leaned into him. He was so near I could feel his warm breath on my cheek, and yet only his hand touched my back. Again his eyes caressed my face, my lips and then glanced lower, admiring the slope of my bosom and the shadow where the lace of my fichu barely covered my skin.

I was aflame with his nearness, and while I longed for more of his touch, I felt that at any moment I would get up and flee. I had not planned this circumstance, and so the deeper I came under his spell, the more I tried to acknowledge the warning that sounded in some distant part of my mind.

Yet when his lips brushed my forehead and he murmured my name, I responded by raising my mouth to his. His lips were warm and soft, and I thrilled at being kissed so. My arm went round his neck and before I knew what had happened, he held me firmly against him. Our kiss deepened, and my mouth opened to the touch of his tongue, my body thrilling at the new sensations. There was not only fire in my veins but I drew comfort from his strength and the firmness of his body against mine.

He raised his head, his fingers coming up to touch my chin. "Rhionna, my dear. You are so lovely. Irrisistible. How can you expect a man to resist such beauty?"

His grasp on me at that moment was loose, and he

60

paused as if now were the moment when I might pull away, straighten, arise and wait for his apology. But none of that occurred. Instead, I simply uttered the words, "I do not know, my lord," in answer to his question.

The passion seemed to well up in him and he must have read my acquiescence, for he again gathered me in his arms, smothering my face with kisses. I threw back my head as he lowered his face to my bosom, the touch of his lips on my naked skin unleashing the fire deep within the center of my body. I did not resist as his fingers came up to toy with the knot in my fichu, finally slipping it off my shoulders. Again came the warnings in my mind, but my body craved more. I was lost to the soaring sensations he created in me and only rejoiced when his fingers cupped my breast. The throbbing between my legs increased to a feverish pitch as his lips played at the edge of my gown.

My hands wandered over his shoulders and I found myself pressing his head against me, as his lips worked their way up to the base of my throat. Finally he brought his face to mine again and kissed me long and deeply. Then he held me against him, his movements slowing as he caressed my hair softly. My heartbeat gradually returned to normal, and we sat thus for some moments, the heat of the fire warming our faces. He helped me rearrange my fichu, but there was no awkwardness about it, and I could not honestly say that I felt shame, only a sort of astonishment at my own exhilaration and the newness of this experience.

I laid my head against his shoulder and the comfort of his hand slowly moving across my hair and shoulder together with the heat from the wood fire in the fireplace lulled me. At long last, he turned his face once more toward mine, his words low, intimate.

"I must see you to your room, my dear."

"Yes," I answered sleepily.

He helped me up and tucked his arm beneath mine, for which I was grateful, still feeling somewhat unsteady on my feet. I felt I must be in some fairyland and that when I awoke tomorrow harsh reality would greet me. But it made me want to hang onto the moment, for I would have this secret to cherish.

There was no one about when we stepped into the dank hallway, and the chill greeted me. We came to the staircase and turned upward, our footsteps scraping on the stone steps. I glanced over my shoulder once to see Jonas, the hunchback with his long extinguisher, putting out the candles behind us as we climbed the stairs. Then when we came to the landing and reached my room, I looked back and again saw Jonas, putting out the light at the stair landing. It occurred to me that Lord Rhyweth would have to find his way in the dark.

His hand was at my waist, and he turned me in his arms.

"Good night, Rhionna. Sleep well. I'll not see you in the morning."

It took me a moment to realize that he meant he would be sleeping, since he must now be going to play his music. But all these thoughts and the vision of his dark eyes appraising my face, my hair, my throat, were muddied in the haze of fatigue that claimed me.

I entered my room, and the rustle of my skirts woke Gwynneth who was dozing in the chair by the fire. She rubbed her eyes and then stumbled toward me to undo the fastenings at my back. I was rather glad that I did not have to face her, for my face was still burning.

She removed the cameo from around my neck and dropped it into her pocket. Then I donned my nightgown and slipped happily between the covers, while Gwynneth extinguished the lamp. Rufus came to nuzzle me and I scratched behind his ears affectionately. I felt strangely blissful, and yet the feeling was transient. For even then I knew the lovely sensations that filled me would not last.

Chapter 5

I awoke still a part of my dreams, and yet as the sun lengthened across the floor at the foot of my bed, my feelings hovered between the sweet sinfulness of the evening before and the quandry of what I would do with the memory. One thing was clear, I would have to leave the castle at once.

With the decision made, I arose, and when Gwynneth came to me, I put on a heliotrope muslin day dress, again loaned by the enigmatic Morwenna. Then I sent for Olga to inform her of my leave-taking.

When she answered my summons, she knotted her brows disapprovingly, but I had made up my mind, and no one could stop me.

"It's time I leave. The doctor has pronounced me fit, and my aunt will be waiting to hear from me. I wish to leave immediately, so that Winifred does not take it upon herself to return here instead."

"Very well. I will see that Elwynd escorts you."

"Is it so far? Could I not walk?"

Her dark eyes flashed, but I could not quite read her expression.

"You would not want to be out alone that distance. You'll be safer with Elwynd." And she left to make the arrangements.

"Who is Elwynd, and what does she mean?" I asked Gwynneth after she left.

"Elwynd is the gamekeeper."

She shrugged as if he were of no special import to her. Or perhaps her gesture meant that he was not good enough for her, for there was something in her eyes that gave me to think she knew this Elwynd better than she let on. Then I remembered hearing the name the night of the wreck. It was Elwynd who had first pulled me upon the beach. I had heard Lord Rhyweth address him so.

"What did she mean about being safer with him? Surely in broad daylight . . ."

Somehow I had imagined that my aunt's cottage would be practically within hailing distance of the castle, or perhaps it was my having been caged up for a number of days that made the thought of a nice long walk in the country especially appealing. And I had no luggage to transport with me.

But Gwynneth went to the wardrobe to pull out the clothing I had been using and set about folding the things.

"You can take these with you," she said. "Mistress Rhyweth said you were to use them until you got your own things."

I hated to continue to rely on these people, but I had no real choice at the moment.

"I'll pack a trunk," said Gwynneth.

"Thank you." But I was not to be put off the track. "Now why would I not be safe traveling alone?" I persisted in asking her.

She shrugged her shoulders as if she did not want to answer. "There've been rumors," she said.

"What kind of rumors?"

"Abductions. They say young women've been missing from these parts. Don't know how much is true, 'course."

"Young women? Who?"

"Well, don't know as I know for sure. But I do know that Mary Beale hasn't been seen for some months, though if you ask me she just ran away from her husband. And then there's Jane Seccombe."

She knotted her brows as she folded my dressing gown. She seemed to have reasoned out Mary Beale's absence satisfactorily, but she did not seem so sure about the second girl.

The sun went in at that moment and I felt the change in the air, as if the weather were an omen of some sort. The mention of the missing girls had evidently affected Gwynneth, but I tried not to let the mood rub off on me. I also reminded myself that the Cornish were very superstitious, and the slightest happening could have grave consequences in their minds, whereas I told myself there was usually a rational explanation for such strange occurrences.

"Yes," I said, attempting to put a good face on it. "They probably ran away."

Rufus chose that moment to bark.

Gwynneth packed what I was taking, and Jonas came to carry the trunk downstairs. It was then that I remembered my letters.

"There's one other thing. I had a packet of letters pinned inside my dress for safekeeping. I believe they were taken to Lord Rhyweth the night of the storm. I would like to have them back."

"I'll go ask Madam Olga," said Gwynneth.

A little while later, Olga herself returned with my folded letters, though the ink had run through the paper. I could see that they had been water-logged.

I took them from her, turning them over. My eyes flew up to hers.

"But there's one missing."

"Oh?" said Olga as she stood primly before me.

My heartbeat quickened as I faced her. "Yes. These are letters from my aunt. There was one other."

"I am sorry," she said. "I know of no other."

My words stuck in my throat. I could hardly tell her who the letter was from, for I did not know myself, but the letter that was missing was the one warning my father.

"Are you sure?" I said.

"I am quite sure. If you like, I will report to Lord Rhyweth that there seems to be a letter missing."

"Could it not have gotten misplaced? Perhaps it fell to the floor when I was being undressed?"

She seemed to take this as an affront to her efficiency, and I was afraid panic was showing, for the disappearance of that letter completely unnerved me.

"We would have found it, miss," said Gwynneth. "I'm sure."

"Yes. I'm sure you would. Still I would like Lord Rhyweth to know that I've missed some pages from a letter in case it turns up."

"Very well."

She left, and there seemed little I could do. I did not believe the letter had fallen out in the sea, though I supposed that was possible. Still, I feared that someone here had taken it and the feeling disturbed me.

I prepared to go.

Gwynneth wished me a fond farewell, and we promised to see each other often. She bent to hug Rufus, who licked her face, and I thought she would surely miss his companionship as much as mine.

I had not been outside the castle in daylight before, and as I stepped out to the courtyard I took a moment to glance around me. Then I looked up at the castle's three towers, several balconies, and parapet. The granite walls and tall narrow windows with thick vines of ivy crawling between them made the place look even more ancient than before.

I think that was the moment when the oddity of what I had experienced struck me fully. I felt as if I had been in some sort of dream or trance ever since I was carried to the castle the night of the storm. It was as if I had been under some sort of spell, and merely breathing the fresh air outside the castle walls helped me separate the life inside Castle Rhyweth from my own life. Yet even here, where I could both smell and hear the sea but could not see it, the damp stillness made me shiver.

Elwynd stood beside a two-seated trap, holding a long rifle under one arm. I recognized him though I had not seen him since the night I was brought to the castle. In the daylight I saw that he was of muscular build, with sandy blond hair, blue eyes, and a blond moustache. He wore knickerbockers, a tweed jacket, and a cloth cap. The sight of the rifle startled me, and then I remembered that he was the gamekeeper, and that would explain the need for a weapon.

Jonas placed the trunk in the back of the trap, and then without a word, he shuffled off in his odd gate. I felt a sense of pity watching him as I remembered what Lord Rhyweth had said about him. Still, the words stuck in my throat when I tried to thank him, and I stood helplessly staring after him as he disappeared down some steps that must lead to a cellar.

I turned back to see Elwynd watching me from where he stood. He nodded slightly, but I still felt ill at ease.

"You must be Elwynd," I said. "I never thanked you for pulling me out of the water."

A corner of his eye twitched as he lifted his chin. "Just following my orders. Lord Rhyweth said to help the survivors and salvage as much from the wreck for the owners as we could."

I raised a brow. "That was good of you. It seemed as if many of the villagers took rather a different view."

He shrugged and tossed his head with an indifferent air. I saw pride in the gesture, and his eyes flashed something that spoke of his Cornish individuality. "Wrecking's a way of life here," he said.

"I see."

He helped me up, and Rufus jumped in beside me. Elwynd climbed up to the driver's seat, placed the rifle at his feet, and picked up the reins. Then with a gidap, we rumbled across the stone courtyard, passing under the gatehouse arch and then across the high bridge that spanned the cleft separating the rock on which the castle stood from the mainland. We came through some trees, then the road passed near enough to the edge of the cliffs that I could see down to the treacherous rocks that had beached our poor ship.

She was still there, and my heart turned over to see her now. Her masts were mostly down, lines tangled, and the bow had pitched forward so that only the stern rose above the water. The tide had tipped her on her starboard side, no more than flotsam, left to nature to complete her disintegration. A white mist was drifting inward in patches and began to cover the wreck like a shroud.

We kept to what Gwynneth had called the Cliff Road, a high road that ran along the edge of the land for several miles. The weather was damp, and the sun was hiding, yet the vista of the sea opening in front of me was magnificent. When the road came too near the edge, however, and I stared down steep, rocky cliffs plunging to a tiny sliver of beach, I held tightly to Rufus and shrank to the far side of the trap as if my weight would prevent us from going off the road.

The road curved again, and now I could see the

gray hamlets of the fishing village spilling away from us down a slope toward the sea.

"Is that Pendeen?" I asked Elwynd.

"That it is," he answered.

Fishermen's cottages clung to the side of a hill that reached outward into the water, docks encircling the whole at the bottom. Now I could see the fishing fleet in the harbor protected by the protruding land, and I shook my head, so different did this quiet cove appear from where our ship chose to beach in the storm.

We passed a fork in the road where one might turn off and descend along a stone walled track to the village. But we took the left fork and our path ascended the rock-bound coast further to a green carpeted landscape where the wind picked up. I could almost feel the presence of King Arthur's knights riding through this countryside. If the legends were true, this would have been a fitting place for them. The place seemed haunted with the glamour of such tales.

We entered a wood, and the trees closed around us surprisingly fast. It was quieter here, so that I was acutely aware of the horse's hooves on the road and the grating of the wheels of the trap in ruts formed by the numerous vehicles that must have passed this way. We slowed. Presently, we came to a path, and Elwynd drew up beside it. I peered at the writing on the stone marker that stood by the side of the road, but I could not see it clearly.

"That way goes to a hermit's cell," said Elwynd. "St. Melan gave his name to the glen up yonder. There's a waterfall some forty feet high. All the visitors to these parts go to see it."

I looked up the small path that soon appeared to wind out of sight. "I should like to see it some time, then."

He glanced back at me, then at the path again. "It's

a steep climb."

I nodded and looked again at the path, but Elwynd seemed disposed to stare at it for some seconds. Finally, he said, "Odd story that."

He had aroused my curiosity in spite of the fact that I should have been getting used to the Cornish love of telling tales. But what he said gave me a chill that was not appealing.

"There were two women once," he said, his voice taking on that low, hypnotic quality of one whose thoughts have turned inward to the story they are telling. "They came to St. Melan's cell when it was a cottage, but after he had died. The villagers knew nothing of the two, they never learnt their names. But they remained in the cottage by the waterfall. They had no servant and no visitors, and they never appeared without each other. They spoke only in whispers to each other, and some said it was the Devil's language they were speaking."

"Oh?"

"At last rumor said that one of them was dead, and so the villagers went up to see if it were true. They found one of the ladies weeping by the bedside of her friend, who was dead. Still the living one would give no information, say nothing. The villagers asked what they should do about the burial, but the other one said nothing, only wept. They took the body of her friend away, but the other stayed. Days passed, but she did not leave the cottage. One day a child looked into the cottage window and saw that she was lying still. She too was dead. So they took her away and buried her, but no one ever knew their names or where they came from."

I waited for more, but there was none. Rufus whined apprehensively, turning around on his seat. After another moment's meditation, Elwynd picked up the reins again and we continued. I stared back at the marker, curiosity mixed with a shiver that came with a gust of cold wind. If all the visitors to this place went to the hermit's cell, perhaps I too would make the pilgrimage, but not on such a day as this.

"Cornwall must have many such eccentrics," I said, thinking that perhaps Elwynd had told me the story to start a conversation, but all he did was glance sidelong at me. I saw him nod, then face forward.

"That it does, miss. That it does."

We came out of the woods, and the road dipped into a hollow and then rose to a clearing, and now I could see the fields divided in their long strips by stone borders. The track wound around the fields. The trees on our right had been blown by Atlantic winds to hang like canopies above us. A little farther and we approached a timber-framed clay-built cottage with a thatched roof. A thatched barn and animal pens sat behind. We pulled up, then Elwynd helped me down and opened the gate in the wooden fence that surrounded the small yard and the rambling garden. Smoke curled upward from the brick chimney, and I began to feel the anticipation of seeing my aunt at last.

The cottage door opened, and a gray-haired woman in a long-sleeved print dress and white apron emerged, holding a birch broom, with which she must have been sweeping.

"Aunt Winifred," I said, for it could be no other than she.

"Yes, my dear niece. It is I."

She held out her thin hands, which I grasped as I gazed into her blue-green eyes. Smiles wreathed both our faces, and then we fell on each other with kisses and hugs.

"My, my, let me look at you," she said at last, standing back for a critical view. "Yes, yes," she shook her head, and for a moment her eyes misted over. "I can see your father in you."

"Yes."

Mutual grief came over us, and then she turned back toward the cottage, wringing her hands. "I can hardly believe he's gone, child. I told myself so many times that I would see him again."

She was slight of build, but a little taller than average, and her grasp was strong. Already I felt the affinity toward her that I knew I would.

We entered the main room of the cottage and faced each other while Elwynd dragged the trunk in and placed it in the center of the room. Rufus followed us. Elwynd glanced quickly at Winifred and then at me.

"I'd best be getting back. I've things to do."

Winifred looked up at him, for he was a strapping man and almost had to stoop to avoid hitting his head on the rafters. "Thank you for bringing her, my boy."

"Yes, thank you, Elwynd," I said.

"I'll be getting on then."

He and Winifred exchanged looks, then his blue eyes flashed a look of something else as he glanced at me. Finally, he went outside.

I glanced around the small, neat cottage, remembering Lord Rhyweth's words. The place was clean, the tables and chairs sturdy, and the large stone fireplace at one end of the cottage had evidently had much use from the looks of the blackened hearth. A bed and a small writing desk with several drawers filled the opposite wall. There was a spinning wheel in the corner, and a door led to another small room at the back of the cottage. It had none of the luxury of the castle, but its hominess was comforting. I was sure I had made the right choice in coming here.

"Oh, Aunt Winifred. I hope you don't mind. I've brought my dog. This is Rufus."

73

He thumped his tail from where he'd curled up on the braided rug in front of the fireplace.

"Of course I don't mind. We could use a good dog around here. Can he herd sheep?"

I thought of Rufus' upbringing in the city and shook my head. "But he's very smart. He could learn."

"Sit down, my dear. I'll put on a pot of tea. It's a chilly day." She moved to the iron cook stove.

I glanced out the small glass-paned window. "Is it always like this, Aunt?"

"The weather, you mean?"

"Yes, it seems mild one minute, then damp with a kind of cold that seems to go right through you. Not like the crisp winters in New York."

She smiled to herself as she poured the boiling water into the teapot. "No, nothing like that."

I took a seat in one of the straight-backed chairs, allowing her to bring the china cups and pour the tea. Then she took a seat opposite me, and I could take all the time I wanted looking at her. For I had been very curious about Aunt Winifred for a very long time.

Though I could see from her lined face and hands that she had led a hard life, there were traces of beauty in her strong angular features. And her posture was not stooped. On the contrary, she seemed to carry herself with quiet pride, pouring the tea as if she were the equal of any lady. I hoped she warmed to me as much as I warmed to her.

"I am glad you look so well, my dear," she said. "I feared for your life those dreadful nights. You looked so pale and," she seemed to shrink at the word, "tormented."

I shook my head. "I too am glad that is past. But you can see I have quite recovered. It was only the shock of falling into the sea. Rufus saved me."

He stood up and wagged his tail at the acknowledgment, and Winifred held out her hand to let him sniff her. He licked her hand and then obediently sat down next to me on the wooden floor, truly the hero of the situation.

I smiled at my aunt. "There is so much I want to ask," I shrugged helplessly. "I hardly know where to begin."

She smiled indulgently. "You were so determined to come to Cornwall, weren't you?"

I had so looked forward to meeting Aunt Winifred, that finding my only living relative had nearly supplanted my original motivation. But her words brought me up hard, and I stared at her. She intimated that she knew something of my reasons for being here, whereas I had told her nothing of them.

"Yes, I, that is, it was a reaction I suppose to Father's death." I fiddled with my hands. "I suppose you may find it foolish, but his death seemed . . . It seemed to me like no accident."

Her expression barely changed, except for a flicker of the eye. "In what way?" she asked.

"He was standing under a crane that was being unloaded at the shipyard. It fell. . . ."

The pictures formed in my mind, recreating the scene as if I were there again. I shut my eyes. I was not even sure Aunt Winifred would want to hear this.

As if reading my thoughts, she said, "Go on. I would like to know how it happened."

"I was there, but too far away to do anything. The crate swung forward and then back again." I swallowed. "I saw Father talking to a man directly beneath the crate. Father was gesturing with his arms, like he was angry. Something forewarned me, I'm not sure what. I yelled and started running forward, and at that instant the cable broke and the crate—" I could not go on. I opened my eyes.

Winifred did not reach for my hand, did not touch me, but I felt as if she saw the scene I described. Her mouth trembled slightly, and I felt her empathy. We sat in silence for a moment, then I shook my head. She raised her cup and sipped her tea.

"It may be," she said slowly. "It may be as you say. Who was the man Leslie was talking to?"

"I don't know. Many people saw the accident and ran over to help, but the man was gone."

She nodded as if to herself. "Do you remember what he looked like?"

I shrugged. "The police asked me, of course. All I remember was that he was large with dark hair and had on a long tweed overcoat and bowler hat. I wasn't close enough to see his face."

"And the crane driver?"

"A workman Father knew well. He was aghast that his equipment was faulty."

Again she gave me a perceptive look. "And so you decided to come to Cornwall, even though your father warned you not to?"

I gasped. "How did you know?"

This was the second person who seemed to know that my father had not wanted me to come here, and yet as far I as knew his conversation with me on the matter had been private.

The light outside began to fade, and Winifred drew her shawl closer around her. "I had several letters from Leslie. I knew how he felt about it. I have to say, I agreed with him. But you came anyway."

My heart turned over. While Winifred had seemed glad to see me, now I had the oddest feeling that she did not want me here. Desolation descended upon me. I felt entirely unwanted by my last living relative and unconsciously reached down to touch Rufus for comfort. He rose and licked my hand then placed his head

76

in my lap as if he knew my feelings.

Winifred seemed also to read my thoughts, for she said, "It's not that you're not welcome here, my dear, it's only that things are not what they used to be in this place. I fear it is not the sort of place a stranger would enjoy visiting."

"Aunt Winifred, how can you consider me a stranger? My father was born here. This is the land of my ancestry."

"That may be, but after we've had a good visit, it might be safer if you returned to America."

I was stunned. I had no more than set foot in my aunt's home and she was asking me to leave. I could only stare at her, my hands clenched in my lap.

"But why?" Other words failed me.

She examined my face and seemed to search for words that would pacify me. Yet her warnings did not cease. "I must tell you the truth, then, since you are so persistent."

"What truth?"

"It is not safe for young women here."

Her words chilled me, while at the same time I could scarcely believe that this conversation was real. It was as if I had entered some dream world beginning with the shipwreck and had not yet awakened. But I leaned forward, my face heated both by the fire in the nearby hearth and by my own blood which leapt through my veins at her words.

"Why is it not safe?"

Her eyes darkened and seemed to fasten on my face as her expression hardened. "Several of the village girls have disappeared from here recently. There's been no explanation."

I wrinkled my brow and sat back. "Gwynneth, the upstairs maid at the castle, told me about that, but is it so unusual for village girls to become disillusioned with life in a place such as this and want to seek their fortunes elsewhere?"

Winifred shook her head almost imperceptibly. "That would not be so unusual. But I do not think these girls have simply run away."

"Why not?"

She paused, looked into space for a moment, and then formed her words. "There have been other things. Things to make one wonder."

"What things?"

Again she gazed into the air over my shoulder rather than at me. "There is a wolf that roams the moors. He does not travel with a pack. Two of the girls were seen to walk abroad at night before they disappeared, both giving the same explanation."

"What?"

"That they had been sleepwalking."

I swallowed, my throat suddenly dry. Her words were puzzling, but I tried to shake myself of the mood that had descended upon me. I still thought that these girls might have gone off with young men. If they had had a tryst with their lover at night, what better excuse than sleepwalking? I said as much to my aunt.

"That may be," she said, her eyes coming back to me again. "That may be."

There was an air of mystery and sadness about Aunt Winifred, and while I truly wanted to believe that she was glad to see me, I felt that there was still some distance between us. I wanted to bridge that distance, but told myself that I had only just arrived. It would take some time to establish our acquaintance and kinship. As I got to know her better, perhaps she would open up more to me. I hesitated to tell my aunt about the missing letter and the warning to my father that he was in danger. I did not want to upset her further. And yet, if I was to discover who wrote the letter, I had to

78

find a way of asking questions.

"There is something else," I said. "There was a letter."

She did not stop stirring but asked, "What letter?"

My voice started to tremble as I told her. "It was a warning to my father that he might be in danger. It came from Cornwall."

"Oh." Her hands had stilled.

"But I do not know who it was from."

Her features relaxed a trace. "You do not?"

"No. It was only a page. The signature was missing."

"I see."

"Well, I thought that if I came here I might find out who sent it. Do you have any idea who it might have been from?"

"No." She shook her head.

I suppose I was disappointed. But then I knew that a simple answer would have been rather unrealistic. Still, my heart felt heavier.

I got up and put away the tea things, then together we began to prepare a meal of salted herring and Kiddley broth, a thick bread soup flavored with bacon and onions. We spoke softly, in harmony with the grayness of the day. I talked of many things. I talked of my father's business and how I had left it in the hands of Henry Lawson. I told her of New York, thinking that she would not like it after the wild, open spaces of Cornwall. And then I told her of my stay at Castle Rhyweth.

This last she listened to with an air of fortitude, as if she were curious. But something seemed to hold her back from asking questions about any of the people I had met there.

When I mentioned the strange hunchback, Jonas, she paused in her work and glanced out the window, murmuring to herself. "Yes, Jonas . . . I remember

79

that time." But she said no more.

Later that day, she showed me her garden, and I admired the tenacity of the vegetables that clung to the rocky soil, aided only by frequent rain and a winter that varied little from summer. Already the air felt like a mild February prolonged to a damp June, and there was the promise of more rain to come. Primroses bloomed against the white-washed fence lending color to the otherwise grayish green surroundings.

She had a milk cow she called Heather and a few woolly sheep that she kept in a pen except for when she let them out to graze on the moor.

When night fell we ate the remains of the Kiddley broth and drank tea. After we had washed the dishes in the dry sink and replaced them on the dish rail, we wrapped up leftovers and I fed Rufus some scraps. Then I went outside to take the jar of jam to the root cellar.

After shutting the door on the cellar, I came back up and stood for a moment outside the cottage. The clouds parted to reveal a full moon which silhouetted Castle Rhyweth, rising on its promontory in the distance. A wreath of fog covered the fields between here and there, blanketing even the thick woods in the valley that lay between this rise of ground and the rock upon which the castle guarded Pendeen's fishing harbor.

Then a wolf howled on the moor above the cottage. The hairs on the back of my neck prickled at the sound as I turned to look toward the highlands. Rufus scratched on the inside of the cottage door, and I hastened to open it. He cried nervously at the dying howl, and I knelt, putting my arms around him.

"It's all right, Rufus. It's only a wolf. It won't bother us."

But my words belied my taut nerves, for the eerie

sound and the ocean of white fog that came almost to the gate frightened me. I fastened my eyes on Castle Rhyweth, feeling strangely drawn to it, remembering that last night I had been in Lord Rhyweth's arms. The memory still warmed my blood, and I felt an answering cry within my heart as if I too were as lonely as the wolf on the moor.

I knew that Lord Rhyweth's dallying with me was only done in a moment of reckless indulgence, and that if I saw him in the light of day I would probably not be able to face him. But at night, gazing at the castle far away, my imagination frightened and yet stirred by the setting, something tugged at me.

I rose, as if in a trance and took a few steps toward the castle. I walked far enough so that the fog began to swirl about my feet. Rufus hung back, pacing and whining, trying to get me to come back to the cottage.

I stood some moments thus, looking out over the strange country I had come to, fearing the dangers that my aunt spoke of and that others had alluded to, yet drawn to it as one is drawn to one's own roots.

Finally, the clouds closed over the moor, and the white fog was hidden by darkness. I turned to follow Rufus into the cottage and sat down beside my aunt who was staring into the turf fire in the hearth, musing to herself. Images danced before my eyes in the flames, and I must have lost all sense of time.

It was quite late when I left my aunt and went sleepily to the small bedroom at the back of the cottage, for Winifred insisted I sleep there. She would sleep in the smaller wooden bed at the side of the main room. Rufus got on the bed next to me, and I did not make him get down. I was glad for his warmth, for when the fire burned down, it was quite cold.

When I closed my eyes I still saw the castle in my mind. I felt as if I floated out of my body and went upon the moors where the wolf howled. And there in my dreams, I met Lord Rhyweth, who was waiting for me.

Chapter 6

Winifred was up early, milking the cow and churning butter. I busied myself gathering eggs from the hen coup and drawing water from the well. Though I was not used to these farm chores, I was determined to be as much help to her as I could, and I knew my muscles would strengthen the more work I did. I suppose in the back of my mind I was striving to impress my aunt with my usefulness, thinking that she would more readily want me to stay on if I proved myself worthy.

In the light of day, the strangeness of the night before seemed less real. Castle Rhyweth still dominated the landscape, but this morning it seemed farther away and more remote. Instead, nature, close at hand, held my attention. I could see that much of the land was unsuitable for anything but rough grazing. But the peasants had sectioned off plots where some cereals and vegetables could be grown. And everywhere there was a fine covering of sand. The predominant westerlies caused the sea to fling its sand up on any possible beaches, then when the sand dried, it was blown inland to come to rest on a dune or blow farther in.

I helped Winifred pull up some weeds from the garden and then we cleaned out the stalls in the barn.

I was inside when I heard a man's voice speaking with Winifred, who was still outside. I looked out the window and saw to my surprise that it was Elwynd. She directed him to the barn. When she came back in, I asked her about Elwynd's appearance.

"You wouldn't know, of course," she said, "but Elwynd spent most of his youth here in this cottage. I raised him from a wee mite, for he had no parents he could call his own."

"You mean he was an orphan."

She nodded.

"That was quite good of you, Aunt Winifred. He seems like a very kind man. He must respect you a great deal."

She seemed to warm to that. "He still helps me with the odd jobs I can't manage myself. I've sent him to see to a wagon wheel I think we'll have to take to the harnessmaker's."

We went about our various tasks, and when Elwynd was done with his examination of the broken wheel he came into the cottage. He hung his cap on a peg by the door, placed his rifle against the wall, and after nodding to me, took a chair at the table where Winifred brought him some pastry she had made filled with beef, potato, onions, and turnip. I took a cup of tea and sat down at the table with him. Elwynd held the pastry in his hand and devoured it from one end to the other.

"Do you ride?" Elwynd asked, after he had finished.

"Why yes," I said. "I rode often in Central Park in New York."

"I'd be willin' to take you for a ride," he said. "You could get to know the land that way, and learn what places to avoid."

"That would be very kind of you," I said, glancing quickly at my aunt to ascertain whether or not she

84

would approve of this plan. She nodded and I turned back to Elwynd.

"I wouldn't want to be imposing on your time, of course," I said, but already the thought of being on horseback exploring the countryside and the moors above Pendeen was taking my fancy, I had felt cooped up during my enforced recovery at the castle. And the smallness of the cottage also made me want to be outdoors as much as possible.

He nodded as if the plan were settled. "I'll fetch you a horse from Lord Rhyweth's stables then.

"Oh, will he mind?"

"Nay. It's my privilege as gamekeeper. He's said as much."

He rose, nodded to Winifred, took his cap and his rifle, then he turned to me. "Would you be wanting to ride tomorrow?"

His eyes were so serious when I met them that I nodded quickly. I felt myself suddenly sympathetic to him, perhaps because of what my aunt had told me about his background. And at that moment, I must have been reaching out for friendship myself, so odd had been my reception here. So I accepted his invitation with a hasty nod.

"Oh yes, that would be lovely. That is if Winifred thinks it is all right."

"You may go, my dear," said Winifred. "Elwynd knows the land hereabouts, so you won't get lost. But you must return before nightfall."

That settled, he left the cottage, mounted the horse he had tied to the post outside, and rode off. I set about helping Winifred with the rest of the day's chores and fell into bed that night utterly exhausted but with a feeling of satisfaction about what I had accomplished.

The next morning Elwynd returned with another

horse named Blackie, a black gelding with very good lines and a white patch on his forehead. I could not help smiling as I fed him some lumps Elwynd gave me and rubbed his nose.

"He is a beauty," I said. "Is he Lord Rhyweth's?"

"That he is."

"Lord Rhyweth is very generous."

Elwynd jerked his chin to the side. "He's free with the horses for his guests."

"But I'm . . ." I began protesting, but the words died on my lips. If Lord Rhyweth considered me a guest enough to let me use his horse, I could not refuse.

I bid Winifred good-bye and told Rufus to stay with her. I would take Rufus out another time, after I had learned the countryside myself. I didn't want to have to worry about him getting caught in briars or chasing off after rabbits today.

I hadn't anything to ride in, but Winifred gave me a warm jacket and a pair of boots. We had tucked my hair under an old cap, though wisps of it seemed to straggle out from under. I thought I must look a queer sight, but I didn't say anything, reminding myself that these peasants were on the whole much poorer than the folk I had been used to in New York, and that what might appear queer to my city-bred sense of dress would not seem queer here where everything was pressed into service as long as possible. I would hardly appear at the castle this way, but I reminded myself that I would not be going there again. I was on a level with the common people now. In this isolated place, these people who struggled for a living from such a wild land paid little attention to things like fashion.

We set off on a track that wound around the fields above the village. From the ridge above the cottage, we could see the ocean. The grayness of yesterday had lifted and the sun shimmered on the water like dazzling pieces of glass. A sullen calm seemed to lay over the landscape. Though the sky was a bright azure, I still felt a sense of oppressiveness about the air as I looked about me at the wind-crippled hawthorne trees that crouched at the edge of the ridge and the brambles clutching the ground that rose toward moorlands yet to be seen.

I let out a deep sigh, expressing some emotion I could not yet name, and looked at Elwynd, awaiting his lead. I thought of the hermit's glen he had told me of in the vale between here and Castle Rhyweth. But that was not the way we went.

Instead, we turned our horses inland, and they picked their way along a rocky path that took us upward and above the wooded descent where the small farms around the village clustered.

"There be quarries yonder," said Elwynd, pointing east. I had noted the many stone fences and cottages, and reasoned that the granite and slate must be plentiful hereabouts.

"My father was born here," I said. "In Pendeen."

Elwynd did not acknowledge my comment, but lifted his chin. After some moments, he said, "Did he speak of it then?"

I shook my head. "Not as much as I would have liked to hear. Have you ever traveled far from here?" I asked him.

He shook his head slowly. "I crossed the Tamar once, into Devon. Lord Rhyweth pressed me into service as coachman at one time. I drove him and his sister to the Earl of Stratton. But that was only once. A Cornishman doesn't like to be away from home much. I've no desire to go anywhere else."

I stared at him curiously, half admiring, half puzzling this tie to the land of which he spoke. I loved New York, but it was hard to feel my roots in such a city.

We were in a very strange place now, and we had left the fields and sea behind. All around were large granite boulders and tors—high rocky crags.

"You must stay away from the bogs there," he told me, pointing to lower ground that looked like smooth low-lying pasture with a few reedy streams.

"It's nothing but sinking marsh. Put your weight on the ground there and it sags beneath you, oozing water. Dangerous place for stray sheep or cattle. A horse can easily twist his foot. There've been many people who've been lost up there. Some return, some don't."

"There, you see." He pointed to a mass of bones bleached white. "A sheep strayed there imprisoned for the winter. Most likely the carcass fed the fox or buzzard."

I shivered. I thought of the missing girls Gwynneth and my aunt had told me about, and wondered if they had met some horrible fate in that place, but I refrained from asking.

I gave one last look at the soggy, treacherous place, glad that Elwynd had pointed it out to me, for I would surely avoid it in the future. We turned the horses back toward higher ground, and Elwynd rode beside me.

"Do most of the villagers make their living by fishing?" I asked.

"Aye. That and the tin. But many of the mines are closed now."

"And Lord Rhyweth's land, is it very good for farming?"

"The tenants get by, but much of it's too rocky, no good for farming."

He gave me another sidelong glance. "Lord Rhyweth's no gentleman farmer, not in the true sense."

"Oh?"

Elwynd was silent, but he had aroused my curiosity.

"Do you mean because he hasn't the knack for farming or because he isn't interested in it?"

He took some time, and when he spoke it was not with the answer. "Lord Rhyweth's a man to stay away from."

I sat up straighter, half frightened by his words, half afraid Elwynd was in accord with my thinking, knew my thoughts. That he might be at all able to perceive that anything had happened between Lord Rhyweth and myself embarrassed me.

"What? Why do you say that?"

Again, the sidelong look before he spoke, his words low but impinging on me. "He's not like ordinary men."

His words chilled me to the bone. Still, from somewhere within me defensiveness arose.

"Perhaps not, but what is wrong with being different?"

"Just that for someone like you, he is best left alone."

I tried to pass it off lightly, covering my reactions with nonchalance, trying not to give away the burning sensation I felt.

"You must mean that he is a solitary man. But he told me that himself. Perhaps he still mourns his late wife."

It was a good thing that the sharp wind had lent color to my cheeks, for I hoped Elwynd was able to evaluate my expression less carefully.

"If he mourns his wife," he said, "he has strange ways of showing it."

"Whatever do you mean?"

The wind whipped around us, and we led the horses nearer a tor that rose from the plain.

"There are rumors about Lord Rhyweth, and his sister, too. Your aunt knows them."

89

"My aunt does not indulge in gossip."

We had stopped under a cliff, and Elwynd gazed about him, his eyes narrow as if he were watching for game to scrabble out from between the rocks and dash for the low scrub.

"He doesn't live like other men," he finally said. "He doesn't sleep in his bed at night."

His words were strange, yet I forced a laugh at him. "He composes music at night. He told me so himself."

I rambled on in explanation, even though I knew that it was not Elwynd I was trying to convince, but myself. In some twisted way I was trying to justify my actions of two nights ago still feeling guilty with my secret. My words and emotions raced out of control, as if they had a life of their own, making me stumble on.

"He said he turned to music because of the sadness of his wife's illness and death. He works at night, when all is quiet. Perhaps it is easier for him to concentrate that way."

Elwynd gazed hard at me now, the glint in his eyes making me feel uneasy. I was also oddly aware of his strength and of our position, alone on the moor. I must have been affected by the strangeness of the stark, lonely setting. I was not used to such surroundings, or the things of which Elwynd was telling me. At that moment, my own Cornish blood came alive and I understood, if only dimly, something of the meaning behind Elwynd's words.

"He may have given you reasons for why he works at night," Elwynd said. "But you cannot know all about his wife's illness. No doctor ever diagnosed it properly."

My eyes widened as I sensed some of the meaning that he was trying to convey to me, and yet the rationed part of my mind refused to comprehend it. "Surely Dr. Pearce saw her," I said.

"Aye, he did. And other specialists traveled here from London. But none of them agreed as to what was the matter with her." He glanced into space again, his look brooding. "But people in these parts guessed at it."

He turned his mount, and I followed. I wanted to pursue his line of conversation, for I felt confused. Somehow I resented his insinuations. It was obvious that he did not like Lord Rhyweth, or that he feared him, and yet he would not come right out and say it. Perhaps it was mere envy, I decided. For Lord Rhyweth was titled, lived comfortably, could do what he pleased. Did not often men of such stations inspire envy in those who were not so fortunate?

However, he would say no more. On the other side of the tor we stopped in a place protected from the wind to eat the lunch Winifred had packed. Elwynd helped me down from my side-saddle. We spread a blanket on level ground and Elwynd brought the satchel from the saddle where he had tied it. He stretched out on the blanket while I unwrapped and sliced the bread and cheese. We ate silently.

"And you," he said after he had satisfied himself. "What do you want in Cornwall?"

His question took me aback. I was slow in answering. "I wanted to see the land of my father's."

"And now that you've seen it?"

"I don't know. I need to stay awhile before I find out if I'm suited for it."

He gave me his easy smile. "And if you are?" He ripped another hunk of bread off with his teeth.

I found it hard to answer him, as if he were invading my privacy. "I don't know yet. I have my father's business to think about."

"Then you've no need to stay here and work as hard as your aunt does."

"I might stay because of that. She's been alone too

long."

His look turned inward and I remembered that she had raised him. "Aye, that she has."

I felt a kinship with him, if only because of what he had shared with my aunt.

"I know she appreciates your company," I said, wanting in some way to reach out to him.

"You don't need to explain," he said. "You're kin. It makes a difference."

"It oughtn't. You know her better."

"She is a good woman, better than most."

I hoped I had not offended him. I did not want to seem a rival in any way. We finished eating, washing the food down with a flask of wine, then we packed up and remounted for it was getting late. The wind had not lessened when we reached the top of the ridge, the sea in the distance looked rough. I thought surely it would rain tonight.

We reached the fields behind my aunt's cottage and approached the road, going silently along the rutted track until we came to the barn where Elwynd got down and then helped me dismount. I was about to hand him the reins, when he stopped me.

"The mount is yours to use while you're here," he said.

"Oh?" I did not know I would get to keep Blackie while I was here. "You must thank Lord Rhyweth for me."

We stabled the horse in the barn, and after I had hung up the tack, Elwynd walked with me into the yard. I did not see Winifred about, but there was smoke coming from the chimney, so I assumed that she had begun to make the evening meal.

We paused outside the cottage door, breathing the damp air. I was aware of so many smells here, and I marveled at how close to nature one was in a place like this.

"Will you come in?" I asked Elwynd, but he shook his head, his eyes on me. His final words harked back to what had gone before, words I was not sure I wanted to hear.

"Did you not know," he said, "that Lord Rhyweth never sets foot inside church or chapel?"

His words startled me. "I—I did not know that. But it is no concern of mine."

"Nor does he eat much."

"I know, I—" I caught myself. The remark seemed irrelevant, and yet I remembered that I had witnessed this very fact when I had dined with Lord Rhyweth myself.

Elwynd stepped closer. There was no mistaking the warning in his words now. "You should be careful not to wander outside at night," he said. "A wolf has been seen howling on the moors. It travels alone."

I backed away a step toward the cottage door.

"My—my aunt told me of the wolf," I stuttered. "I will be careful. But what has all this to do with Lord Rhyweth?"

Elwynd stared hard at me. "You know perhaps of the village girls who've been abducted from here?"

My heart began to pound in my chest as the words came home to me. "I've heard there were girls who were missing, but I've heard of no proof that they were abducted."

"I'd beware if I were you, miss. More than one of them was seen meeting Lord Rhyweth before they disappeared."

Beware, the same word used in the mysterious letter to my father. My words came out a whisper. "Surely you do not accuse Lord Rhyweth?"

Elwynd did not answer, he only grilled me with his blue eyes. Then he turned and mounted his horse. I had the irrational urge to run after him insisting he answer me. I could not believe that he was implicating Lord Rhyweth in whatever had happened to the mysteriously missing girls, but that was exactly what he was doing.

He faced me once more before riding off, his horse dancing sideways. "Beware. Lord Rhyweth has many strange habits," he said to me. "Such men do not die."

I could only stare after him, puzzled and astonished as he turned and rode down that path that led to the rutted road for Castle Rhyweth, for I did not know what he meant.

The cottage door opened, and Rufus bounded out to meet me, obviously pleased that I had returned. I knelt to pet him and let him lick my face.

"Did you miss me?" I said to my dog. "Good boy."

I gave him a good scratching behind the ears, and he leapt and danced in front of me as we returned to the cottage, and I thought how glad I was for his companionship, more so now than ever since we had come to this strange land where I seemed to understand no one and had somehow gotten thrown into a village full of fears and strange goings on.

I did not want to think there was anything much to the stories of the missing village girls, but something at the back of my mind stirred, a tiny recognition that there might be some truth to Elwynd's warnings. Elwynd's words rang a bell deep within my memory. It was not a clear memory, more like a myth he had touched on.

That evening after we had eaten our simple meal, Winifred and I sat by the fire which burned the smoky sweet moorland turf cut for fuel. Winifred showed me the wool she had washed. It was a dingy grayish buff color. She worked quickly with the carder, dragging one card through the tangled mass until the strands lay

94

in the same direction. Then she loosened the wool from the carder and rolled it off the cards, ready to spin.

She handed me the roll of wool and showed me how to pull a few strands of the wool and twist it tight. I drew the fibers from one end, twisting it into strands with which Winifred threaded the spinning wheel, and as I held the wool, continuing to draw the fibers from the tuft, she began to spin. It was then that I brought up what Elwynd had told me. Winifred did not meet my gaze, continuing to spin.

"I've never been one to indulge in foolish village gossip," she finally said. "But I have heard the rumors that there was some connection between one or more of the girls and Lord Rhyweth. But who can say it's true? I tell you only for your own good. It is not unlikely that his eye might turn toward a comely young woman like yourself. You must be careful."

My face warmed. If it were true that one of the village girls had become his mistress and then had later mysteriously disappeared, did it not bring the matter closer to home than Winifred could realize? I could not tell her how shamefully I had acted with Lord Rhyweth when we had dined together only two nights ago. I had found him irresistible, had I not? Was I no better than an ignorant peasant who could easily be overwhelmed by the enchantment of such a man?

I pulled the wool furiously, waiting for my temples to stop throbbing, trying to think about the situation reasonably. With no wife to love, I could see easily how Lord Rhyweth might turn to a handsome village maiden to satisfy his appetite. Did he not allude to that very appetite the night he had dined with me? I knew such arrangements were not uncommon. Being brought up by my father in New York, I was not as protected as were other young women my age, and I was aware of the habits men had, especially virile men like Lord Rhyweth with dark handsome looks and charms that could set a girl's blood on fire.

I was embarrassed by the emotions such thoughts stirred in me, for even though ashamed of my actions, there was still something delicious about the memory of his touch. The warnings I had received were not misplaced, for I could not allow such a thing to happen again. However, I had little fear of that. I was living here with my aunt now, and would have no reason to return to the castle. There would be no cause for a man of Lord Rhyweth's station to have business with the niece of one of his tenants.

I realized that we had been silent for some time, and perhaps my aunt suspected that I had been mulling over her words. Though unspoken, she also may have understood something of my feelings, for I felt she had that Cornish knack of perceiving in special ways.

"I will heed your warning, Aunt," I said. "I will keep my distance from Lord Rhyweth. Though I do find it hard to believe that he is actually a dangerous man."

" 'Twould be better still were you to return to New York," she said. "Though I hate to say it, it isn't safe here. Things aren't what they used to be. You'd best take care."

As usual, when told what to do, my resolve to the contrary hardened.

"I've determined to stay. There's still the matter of my father's letter. Have you no idea who might have written it?"

She pursed her lips, concentrating on the clockwise motion of the wheel. "No matter what you do, Rhionna, it won't bring Leslie back. It might be best to let the matter lie."

I frowned. "I know it won't bring him back. But I

have to satisfy myself. I want to know if someone wanted my father dead and the reason why."

She stopped the treadle and fixed me with her gaze. "And what would you do then?"

I met her look, but I could not find the answer within myself. "I . . . I don't know exactly. I don't know what I could do. But whoever wrote that letter was trying to warn him. I need to know why."

"There you see. Then there's no reason to look for something that can be of no concern to you."

I did not entirely agree with her and yet I could not find it within myself to argue. I had great clumps of wool on my lap and it took some time to straighten them and separate the strands before Winifred could spin again. After a while, the fire burned down, and finally we prepared for bed.

I lay on my bed, staring out the glass-paned window at the moon until my lids got heavy. Then Lord Rhyweth's face came to me again. I was not sure where waking thought left off and dreams began. But I walked with him on the moor, while somewhere distant, the wolf cried. It seemed the more I tried to turn from him, the more he drew me near. His fingers reached out to caress my skin, and my hair loosened and flew behind me in the breezes. Then he lowered his lips to my white throat as I arched myself toward him.

Chapter 7

The next day was Sunday, and we attended chapel in the village. I put on the day dress that Morwenna had lent me and wound my hair in a plait round my head, covering it with a poke bonnet that my aunt had saved. Though it was quite out of fashion, I knew that would not matter.

Elwynd came for us, dressed in his Sunday black suit. He harnessed my aunt's horse, Nedda, to the wagon. Then we hitched up our skirts and climbed up to the seat. Elwynd rode his horse, while Winifred drove the wagon, handling the reins with ease. When I complimented her on her driving, she chuckled.

"Nedda knows the way. The wagon's never been outside the parish, and then mostly to the village and back."

I returned her smile. "Yes, but when we reach the village we must get to chapel. Does she know it's Sunday?"

The road wound down through the fields, past a few other cottages until we rounded the hill, the road lined with stone fences on either side, and we approached the village. Other villagers in their Sunday best were making their way along the road, and some raised their caps as we passed.

We passed the smithy's, the public house, and several small shops. Here the cobbled main street fell steeply to the harbor, the ground floor of some of the cottages on a level with the roof of the one next.

We turned south. The chapel lay at the end of the village on a spit of land that rose toward a copse. My eye was drawn to the markers, some of which must surely have been left from Saxon times, crosses with broad elaborately carved shafts. Celtic crosses with arms enclosed in a circle gave witness to even earlier settlers.

The chapel itself was of the familiar granite quarried nearby, with its slate roof, simple and plain as the rugged landscape that had begot it. But the perpendicular windows had fine leaded stained glass. Gnarled trees guarded the cemetery behind. We tied Nedda and followed the others inside, taking seats on one of the hard pews. There were very few adornments inside, though the sun shining in the tall arched windows fell on the altar in a lovely way.

I knew little of Methodism, though I had heard of the great John Wesley who had traveled through Cornwall in the middle of the last century, shaking people into a spirited sense of their sins as well as their worth. And there was still something of this in the sermon we heard this day.

"Repent, repent," the preacher entreated his flock. The lake of brimstone awaited those who would not hear the Word. But for those who put away the horror of sin, confessed their iniquities, there could be mercy and forgiveness in the everlasting arms.

But the sermon lacked inspiration. Hellfire was in evidence, but forgiveness and neighbourly love less so. I glanced sidelong at the sober faces of the respectable villagers around me. There were no faces aglow with zeal here. "Thou shalt," had become "Thou shalt not."

I thought again of my father's view of religion as something that evolved over the great periods of history. I was thankful for his enlightenment, and the many fascinating things he had taught me in this vein, for surely he had been before his time when it had come to the common man's philosophy.

Then another thought penetrated the repetitive words of the sour-faced minister in the pulpit. *Lord Rhyweth does not set foot in church or chapel.* I could see why, if the only religion he knew was this hopeless. It made me curious again about the man I had vowed I would never see again. He was not only a man of much magnetism, but perhaps a man of depth. Did he not compose music? Perhaps he too had given some thought to matters of the mind and spirit, of religion and philosophy.

Most men did not discuss such things with women, and I was sure he would not choose to do so with me. And since my father had gone, there was no one I could turn to for such discussion. I sighed, rather louder than I meant to, and immediately shrank back into my pew, hoping no one had noticed. For the first time I considered my aunt's persuasion that I should leave Cornwall, and in one thing I knew she might be right.

Coming from a cosmopolitan city I was used to rubbing shoulders with people of many walks of life. Now I was limited to peasants in a provincial, isolated place, people set in their ways and beliefs. Would I not find them too narrow? Only time would tell, for I still had much to learn of them. I still had to find out if there was any merit to my suspicions. Only after that could I return to my father's business in New York. Or perhaps go home and marry, if I found someone with whom I thought I could live.

My thoughts became more and more introspective,

so that when the service was over, I was glad to step outside and once again breathe the moist sea air as the rest of the congregation poured through the doors. I recognized many of the servants from Castle Rhyweth, evidence that indeed there was no service held in the chapel I had glimpsed there.

A shyly smiling curly-headed figure who was dressed in a blue print dress with white lace at collar and cuffs emerged from the crowd and came to greet me.

"Gwynneth," I said, taking her hands. "You look lovely. It is good to see you."

"And you, miss. I hope you and your aunt are getting on well."

"Yes, very well, though I'm sure we could use some company now and then. You must pay us a visit on your day off."

She seemed flattered by the invitation. "I will do that, miss, if you really want me to. I hardly ever have a place to go on my day off except to take a walk along the cliff road."

"Then you must come to us. My aunt would be pleased."

Elwynd was watching us from some distance. Gwynneth became aware of his stare at the same time and looked his way, then turned back, a blush on her cheek.

"Well, I must be getting back, miss. I promise I'll come to see you."

Elwynd's eyes followed Gwynneth as she joined a few of the others who set off on foot back through the village. I suddenly recognized the emotion I saw in his eyes and turned away in embarrassment. His lust was evident. Was I so quick to recognize that emotion because I myself was guilty of it? I made a point of keeping my back to him, for I did not want him to know I had guessed his secret.

Sunday was a day of rest. We would do no work today, but could have no amusement either. There would be no reading of any book but the Bible. So when we returned to the cottage, I told my aunt that I might take Rufus for a walk to the hermit's cell, and I put on the simpler dress I had been using for work and a pair of sturdy boots from my aunt's trunk.

The day was fine. That is, it was fine by Cornwall's standards, for I was quickly learning that even though the sun might be high at the middle of the day, that was no reason a cold wind might not blow in that evening, bringing rain behind it.

Telling my aunt good-bye, Rufus and I set off down the track we had traveled when we'd first arrived at the cottage, and unconsciously I headed toward the little stone marker that pointed the way to the hermit's glen. I had promised my aunt that I would be back before nightfall, but I could see no difficulty with that. From what Elwynd had said, the place where the hermit had dwelled was only a short distance, though probably somewhat of a climb. Rufus bounded ahead of me, stopping every few feet to investigate a new smell. Already he was accumulating dirt and twigs in his coat and I could see that I would have a fine job of brushing him when we got back.

I found the marker by the road and turned into the trees. The path wound upward with comparative ease at first, coming out on a ledge where I looked back to the sea, and even when I could not see it, I could hear its waves splashing up the beaches far below. Then the ascent turned steeper, the cliffs jutting out on either side, so that my heart began to pound from the exertion, my limbs to strain.

At last the sound of a rushing stream replaced the pounding of the far away surf, and both Rufus and I

102

egan to crane forward to get a glimpse of it. The
water looked so inviting that I left the path and made
my way to where it was rushing over a little falls. My
oot slipped on a rock surface, but I caught hold of a
ree limb, thus saving myself from a spill.

"Get back, Rufus. It's slippery here." Though Rufus
was sure-footed, I did not want to see him spilling
down those rocks.

Dark cliffs towered above us now, and I could see the
narrow gorge that impelled the water, white with foam
as it tumbled over its stony bed, down the canyon to
where it plunged to the open sea. As I went higher, the
rees closed in, growing thicker and more dense, so
hat it was impossible to leave the path now. The air
was oppressive, heavy and damp. I took the stepping
stones that forded the stream at intervals, but some
must have become dislodged, and once I had to leap
he stream itself, with the help of an overhanging
oranch.

Something told me I should turn back, for the going
was more difficult than I expected, and it was taking
me longer than I had planned to reach the top. But
Rufus seemed to pay the ascent no mind. He slipped
and slid off the stepping stones, splashing into the cold
water and coming out on the opposite bank with a look
of glee. But I was city-bred and not used to such a
climb. I told myself it was only a matter of strengthen-
ing weak muscles. Before long I would be able to
match the country folk in exertion.

We left the stream behind as the path led on upward
toward the waterfall. I had to step carefully now to
avoid rotting stinking trunks. What path there was was
overlaid with briars. And it was darker here in the
woods than it was in the open. Despair set in. Yet the
path led still upward following the sound of the falls,
which were nearer now.

At last I rounded a point and looked straight down, drawing in my breath at the sight which opened below me. Water rushed down in a solid white sheet. There was no cove at the bottom to receive the fall, no spit of shore. Rather, the full surge of the Atlantic swept against shore far below me, turbulent and gray, like the rocks that had spelled disaster for the ship that had brought me here.

Getting my second wind, I went farther up, leaving the foliage and the falls below, and finally came out above the falls on a barren plane. This was where the hermit had meditated years ago. The ceaseless sound of the water must have been the same. The tumbling of foam into the sea sounded distant now. Here no gulls perched to silently answer one's speculations, no sheep grazed on the headlands beyond. It was truly a lonely place, full of the indifference of nature. Large boulders abounded, and it made me more curious as to the inspiration the hermit had received here.

But a trail was still marked, if you could call it that, and a little farther on I came to the remains of the cottage and envisioned the two women that Elwynd had told me about. Though the story was probably mostly legend, it was not hard to imagine two women living here who seldom got down to the village. Still, it made me wonder how they lived. How did they get supplies? For there seemed to be no other way down except the way I had come up.

I heard a tumble of rock behind me and Rufus began to bark. Though it was still light, the loneliness of the setting and the apprehension that it would take us some time to get down had set my nerves on edge.

I knelt "Quiet Rufus."

He quieted, but continued a low growl. "Come," I said. "We must start back or else we'll never get down from this place before it is dark."

104

The thought of spending the night on this barren plateau gave me the shivers. I looked about, seeing no movement at first. Then a hare darted out from a rock and dashed across the ground, and Rufus barked again. The Cornish believed that if a hare did not contain the spirit of a dead man or woman then it was the metamorphosis of a witch. And in this strange place, I could almost believe it.

We crossed the boulder field and started back down the path, and I was thankful that it was clearly marked, for nothing looked the same now. A fallen trunk that I thought I surely would remember was not there. There seemed to be fewer stepping stones than before, and I felt my arms shaking as I clung to branches, praying that they would not break as I swung myself across the little stream. More than once I heard something that sounded like a footfall far above me, but with the noise of the rushing stream and my own pounding heart I could not tell.

Once, timidly, I called out, "Hello, who's there?"

But as I counted the seconds while I waited, I knew I hoped no one would answer, that the odd premonition that someone was watching me was all my imagination, which was easily stirred up in a place of such great superstition.

We came to the promontory where I had cautioned Rufus earlier, and I tried to tell myself that the way would go easier now. But even as I set my foot on a large flat rock the cracking of boughs above startled me. Then there was a woosh of air, and something hit me on the left shoulder. I cried out and pitched forward. My hands slid across the rocks as I tumbled down the path. Rufus ran toward the woods barking, but then turned and came to me, whining, his nose next to my face, as he was obviously concerned that I had hurt myself.

My hands were scraped, and I was winded, but after lying there for a moment, I decided I was not seriously hurt. I raised myself to my knees.

"It's all right, Rufus. I'm all right."

I looked about at what could have knocked me off balance, and I saw a broken branch lying on the rocks where I had fallen. I got up and limped back to examine it. If I had had my wits about me and if I had known what to look for, I might have been able to ascertain if the branch had broken of its own accord or if it had been torn. But I was too frightened and bruised to give it much attention.

I turned and hobbled down the path, Rufus at my heels. Panic now filled me at the lateness of the day and my promise to return to the cottage before nightfall. The going was difficult, and only the fact that the path was so well marked through the dense wood kept me from losing my way.

When we reached the bottom and came out of the trees, I collapsed to the ground, my heart pounding as I panted in relief. Here was the stone marker, there the rutted road. Though there was still a ways to go, and dusk was closing in, I knew the way from there.

"Oh, Rufus," I said, hugging his shaggy head. "We had quite a scare, didn't we? But It's all over now."

I got unsteadily to my feet and walked quickly along the road. I don't know why I should have felt safer there. If someone had been following me or had wanted to harm me, they could still do so here, for the road was isolated. Soon, however we came out of the woods, and then I could see the cottage, still a distance away. However, with familiarity comes relief, and already I was looking back on my mishap with a more objective view.

I should have left earlier, for such a climb would have taken longer than if the same distance had lain on a straight path. In my panic I hadn't taken the time to examine the branch that had fallen on me. In all likelihood, it had been partially broken, or perhaps an animal had climbed on it, sending it crashing down on my head. Rufus had most likely wanted to give chase to the creature, but his first loyalty had been to me.

I was not fully convinced that I was right, but some form of self-preservation made me think of the most logical explanation. Something about the way the day had gone still bothered me, and it was not until I lay in bed that night, the moonlight spilling in the window across the foot of my bed that I thought of it.

Surely Winifred had known how far the hermit's cell had been, and yet she had not objected when I had set out so late in the morning. Why had she not warned me that the way was difficult and far, and that I ought to go on a day when I could start earlier than on Sunday, when I had had to attend services first?

The next few days took on a comfortable routine. I put the matter of my accident aside, telling Winifred that I had scraped my hands when I had fallen, missing one of the stepping stones over the stream. For my abrasions, she gave me a soothing unguent made from the bark of wild plum roots and made me wear work gloves so as not to scrape them further, and we said no more about it.

On Thursday, my aunt and I harnessed Nedda to the wagon and made the journey to St. Ives, for it was past time I took care of the business I needed to attend to there. A damp cold hung over the land that morning, and as we got into the wagon, I pulled the cloak Morwenna had lent me tightly around my shoulders. At least the woolen stockings of my aunt's kept my feet warm inside my boots.

The track led through a rough landscape with low scrub. Below us in the folds between the hills, a few dwellings hid among the trees, and sheep on the highland stopped their grazing to watch us pass. The sea seemed never far away, for we could either see or hear it during most of our journey.

My aunt pointed out the lighthouse that should have directed us to St. Ives the night of the storm, and not far from that a mine that was still producing some tin.

At length we came to the outcropping of greenstone, contrasting with the ever present granite. The town of St. Ives had been built on the greenstone. From our approach, I could see that the harbor was overcrowded with sailing vessels of all kinds, as well as what looked to me like several hundred fishing boats. Fishermen's cottages built of great blocks of granite huddled together in narrow alleyways. And we were assailed with the strong smell of fish.

"That's the pilchard cellars, and the smoke kilns where the herrings are kippered," said Winifred.

And she pointed to a large building that housed the net factory. We came into town, turned into a cobbled street, and found space for our wagon. Then my aunt led me to the telegraph office where I wrote out a telegram to Henry Lawson, in whose capable hands I had left my father's business.

Arrived safely Pendeen. Shipwreck took all belongings. Please wire funds to St. Ives Bank & Trust Co. Advise Elsa all is well. Rhionna.

I also mailed a personal letter to Elsa, but since that would take several weeks to get there, I didn't want her to worry in the meantime.

Next we entered a dress shop where I was fortunate in that several ready-mades fit me well enough and I chose a tailored riding habit in dark green. When Winifred explained my situation to the shop owner,

108

she was only too anxious to let me have the dresses on credit.

"Don't worry child," the woman told me. "Take these so you won't have to go about naked. You'll pay me when your money comes."

"Thank you so much," I said. "You are very helpful."

We selected some high-top boots that buttoned up the side, and my eye fell on a pair of white satin slippers beaded with pearls. It was an extravagance, and I was sure I would not need them for working at the cottage, but they were so lovely I could hardly put them down. I felt a great longing for something pretty in addition to all the practical things I was getting for my wardrobe, so I added them to my purchases.

A selection of underclothing completed our errands, and by the time we were finished, the back of the wagon was quite full of packages. We were hungry by then, and my aunt led me to a small tea shop on a side street just up from the pubs that lined the harbor. The smell of fish was even stronger here, but the shop was cozy and the tea and muffins delicious.

I enjoyed the hustle and bustle of the busy port and regretted turning our wagon around and setting our faces once again toward Pendeen Village, which was truly isolated by comparison. But I had things to wear now and would not have to go about in borrowed clothes, and soon we would have funds with which to buy extra things that we needed. Though I knew Winifred would never take charity, surely she would let me contribute something to her household in exchange for letting me stay with her.

I set my mind for the routine I knew awaited me, and though the outing had refreshed me, I was ready to tuck myself into bed in the cottage that night, Rufus, huddled on top of the covers, next to my feet.

Though my muscles still ached from work I was unused to, I rather enjoyed throwing myself into the tasks that needed doing everyday when one had to live so self-sufficiently. I had promised to forget about Lord Rhyweth and his castle, but the more I tried to forget him, the more my thoughts seemed to turn in that direction and the more my eyes strayed toward the horizon, watching as clouds descended about the castle, or as mist rose up around it.

It was with a great deal of restrained curiosity that I looked up one day to see Jonas standing at the cottage door. My aunt was sweeping ashes from the brick oven, so I went to meet him.

"Hello, Jonas," I said. "Have you come from the castle?" I looked helplessly at Winifred, hardly knowing what to expect from the hunchback. She straightened from her task but when I turned back to him he wordlessly handed me an envelope with a thick seal on it.

My fingers caressed the heavy vellum, but I held it out for Winifred. She took it, then handed it back to me.

"You open it," she said.

I did so with shaking hands, and as I read the even scrawl on the folded paper, my pulse began to quicken. I could not help my excitement.

"Lord Rhyweth has invited both of us to supper tomorrow evening," I said.

Winifred looked straight at me then toward the window. "We should not go."

My heart fell, and I glanced at Jonas, thinking I would have to send him away, the invitation refused. He must have seen that we were undecided, and so he turned his back and went a few paces into the yard and sat down on a wooden crate.

110

"See," I said, trying not to sound like a spoiled child, "he's going to wait for our reply."

I could see Winifred's determined expression, and while conflict ripped me, I knew I could do little about the decision. I had promised not to go to the castle again, and yet there were reasons I could justify going. Somehow I found the words I needed.

"Aunt Winifred, would it not be best to go? I have not had a chance to speak with Lord Rhyweth about my father's death. Perhaps he knows something that might help me. I know you think it's foolish to ask but . . ." I was kneading my woolen skirt nervously, still trying not to let my true feelings show.

Winifred seemed to be struggling with herself as well. It was almost as if behind her resolve to keep me from the dangerous Lord Rhyweth lay some sort of recognition of the spirit of youth. I felt in that instant as if she knew what I felt, that in some way she had experienced these turbulent emotions in her own past, though at the time I could not begin to understand it. Her words bore me out.

She gripped the back of a chair with her hand. "I curse the fact that you will not listen to my advice and return to America." She turned imploring eyes on me. "I am torn inside. Of course you must know how good it is to have my niece near me. You bring gladness into these mournful surroundings."

Her words gave me hope, and I looked into bright blue eyes that belied her age. "Oh, dear Aunt, do not send me away. For I too have joy in being near you. If there is danger, is it not best to discover its source and banish it rather than to run away from it?" My words were brave even if my feelings at that moment were not.

I saw her tremble and knew that while she wanted to refuse Lord Rhyweth's invitation and send me away,

she would not. Neither would she disappoint my en
treaties. She seemed to give up her posture of defense

"Very well. I see I cannot hold you back. I suppose
we shall be safe enough going there together. And I
will make sure Elwynd knows of it."

"Yes, of course. Everyone will know of it. There car
be no danger."

We quickly got out a sheet of white paper tha
Winifred kept in her small writing desk. We got out
pen and ink and I sat down to write. In my best hand,
I scrawled a message. *Misses Winifred and Rhionna Fow
ley will be pleased to accept Lord Rhyweth's invitation to din
tomorrow evening.* Then I folded it and hurried out tc
where Jonas sat in the sun.

"Here, Jonas," I said, handing him the folded note.
"Please take this to your master. It is our reply."

He nodded, stuck the note inside his shirt, and then
without looking up at me, lumbered off. I watched
him go, my heart full of the pity I had felt when I had
first learned of his acquaintance with Lord Rhyweth,
though I had trouble gazing on his deformed body
without flinching. I did not want to believe that such
looks denoted an evil spirit within, but I could easily
see how those with a bent toward superstition might
think so.

I could not help but wonder how he could hoist his
crippled form onto the wagon seat. Then I saw that the
wagon was equipped with steps that hung down from
the driver's side and guessed that Lord Rhyweth had
installed these for his faithful servant.

I went back in, finding it hard to suppress my
smiles. Already my step was lighter. At least it would
be a change of scene, and I felt I deserved a reward for
all my hard work of late. I looked at my cracked hands
and broken nails and determined to put something on
them this evening to help heal them.

"There," I said to Winifred. "It's done."

"So it is, my child, so it is." She sighed.

She had a faraway look in her eye, as if she were herself envisioning Castle Rhyweth, and I suddenly wondered if she'd been there before as an invited guest, though I did not see how.

"Perhaps you are right, Rhionna," she said. "One listens too much to village gossip that may mean nothing. I have always regarded myself as a practical woman. And haven't I known the Wyckes all my life? How quickly the people here forget Lord Rhyweth's generosity in times of hardship and the way he and his father Arthur always aided those in need, not pressing for rents in bad years, but sharing the hardships."

She nodded as if convincing herself. "Yes, it is very quickly that we forget such kindnesses."

Her words made me curious about my aunt's relationship with her landlords, and I promised myself that I would ask more about it when the time was right. For now I was glad she had changed her mind about the supper. I went immediately to my room and took the new slippers out of the trunk. To me they seemed like magic slippers, ready to make my feet dance and I was only too anxious to wear them.

Chapter 8

The very next morning, Winifred did not rise from her bed. "It's the dizziness," she told me when I went to see what I could do. "It sets on me sometimes when I least expect it.

"Is there no remedy?" I asked, feeling great concern.

She shook her head. "Help me up a little. I'll just rest here, though there's no telling how long it'll last."

I fluffed the pillows up behind her. "Shall I send for the doctor?"

"No. There's naught he can do. Though Hannelore Treleaven sometimes brews me a drink from some of her herbs that help steady me."

"I'll get her then."

"Elwynd can do that. He'll come this morning. Tell him to fetch Hannelore and for her to bring the herbs for my dizzy spells."

When Elwynd came to do the heavy chores, I sent him on his errand and then did what I could to make Winifred comfortable. By midday she was little better, and I realized that now we would not be able to go to the castle for dinner.

"Shall I send a message to the castle telling them that we will not be able to go to dinner?" I asked Winifred after serving her some soup.

She shook her head slowly. "Though I am loathe for you to go alone, I will not go back on my word. I can hardly allow my illness to spoil your evening. It would not be fair to you after I agreed that you could go."

"Oh, Aunt. Do not concern yourself with me. There will be another time."

Though my words were appropriate, I already felt my anticipation mounting. I hated to admit how much I looked forward to returning to the castle. And I was afraid to protest too strongly for fear she would agree with me and say I should not go. And so it was decided that I should go and take Rufus for protection.

I put on the velvet gown I had worn to dinner before, adding the new slippers, and for jewelry, not a cameo this time but a ruby brooch of my aunt's.

"This is beautiful," I exclaimed when she showed it to me.

She had kept it in a beautifully carved wooden box by her bed, and I knew that it must have been one of her special treasures. Indeed, I was curious to know where she had gotten it, for I knew that her situation would never have allowed her to buy it for herself. I wondered if perhaps my father had sent it.

"You must treasure this," I said, watching the light glance off its surface, enhancing its fiery depths. "Was it a gift?"

Her smile had a touch of reminiscence in it as she said, "Yes, it was a gift. A very long time ago."

Something about the way she said it made me refrain from asking from whom the gift had come. If she wanted me to know, she would tell me.

"How does it look?" I asked, as I pinned it to my bodice. She looked me over from head to toe, and then nodded, smiling more to herself than to me.

"Lovely, very lovely. I am sure Lord Rhyweth will be pleased."

I kissed her good-bye and turned to go. I tried to still the beating of my heart as I wrapped a heavy woolen shawl about me and stepped outside at the appointed time. Lord Rhyweth had sent his carriage, a polished black brougham with curved glass front window. The driver, in black livery, introduced himself as Malcolm, and held the door for me, making me feel quite the lady as he helped me in. Rufus leapt up to the box to sit next to Malcolm.

The clouds were moving slowly across the sky, and from the puffs of wind and the strong smell of rain, I could tell that a storm was on its way. As we rumbled toward the castle, I was again filled with the sense that I was drawn toward it in some mysterious way that was beyond my control. I clung to the strap, feeling almost guilty to be sitting on the plush velvet seat, gazing out the glass at the moonlight above and the flickering brass lamps affixed to the box.

As had happened before, in the lamplit courtyard of the castle, dressed for the elegant entertainment that I was sure awaited me, I felt more reckless that I would have in the light of day.

Malcolm came around to open the door to me, and I got down and was greeted by Godreven.

"Good evening, miss," he said in his sober, formal way, his eyes never glancing below my face. "You are expected."

"Thank you, Godreven. Would you please have Gwynneth give Rufus something to eat in the kitchen?"

"Very well, Miss Fowley. Andrew will take the dog to the kitchen." He issued the order to the groom who appeared, and Rufus went off with him.

Godreven led me in, and I followed him along the drafty halls to the formal parlor. I was announced, and when I entered the parlor, I was strongly aware of the foolish beating of my heart when I saw Lord Rhyweth, his dark looks as handsome as they had been before, even more so. There was another gentleman present, a tall

116

blond man with brilliant blue eyes. He was dressed in cutaway with satin lapels and red cummerbund.

Morwenna greeted me with outstretched hand and cool appraising gaze.

"The dress looks well on you," she said. "I am glad."

My cheeks colored. "I do so appreciate your allowing me to wear it. I will gladly return the dress as soon as my funds have arrived from New York."

But she waved this away. "There is no need. I have more gowns that I can wear. That color was never good for me in any case."

"But it is quite fetching on Rhionna."

I blushed at Lord Rhyweth's comment, glad now that Morwenna and the other gentleman were with us. It enforced a protective formality that saved me from struggling with how I should behave after my most embarrassing encounter with his lordship on the only other evening I had dined with him.

"Thank you, my lord," I managed. "I am glad you like it."

"And what is this?" He came nearer and gazed on the ruby, the fire in its depth reflecting in his eyes.

"A brooch of my aunt's," I said. "She loaned it to me."

He fingered the brooch, the back of his hands brushing the skin of my bosom, making me shiver, and I wondered if it was deliberate on his part. "It is quite lovely. And valuable, I would guess."

"She said it was a gift."

"Indeed." He gazed at the jewel speculatively, then his gaze raked my face.

I tried to smile, but decided to turn my attention elsewhere. I had felt rather reckless coming here this evening, but I was not prepared for the way Lord Rhyweth's dark eyes turned my knees to jelly.

He gazed at me a moment longer, then said, "But I am forgetting," he said. "You must meet our good friend.

117

Enys Northcote, the Earl of Stratton. May I present Miss Rhionna Fowley."

The blond gentleman, who was as tall as Lord Rhyweth, crossed the room and bowed before me. "The pleasure is mine," he said in a mellifluous voice.

When he raised his head, blue eyes sparkled at me, and I could not help but return his smile. I instinctively gave a little curtsy. It seemed instinctively the right thing to do before an earl, though I was not schooled in such things.

"I am glad to meet you, my lord," I said.

"I understand you are a heroine, reclaimed from the sea."

I blushed. "I am grateful for my fate. Lord Rhyweth and Mistress Wycke were most hospitable."

He grinned at me. "How fortunate for them."

Dinner was announced, and we went in. This time Morwenna sat opposite me, with Lord Rhyweth at the head of the table and Lord Stratton at the foot. The first course was a thick bouillabaisse with lobster, mussels, red mullet, and other ingredients I could not name. But I let the juices run down my throat, appreciating the expertise of the Wyckes' cook. The food I had been having at Winifred's cottage was sturdy and healthy, but she had little time to spend on special sauces, and it was obvious to my tongue that the Wyckes had access to spices not available to the peasants.

By the time Godreven removed our dishes, we all seemed to have satisfied our hunger enough to indulge in conversation.

"I am sorry your aunt could not join us," Lord Rhyweth said. "I hope she is not seriously ill."

"She has dizzy spells. She says the doctor can do nothing, but she asked for the herb woman."

Something flickered in his eyes, but then he smiled kindly. "Ah yes, Hannelore."

"Is she very skilled?" I could not help but think of the erb mixture I had poured down the walls. That may ave been overly cautious of me, but in any case I had ecovered. If my aunt had faith in the woman then that vas another matter.

Lord Rhyweth studied his wine. "She has quite a reputation among the peasants. They seem to swear by her emedies."

"I believe I took a remedy of hers when I had a cough he last time I was here," said Lord Stratton.

"That is true," teased Lord Rhyweth. "I remember how ve had to nurse you back to health. I believe you sat for a lay in the sitting room, a towel round your throat and ad Morwenna read to you."

Morwenna gave her brother an annoyed look, but ord Stratton rained his smile on her.

"Yes, she was a very good nurse. I recovered quite vell."

"And how have you been spending your time, Rhionna, when you are not helping your aunt, that is?" Morwenna asked, deliberately changing the subject.

"I went riding with Elwynd. He took me up to the moor. It was quite fascinating. And he showed me the places to avoid."

"That was kind of him," she said, and I thought I noticed a trace of sarcasm in her voice.

Lord Rhyweth turned to me. "I was aware that Elwynd took you one of my horses. I did not know the extent of the ride."

I did not know how to answer this, wondering if Elwynd had been doing something not entirely approved of by his employer. "I wish to thank you for the use of the mount. He is a beauty."

"I am glad you have enjoyed him."

Then his eyes took on something like warning. "However, I caution you never to ride about these parts alone.

119

And always go by well-marked tracks."

"I will."

"You should go with Morwenna," put in Lord Stratton. "She knows the moors like the back of her hand."

I wanted to ask further questions but was unsure how to begin.

"Tell me, how long has Elwynd been your game-keeper?"

We had finished a course of meat pies and waited until Godreven had removed our plates.

"My father hired him. You may know that he was the illegitimate son of some village girl who gave him to Hannelore Treleaven and ran away after he was born. I hope I do not embarrass your sensibilities by discussing such a matter."

I blushed. "Of course not, Lord Rhyweth. I was not overprotected by my father as I grew up. And besides, my aunt has already told me."

"Yes. Hannelore gave him to your aunt for upbringing, I believe."

Again, I tried to launch my questions. "When was the castle built?" I asked after a pause. "It must be very old."

Lord Rhyweth glanced about the room as if seeing the past. "The Duchy of Cornwall gave permission to the Godolphin family to build here in 1482 to guard the coast. That family was driven into exile when Parliament ruled, but Charles II restored the place to the family. However, they became impoverished in a few generations and sold the place to my ancestor, the first Viscount Rhyweth. Our family wealth was squandered as well before the title was handed down many times, thus the necessity of my father to make a wealthy match."

He lifted his glass at the end of this recital to take a sip. "I am the younger son."

This made me curious. "There is an older son?"

"He is dead." He did not elaborate.

120

I glanced at Morwenna and then at Lord Stratton, but both of them looked at each other and then away. I thought I saw Lord Stratton frown and realized that this subject was not one they were fond of discussing.

I could see that this cliff-guarded stronghold was in the most obvious position to command a fief while at the same time guard the small harbor of the fishing village. I could see why the Godolphins had built here.

Our conversation was stilted, and I was glad when Morwenna excused herself after dessert. Though she had seemed withdrawn during the meal, she seemed more relaxed as she bid me goodnight.

"You must excuse me," she said. "I am rather tired. My brother will tell you that evening is not my best time. Please enjoy yourself."

"Thank you, Morwenna. I hope that at another time you will feel more like conversing."

It was on the tip of my tongue to say that I hoped there were many things that we could share, though I don't know why I wanted to say that. I scarcely knew the woman.

For a moment, the shield around her seem to drop, or perhaps it was merely the relief that she could leave us and go about her business. I wondered about the relationship between brother and sister, and while I did not dislike Morwenna, I found her a strange person. I did not think she was merely spoiled, rather there was an air of mystery about her that made me curious, and I wondered in that moment if we could ever be friends.

She gave my hand a quick squeeze. "I shall feel better another time. You must visit me one afternoon, or perhaps I shall take you riding. I can show you places Elwynd does not know of."

"I will see you to your room, Morwenna," said Lord Stratton, and she turned quickly to him as if surprised at his offer. She gave a little shrug.

121

"Very well."

He bowed in our direction. "If you will excuse me." I saw his blond eyebrow raise just a trace as he looked at his friend.

Lord Rhyweth nodded. "By all means."

They left us, and I was at once aware that the strain I had felt before relaxed a bit. Though Lord Rhyweth still made me nervous, there was something more familiar now, some deeply seated pleasure I experienced when I was alone with him, though I could not yet look him in the face.

He led me to the parlor where a fire blazed in the marble fireplace, and this time I seated myself safely in a red plush chair. I had formed questions that I wished to put to him. Questions from the strange insinuations I had gathered from Elwynd and Winifred, and I suppose I wanted to put them to rest.

"My aunt took me to chapel on Sunday," I began. "It was very different from any sort of service I had been to before. But then I must admit, my father's views were uncommon."

Lord Rhyweth stood before the fireplace, his hands clasped behind his back, flexing his long fingers.

"I see. And do you share your father's uncommon views, whatever they may be?"

"Perhaps." I paused, my heart accelerating as I said, "I heard it said that you do not attend religious services. Is this true?"

His amusement was apparent as he turned toward me, drew up one brow, and twisted the corners of his mouth into a teasing expression.

"It is very much true. But then I have become disillusioned with religion."

I remembered what Elwynd had said, but somehow Lord Rhyweth's remark did little to set my mind at ease.

"But come now, let us not dwell on so dreary a subject.

My fingers have been itching for a little music all evening. Would you mind very much if I played? You might even enjoy it if I can play decently tonight."

"Please do," I said. "I would like that."

In truth I was vastly curious about the organ that was installed somewhere in the castle, but he did not make a move to lead me there. Instead he crossed to the harpsichord that sat at an angle filling one corner of the room.

He seated himself and laid his fingers on the wooden keys. Then he began to play, and I was struck by the sweet sound he brought forth from the plucked strings. I watched entranced as his hands danced along the keyboard. I stared at his long, nimble fingers, becoming enchanted with the music, which seemed to vibrate from within him as much as it came from the obviously well-crafted instrument, and I was impressed that his gift was so great as to move me thus.

When he finished, I applauded. "That was very good. You are a man of talent, Lord Rhyweth," I said.

"Oh no," he said with a wave of his hand, turning from the keyboard to face me. "I would not go that far. I am satisfied if I please those I play for."

"The pleasure is mine."

"Then," he said, his voice taking on a more intimate tone. "Let us drop the formality. You must call me by my given name, Geoffrey."

He sat very still, and our eyes met across the room. I felt so in accord with him at that moment that I would not have been surprised if he could have read my mind. Then I nodded modestly, and he returned to the keyboard to play again. This time the piece was full of dissonance. Yet it came together in the end if in an unsettling resolution.

"That was an unusual piece," I said. "Who wrote it?"

"I composed it myself."

"It was . . . haunting," I said when he had finished.

I had only heard a harpsichord once before, when my father took me to visit a friend of his who collected old instruments, and I did not know that it was capable of such emotion. I was no musician, but I could tell that Lord Rhyweth's execution was flawless. And at the same time, I felt I learned more of him from the music than if he had spoken aloud.

The music allowed me to see something of a troubled soul. That was the only word I could put to it. I thought of other, darker words and felt a slight prickling sensation on my skin. I wondered if perhaps it was true that Lord Rhyweth was not an ordinary man, and that things were not quite as they seemed at Castle Rhyweth.

Whereas a moment ago I had felt only nervous agitation and a nearly willing subject of his magnetism, now I felt a sense of unease, as if I were being drawn into a trap of his making. I had the urge to leave, and yet I felt weighted to the chair as if I could not go until he decided it.

"Perhaps you have had enough music," he finally said.

Without waiting for an answer, he rose and held out a hand indicating that I should rise. "Would you like to see some of the paintings in the picture gallery? I remember your interest in my family history. Perhaps you would like to see some of my ancestors."

I nodded, mumbling acquiescence, feeling that what was needed was movement. We passed through several anterooms and then into a long gallery on the north side of the castle. The gloom here was only partially dispelled by oil lamps in wall sconces set between every few paintings.

"This is quite a collection," I said, looking at the rows of dark oils on two long walls. "Some of them must be very old."

He lit a candle in a hurricane lamp that stood on a small side table and held it aloft so we could better see the pictures as we strolled by them.

"They reflect the history of the castle itself," he said.

We stopped in front of one oil. "Henry Rhyweth, the Viscount Rhyweth. The first of my ancestors to live here."

He was a stern-looking man, tall and thin with no warmth that I could perceive. I thought I saw Morwenna's face in his, but oddly enough not Geoffrey's.

"Here is my grandfather," Geoffrey said, moving along. His hand brushed mine as we stopped, and a spark seemed to fly along my veins.

I gazed at the painting, quite fascinated by becoming better acquainted with the Lord Rhyweths. He showed me a small portrait of a young man that looked quite a bit like Geoffrey. I guessed that this must be Geoffrey's older brother, and I ventured to ask how he died.

"He was never healthy. Perhaps he inherited his mother's constitution. Never recovered from a chest cold one particularly bad winter. It turned into pneumonia and he never got well."

It saddened me to think that such a rosy-cheeked boy had not lived a full life.

"And this is my late wife."

"Ah."

He led me to a large portrait done in soft pastels, and I gazed at the delicate features framed by curls of gold. Her hand was on a plush red upholstered chair, and she was looking back over her shoulder at us as if she'd just heard her name called.

"She was very beautiful," I said.

"Alas, her spirit did not match her physical beauty."

I thought I detected a trace of bitterness in his voice.

"I'm sorry." It was an honest reaction.

We walked further. "My mother." The face seemed somehow familiar.

"The artist has made her very real," I said. "It's almost

125

as if she were about to speak."

"I would hope not."

I looked at Geoffrey curiously, wondering why he would say that. Again I sensed that there were things he would share with no one. What could his secrets be, that he had so shut them within himself?

"Is there no portrait of yourself?" I asked him.

"I do not like images of myself."

As we looked at the paintings, it occurred to me that we were very much alone. Nothing threatened me, and yet I felt threatened by something. I gazed about me. Perhaps the rumors were true. There was something odd about this castle, some evil presence lurking in the shadows.

I had felt it before. Fanned by the flames of the warnings I had received, I began to feel frightened by it. A premonition of something to come. Still, I tried to appear calm. It would do no good to suddenly take the notion to flee.

As if reading my mind, Lord Rhyweth's fingers closed on my elbow, and he steered me toward the bay windows. I stood trembling beside him as we gazed out at the moon rising over the glittering sea.

"You're trembling," he said, his hand coming up to my shoulder. "Are you cold?"

"Um, yes, a little."

His hand drifted along my shoulders, floating over my hair and down my back. I trembled at his touch, but this time from something other than fear. As frightened as I was of Lord Rhyweth's intentions regarding me, I came under his spell once again as he pulled me toward him.

"Let me warm you," he said in a voice that caressed and entranced me. I felt powerless in the mantle of enchantment he threw about me. And my mind seemed to take flight as he lowered his lips to the base of my throat.

Chapter 9

At the first touch of his lips to my skin, I trembled inwardly, my hand straying toward his shoulder. He raised his head, gazed intently at my parted lips, to which he lowered his own.

Then a loud knocking sent my heart leaping into my throat, and we both jumped.

"What the devil," he muttered.

Then setting me aside, he strode along the gallery to open the heavy oak door which had closed behind us. Olga stood in the doorway, silhouetted by the light cast from the oil lamps behind her.

"I beg your pardon, sir, but something's happened." She glanced at me and then back at him.

"Go ahead," he said. "What is it?"

"A girl's body has been found in the field above Penhallow cove.

"And?"

"She's dead."

I came up to them and stood with my mouth agape, my eyes wide.

"Dead," I whispered.

"Does anyone know who she was?" he asked.

Olga shook her head. "It seems she wasn't a local girl. She was from somewhere else."

Geoffrey stiffened. "I see," he said.

He turned to me, and I saw the tautness in his face.

His mouth, full and sensual a moment ago, now pulled into a grim line.

"You must stay here under the circumstances. Jonas will take word to your aunt. I must go to the scene of this latest tragedy and see what can be done."

I was too stunned to refuse. Still envisioning the horror of a girl lying dead in a field, I meekly followed Olga off to the same room I had used before. In a daze I allowed her to turn down the bed and lay out a dressing gown. I realized that she was standing by the door waiting for a reply, but I had not heard the question.

"I'm sorry," I said. "It is so terrible, this death. Is there anything I can do?"

She shook her head. "Lord Rhyweth will take care of everything. Would you like anything else?"

"Could I have my dog with me? Gwynneth has him in the kitchen."

The words were out of my mouth before I remembered that Olga did not approve of this. True to form, she merely sniffed at this request.

"The master does not allow animals upstairs. Your dog will be perfectly well cared for in the kitchens and put to bed in the stable." The corners of her lips turned down in a slightly disdainful manner, and she left me.

I felt suddenly desolate and frightened. Some poor girl lay dead in a field, and I knew nothing of the cause. I was shaking from head to toe, hating being shut up in this room again. I paced back and forth, looking out once, but the night was black, for clouds had covered the moonlit view, and the darkness made me shiver even more.

Where was Gwynneth? If she would come to me at least I would have someone to talk to. I thought of leaving the castle. How did I know that Jonas would deliver the message to Aunt Winifred? But the thought of venturing out into this black night was too awful to contemplate.

However, I had to do something. If Olga would not bring me Rufus, I would go get him myself. Inaction was impossible. I could not simply stay in this bedchamber all alone. I went to the wardrobe and pulled down a shawl, which I threw around my shoulders.

Venturing out into the corridor, I saw that no one was about. I hurried along, the flames in the oil lamps flickering as I rushed past toward the main stairway and went down the circular stairs, my dress billowing behind me. When I reached the main entrance, I stopped. I only then realized that I hadn't the slightest idea where the kitchens were. I tried to reason. In medieval castles the kitchens were often in a separate building. Approaching the front doors, I saw the butler.

"Godreven," I said. "Would you be good enough to direct me to the kitchens?" I said. "I must see about my dog there."

He narrowed his gaze, but gave me the directions I needed. Then, feeling his gaze on my back, I turned and made my way down a drafty corridor that led along the north wing and finally to a smaller door, which I pushed open.

The wind slammed the door shut behind me, and for a moment I feared that I would be locked out. But I tried to shake some sense into myself and hurried across the courtyard to the building that fit the description Godreven had given me of the outbuilding. Smoke rose from a chimney in its roof.

I pushed open a heavy wooden door and sighed in relief that I had come to the right place. Several servants bustled about in the large kitchen, and across the room I could see Gwynneth petting Rufus as he ate something from a bowl.

I closed the door behind me and as I was about to continue on my way, I stopped. There was a dark passage behind Gwynneth, leading I knew not where, but as I looked that way I saw to my surprise that Elwynd was standing in the shadows watching the maid feed my dog. Some instinct made me step behind a post, out of sight.

I could see that Gwynneth and Rufus had renewed their friendship, and this made me glad. I knew that once Rufus made a friend he remained forever loyal, and the girl seemed deserving of his friendly attentions. But something about the furtive manner in which Elwynd stared at her made me uneasy. I saw the way his eyes narrowed, and the way he flexed his hands. Then, to my embarrassment I saw the bulge that formed in his trousers as he watched her pet Rufus, as if he envied the caresses she gave the dog.

I swallowed in shame. The firelight reflected in his eyes, and there was no mistaking the lust I saw there. I remembered him watching Gwynneth at the church, and it was evident that he wanted the girl. Or was it simply my own guilt at a similar emotion that led me to guess his desires?

Now he emerged from the shadows and approached Gwynneth, who stood to speak with him. I do not know what he said, but I saw her cast her eyes downward. I saw the muscles in his jaw tense, and again it was as if I read his thoughts. I could see that he was determined to have his way with Gwynneth. But my heart leapt to my throat when I saw the expression that he cast in Rufus' direction. He was obviously jealous of the attention she was giving the dog, and I feared that he might be desperate enough to do whatever he had to do to turn that attention his way.

I tried to get ahold of my feelings while I waited until Elwynd left, going back the same way he had come. Then I came out of the shadows and, dodging the scullery maids who were washing up, I crossed to Gwynneth.

"Why hello, miss," she said when she saw me. "Come for your dog?"

I knelt and accepted the licks Rufus gave me. He was all tail wags now, obviously in heaven since he was well fed, warm, and between mistress and newfound friend.

"Yes," I said. "I'm staying the night."

She lowered her voice as if not wanting the other servants in the kitchen to hear. "I heard what happened. Terrible thing."

I swallowed. "Was it anyone . . . you knew?"

She shook her head. "They say she wasn't from around here."

I knew that the girl may have only been dead a short time, but that the grapevine would have already passed the news.

"They say she was wounded in the throat. Awful thing if you ask me."

I could think of nothing to say, but let my hand rub Rufus' head, his furry coat and warmth giving me some comfort.

" 'Tis a good thing you're staying here tonight," said Gwynneth, leaning over to warm her hands by the blazing fire in the hearth. " 'Twouldn't be safe out."

I pulled my shawl closer. "Have they any idea who did it?"

"No, no they haven't."

"I wonder if the poor girl might have been killed by the wolf that wanders the moor."

She gave me a queer look. "No telling," she said.

It made me shiver to think that the wolf might come down as far as the fields between here and my aunt's cottage.

We left the kitchens, and Gwynneth led me across the courtyard and upstairs following a narrow twisting stone stairway that I had not used before. I felt very furtive as we climbed upwards, Rufus on our heels. But we reached my bedchamber and shut the door behind us. Gwynneth poked up the fire then helped me get undressed and into a frilly nightgown. She tucked me in, then squeezed my hands.

"You try to rest now, miss. And try not to trouble yourself too much over that poor dead girl. There's nothing you can do now."

"No, nothing, I suppose."

She bid me goodnight, and I was left alone. But I was too restless to sleep, so I rose again and went to look out the window. Several riders came into the courtyard below, and I saw Geoffrey dismount and hand his horse to the groom. Then he swept up the stone steps and into the castle, his long cape flowing behind him. Whatever had been done about the dead girl, I would have to wait until morning to find out.

Then I looked over the parapet and out to sea where a thick driving mist was rolling in. The moon's light, diffracted by the fog, spread a ghostly glow from behind the clouds. I thought idly of the French pirates that had sometimes rounded Land's End and launched their raids upon this coast, raids this castle had been built to repel. Then, as if to punctuate my imaginings, a ghostly shape slipped through the gloom.

Cutting through the fog like the wing of a bird, came a white sail, then another. Then the outline of a three-masted schooner slid across the water, faintly outlined by the moon.

At first I thought it had no light, and then I saw a lantern that hung from its bow and one from its stern. Still, I could not fathom where a ship would be going at night and in this weather. She slid slowly out to sea and then as suddenly as I had seen her, she disappeared. For a moment, I wondered if it were an illusion, and I wondered if anyone else had seen it.

I was finally tired enough to sleep and sought the comfort of my bed while Rufus took up his position on the braided rug beside me. I drifted off, but awoke a few hours later to hear haunting chords coming from the depths of the castle. But now I knew the music was not part of my dreams, it must be Geoffrey playing. The music was dissonant, disturbing. It was not consoling music. Not music I wanted to hear.

I turned over, placed the pillows about my ears and went back to sleep.

I did not see Geoffrey or Morwenna in the morning, but took my leave of Gwynneth and Olga.

As I came down the main staircase, Rufus at my heels, Lord Stratton emerged from the antique weapons collection room.

"Ah, Miss Fowley, I see you are leaving. Awful thing, what with the murder and all."

I lifted an eyebrow. "You are the first person I have heard call it thus."

"What else could it be? So horrible a death."

"It could have been an accident, could it not?" I asked. "I've heard a wolf roams about at night."

"Oh yes. I see what you mean."

I studied him carefully. It was on the tip of my tongue to ask him where he had been last night, but I could not find it in me to speak thusly to a man of his station. He followed me out to the carriage and held the door for me.

"I must go up to London today," he said as I got in. "I hope I shall see you next time I am this way."

I gave him a half smile. "I do not know," I said to his polite inquiry. "I am not often at the castle."

"Then that is a shame." He shut the carriage door.

I turned again and saw Godreven watching us from the top of the stone steps, and then Malcolm snapped the reins over the horses' heads, and we were away.

We rumbled across the courtyard, past the gatehouse, and out into the countryside. I thought again of the tragedy of the night before in the field above Penhallow Cove. The damp air felt oppressive, and I still could not shake off the feeling that some great weight dragged at me.

When I reached my aunt's cottage I got out and thanked Malcolm, who helped me down. He nodded without a word, but got back onto the box and turned his team around, the air snapping under his whip as he raced them back toward the road that wound through the woods to the castle.

I turned and was about to step into the cottage, when I paused curiously. Several pots of very strong-smelling plants sat on either side of the door and under the window. It took me a moment to realize they were garlic plants. The tall, green stalks emitted a very pungent odor, and I went in to ask my aunt about them.

I found not only my aunt waiting for me, but a smaller, wizened-looking woman in a print dress with a yellow scarf tied around her white hair. She sat in my aunt's rocker, while Winifred was seated in one of the straight-backed chairs.

"Aunt Winifred," I said. "You must be feeling better. Is the dizziness gone?"

"Yes, child. And I am glad you have returned safely. Hannelore brought me her life-giving herbs and has stayed with me through the night." She gestured to the other women.

"This is Hannelore Treleaven. Hannelore, my niece, Rhionna Fowley."

Hannelore eyed me curiously. " 'Tis a good thing you've returned," she said. "With so much evil about."

The way she said it made me feel ill at ease. I could not get used to her sharp, penetrating eyes, like small black beads set in her tiny wrinkled face.

"We had quite a fright last night when the news came about that girl," said Winifred.

"Yes, it must have been gruesome," I said. "Then Jonas did bring word to you that I was to stay at the castle?"

Winifred nodded, but the apprehension had not left her eyes.

"I was," I paused, "quite safe there."

Winifred and Hannelore exchanged quick glances.

"I'm not sure about that," said Hannelore. "I was just reprimanding your aunt for allowing you to go there. Once there, it was the choice between two evils. Remaining and traveling about at night."

"Why the strong-smelling plants outside?" I asked.

Winifred would not meet my gaze. "Garlic. Hannelore brought them."

"But why something that smells so?"

"Protection," said Hannelore now rising from her chair. "The plants yield a medicinal oil. The bruised bulbs can be used as a poultice for pneumonia."

My eyes widened. "My goodness, I hope my aunt doesn't have pneumonia."

"No, no," Winifred said hastily. "Nothing like that. Just a remedy for colds and coughs. You boil the garlic cloves in water for half a day."

Hannelore pushed herself out of the rocking chair. "It's time I went about my business," she said. "There's much to do."

I thought she was a strange little woman, dour of countenance, even if she did possess great knowledge about plants. Still, it was said that she had many skills, and if she had helped my aunt, I was grateful.

"Thank you for staying with my aunt," I said. "I was worried last night."

"So were we all," said Hannelore. "So were we all. I'm

135

an old woman and haven't much time left. And I can't say I'll be that sorry to leave this world."

"Hannelore," said Winifred. "You're a woman of many gifts. You shouldn't say such things. You will be missed, I'm sure."

"That may be, that may be." She glanced at me again but spoke to my aunt. "Mind what I told you, Winifred."

"We will."

I bid the herb woman good-bye, and we watched as she left, her figure bent, her yellow kerchief like a butterfly on her head.

"Does she live far?" I asked.

"On the moor," said Winifred. " 'Tis gloomy where she lives." She looked at me. "You weren't far from it the day you visited the hermit's glen.

"Oh," I said. "I didn't know."

And why hadn't my aunt told me that? But the words stuck in my throat. Instead I said, "She seems a strange one, but if you have faith in her skills, then I'm sure they must have merit."

I meant what I said, for was I not witness to the fact that my aunt's dizziness had left her and she was now up and about?

"But why did she bring the garlic flowers?"

Winifred shook her head. "I did not want to frighten you, girl, but Hannelore sets store by them." She shrugged, not looking at me. "And I did not want to hurt her feelings."

We spoke no more of Hannelore, but I told her of my dinner at the castle. I told her that Lord Rhyweth had played for me, avoiding, of course, any discussion of my personal feelings. I turned the conversation to his sister, speaking of the confusion I felt over her strange behavior toward me.

"I did not think she liked me at first," I said. "But then she seemed as if she wanted my friendship."

"Perhaps she likes you, child. It is just that she has not had the opportunity for friendship. You must understand, she grew up in a castle with no one but a brother for companionship."

I nodded, trying to envision such a life. "I do not suppose she made friends with any of the peasant girls."

"No, she did not. Morwenna has always kept to herself."

"Indeed. I do not know what she thinks of me. Neither am I of her station in life."

"You are an American," said Winifred, considering. "That is different."

The next day was market day in the village, and for once the sun was shining. We took eggs and milk in the wagon into the village, which Winifred exchanged for salt herring and pilchards.

As I strolled along the street, I caught snatches of conversation that floated between the villagers standing about in the sun, for it was an exceptionally fine day. But the rumors were rampant.

I could see in the women's faces that they were all frightened for their own daughters, and the young men stood in groups talking in hushed voices among themselves. I caught the gist of their determined rumblings. But the dilemma was more felt that heard. How could they fight an enemy they did not know?

Truly this part of Cornwall did not feel safe, but I still tried to tell myself there were rational explanations for all these happenings. The excitable and imaginative Cornish were more likely than anyone to see ghosts in every corner. Yet their fears were real to them. I read it in the eyes that flicked everywhere but failed to meet mine—nervously, as though death lurked over their shoulders.

At the end of the day we entered the dilapidated little tea shop where we found Hannelore sitting sipping from a cup of tea near a cold fireplace. Talk turned immediately to the speculations about the missing young women and then the death of two nights before.

"Those who can afford it are sending their daughters to relatives in other parts of the country," Hannelore said.

She pinned me with her gaze. "If you knew what was best for you, young woman, you'd book passage on the next ship out of St. Ives. You're better off in America. You've no more reason to be here now that you've seen your aunt."

I did not want to tell her my real reason for being here, but said, "Surely running away cannot solve anything. If this was truly murder, will not the authorities investigate and the murderer be caught?"

Hannelore's words took on a singsong quality. "It's not so easy to catch a murderer. The evil doer would have to be caught in the act, wouldn't he? And until such evidence is discovered, who will the next victim be?"

This time her meaning was clear, and I swallowed hard at the way she stared at me as if picturing me the victim of the next crime.

"But surely no one has reason to harm me," I said in a meek voice.

For though I tried to remain determined in my views, something about the herb woman's manner intimidated me. It was all the more disconcerting because there was something covert in the way her eyes shifted, now penetrating mine, now hiding their true meaning.

She leaned closer, her black eyes seeming to draw me in. "The girl that died was sister to one of the scullery maids at the castle. She was visiting her there."

I felt a chill at the back of my neck. Again the association with Castle Rhyweth. "But surely . . ." I found myself saying, but with no explanation to offer.

Hannelore's voice droned on. "If you ask me, Lord Rhyweth's got a hand in this. She wasn't the first girl who'd gone to that castle under cover of darkness only to disappear."

"Lord Rhyweth had nothing to do with this occurrence," I said, my face becoming flushed. "He was—"

I stopped, reforming the words that came to my lips, for I very well remembered what he was about to do when we were interrupted with the news of the tragedy.

"I dined with Lord Rhyweth and his sister that night. He could not have done it. In any case, I cannot believe he is a murderer."

I shut my mouth. Having to face my aunt's and Hannelore's accusing eyes was enough. I did not want to further reveal just how far I had come under Lord Rhyweth's influence, which was the very thing they feared. But my feelings must have been transparent.

"Ah, so he has cast his spell already," said Hannelore in a droning voice.

Suddenly her gnarled hand reached across the splintery table and pinched my arm. "It was as I feared. It is what I warned your aunt. You must heed these warnings. That is, if it is not too late."

If it is not too late. Was it too late then for me? Was the real reason I was not ready to leave Cornwall because I had become infatuated with Geoffrey Wycke? And yet where could such infatuation lead? To death on a dark night in a lonely field? I shuddered at the thought.

I felt confused and frightened. Outside the wind gusted, and we could hear the waves lapping at the fishing boats. I felt cold, even though the matronly hostess had started up the fire in the hearth to chase away the coolness brought on by the coming of evening.

I did what I could to summon up my own defenses, half driven by my pride.

"It may be true that Lord Rhyweth dallied with the village girls after his wife died. Like most men, he may not be perfect. But that does not mean he is a murderer."

I could easily picture him taking his pleasure in the arms of a village wench, but my mind could not make the leap from that to slitting a girl's throat or hiding her in his dungeon. In spite of the morbid atmosphere that pervaded everyone's thoughts, I still believed that there was something basically good in Geoffrey Wycke's character.

It had grown later than we thought, and by the time we came out of the tea shop and walked up the hill to our wagon, the clouds were banking up against the setting sun, and it had grown dark earlier than usual.

"There's a storm coming," said Winifred. "We must hurry."

We placed our bundles in the back of the wagon and climbed onto the seat. I had gotten more proficient at driving, so I picked up the reins, and we set off, leaving the village behind.

The wind whipped up, and as we drove along, the darkness seemed to close in around us. We entered the woods and wound through them. But we rumbled on and came to the hollow on the other side. As Nedda plunged down it, I heard a screech. Something flapped above me, and I fought to keep control of the reins.

Suddenly something was tearing at my hair and face, and I dropped the reins and screamed. Nedda reared and the wagon tipped, nearly throwing me out. Then the horse bolted, and I grabbed the side of the wagon seat, holding on for dear life. We were tearing down the track, headed for the gate to our field, and I feared we would run right through it.

"Winifred!" I screamed, aware that she had somehow clung to her seat as well.

But Nedda turned before she ran into the gate, and as

the wagon flew off the road, she came loose from her traces and we bounced to a stop. I was shaking, but relatively unhurt and I turned to Winifred, fearing the worst.

We fell into each other's arms, each making sure the other was all right. When she touched my forehead, her finger came away with blood on it.

"Bats inhabit that hollow," she said grimly. "Best not to go there after dark."

Assuring her that my cuts were minor, we got down to inspect the damage to the wagon. I was not versed in harness-making, but she was, and as she looked at the broken black straps, her lips set in a grim line.

"Been cut through," she said, and she showed me where a clean slice had separated all but a piece of the traces on both sides.

"You mean someone cut them on purpose?"

My heart was still pounding in my chest, and now my eyes widened at this new horror.

She nodded slowly, looking at the mare where she stood nearby, half harnessed, now over her fright.

"I cannot believe it."

I stared at my aunt and then at the broken harness, my gaze flitting over the dark landscape. From the hollow an owl hooted.

The implications were that someone had planned our accident. But who? Who would know that we would leave the village late enough for our horse to be frightened by a bat?

Hannelore Treleaven had kept us at the tea shop until after dark. I narrowed my gaze, thinking. There was something about Hannelore that I did not trust. Her fingers would not have been strong enough to cut through leather traces, but she could have had someone do it for her. But why? Had she not warned me to leave Cornwall? If she wanted to harm me, would she warn me first? And what could she possibly gain by hurting my aunt?

Winifred whistled to Nedda, and she came trotting to her owner. She was still jittery, but Winifred rubbed her nose, speaking to her in low tones until she quieted. Then with each of us taking one side of her harness, we led the horse home, leaving the wagon until morning.

Chapter 10

We got to the cottage just before sheets of rain began to come down outside. Once again, we removed Nedda's broken harness and put it away. I stopped by Blackie's stall and fed him some oats, then we ran back through the rain to the cottage. While the wind battered at the door, we saw to my scratches. The wounds were not deep, and I would heal without any scars. I was probably more frightened than hurt. While Winifred put away the bandages, I got the fire going in the hearth.

I had been so distracted that I had not noticed a small morocco-bound book that was lying on the center of the table. Finally Winifred paused by the table and bent over it.

"What is this?" she said.

"What?"

"This book. Someone must have left it here."

She picked it up and a piece of paper fell out, which I bent over to pick up from the floor. When I unfolded it, I saw that someone had scrawled my name on it.

"Why," I said in surprise, "it looks as if they meant it for me."

I reached for it, but now my aunt held it, reading the title with a pinched expression on her face. I still held out my hand, expecting her to give it to me, but instead she looked up.

"What is it?" I asked, growing more curious every moment.

She neither offered it to me nor held onto it when I slipped the little volume out of her hands. I brought it over to the firelight and sat down on the stool by the fire. The book seemed very old, and I could not read the title from the cover. Opening to the yellowed title page I read, *True Stories of the Undead.*

My eyes widened, and I turned to the first page. Skimming over the paragraphs I discovered that it was a little book about condemned creatures who roamed at night. It was a tale about vampires.

I was hardly aware of my aunt's presence as she got ready for bed, and I did not know how long I sat by the fire reading, but something drew me on, and I moved to the rocking chair when my back got stiff from hunching over on the stool.

As I turned the pages incidents began to come together in my mind. Now I remembered where I had heard about those who did not like the sun, who stayed up at night, who ate little or nothing and who did not set foot in sacred places. It was as if I heard Elwynd speaking to me, and I remembered his words about Lord Rhyweth.

I finally closed the book and stared at the dying embers. Surely such a thing could not be. Surely this was folklore. And then other thoughts came unbidden. I remembered my father's notion that many legends had some basis in fact. While I tried not to let my own horrors cloud my judgment, I could not bring myself to agree with the wild superstitions of the Cornish peasants, for the Celts had been given to myth and legend for centuries. I could hardly expect them to be objective about the truth.

And yet I had proved a very poor investigator, had I not? I had found no answers to my questions about my own father's death. And there was some sort of link between Lord Rhyweth and the girls who had come to a bad end, or at least uncertain ones in the cases of the maidens who had simply disappeared.

I closed the book and leaned back in the rocking chair. My aunt was sleeping soundly in her bed on the other side of the room. I tried to gather my wits and sort through things. I had been foolish to have enjoyed Lord Rhyweth's company so much that I had not pursued my purpose in being there. It was true that to find out what I wanted to know about my father's death and other matters, I would have to return to Castle Rhyweth, but I could not afford to surrender so completely to Lord Rhyweth's spell.

Perhaps he did have some evil powers, I thought with a shiver of fear. For I considered myself a rather self-determined person, yet when I was with him my thoughts and feelings gave way to the magic he wove about me. I stared at the little book before me. Could it be true? Could something so horrible as this truly exist in our own day and time? The consequences were simply too awful to contemplate.

The last chapter of the book contained the only sure methods for disposing of vampires, but I only glanced at it. Even then I knew that my imagination was perhaps running away with me. Such things should be considered in the light of day, not when I was too tired to think straight. Not when it was dark and the wind was howling about the cottage outside.

I put the book on the floor and went off to bed. Rufus climbed up on top of the covers, nuzzling me with his nose.

"Rufus, old boy," I said, petting his long black fur. "It's a strange place we've come to, that's for sure."

I did not think I would sleep at all, my mind was so wrapped up in the evil images created by the little book, and the storm still raged outside, a branch of the big oak tree beating incessantly against the window. I wondered why Winifred had not had Elwynd take it down. Finally I

145

slept, just when the night seemed its darkest.

The storm spent itself at dawn, and when I woke and dressed, I went outside to a sullen calm. I stayed near the cottage that day, deciding to do a thorough cleaning. I swept every corner and then took a pail with water and scrubbed everywhere, the physical work doing something for my mental state as well as making hitherto lazy muscles work. By mid-morning I was feeling much better and looked around the sparkling room with a sense of accomplishment. Equally banished were the thoughts of the night before, and I put the little book in a drawer in the writing desk.

I was cleaning the same desk when two folded sheets of paper fell out of a slot and onto the floor. I bent to pick them up and noted that it was a letter from my father to Winifred. I did not mean to invade my aunt's privacy, but I could not help my curiosity, and my eye fell on the contents. As I scanned the page, I saw Elwynd's name.

I frowned and read the sentence. In it my father asked of Elwynd's current activities. Something about the wording reminded me of the letter I had brought with me from New York, the letter I had lost.

Somehow a link was forged in my mind, though I could not see the logic to it. But I decided to ask Elwynd or my aunt about it later.

The opportunity arose that afternoon when Elwynd came to get the broken harness and take it to the harness-maker in the village. I was in the garden and I strolled to the barn to meet him. He was examining the harness where it had been broken, frowning over it.

"Good morning, Elwynd," I said.

He straightened and removed his cap as I approached him.

"I heard about your accident," he said. " 'Twas a good

146

hing you were not hurt." He looked concerned, his eyes flickering over the bandage still tied around my head.

"Yes, we were lucky. Do you think the harness can be fixed?"

He nodded. "Uther Carn is very skilled in leatherwork."

"Look," I said, pointing to where the traces had been deliberately cut. "Do you have any idea who could have done this?"

He shook his head, pondering, then he took refuge in the general forboding that everyone seemed to fall back on rather than commit to a specific accusation. "Evil things are afoot these days. No one's safe."

I read the fear in his eyes, and I changed the subject. "Tell me something, Elwynd. Did you know my father Leslie Fowley? When you were a boy I mean?"

He nodded slowly as we left the barn and approached the wagon where he heaved the broken harness into the wagon bed.

"I knew him. I was a wee mite when he left Cornwall. But yes, I remember him. Big man with bushy blond whiskers."

I smiled at the description, for it exactly fit my father when he was younger. "Yes, that's him."

Elwynd grunted. "He did do well in America then?"

"He did well enough, I suppose. But I am curious. I believe he imported goods made in Cornwall at one time. Did you know of it?"

Elwynd readjusted some bags of feed in the back of the wagon, then faced me and nodded.

"Arthur Wycke sent him handmade articles made here by the village women. Woven cloth, carvings, and such. It brought some money to the village."

"I see."

Then my father had done business with Arthur Wycke.

147

I pressed on. "Then did you know my father well?"

He shrugged. "Only as well as a wee tot remembers a man he once looked up to."

His look became more serious as his eyes swept my face.

"If you mean did I know him after I had become a man, the answer is no. I did not know he had such a comely daughter."

I flushed, not knowing what else to ask him, and made my modest excuses. I stepped back and watched him climb upon the seat and turn the wagon down the track, heading for the village.

I mulled over what Elwynd had said as I finished my cleaning, and when Winifred came back from her visit to Hannelore, her eyes lit with pride as she inspected the job I had done.

She shook her head. "What can I say? It fills my heart to see you put yourself out so, and yet I know that I should send you away. What bittersweetness it is to have a niece."

"Oh, Aunt. Do you not know that you could not send me away? I am as strong headed as the rest of our family, and nothing will make me leave until I am ready."

Then my tone became more serious. "Besides, if I left it would be only to save my own skin. Who knows, by staying I might be able to prove either that that poor girl's death was an accident or else help discover who is at fault so the person can be captured."

Winifred cocked her head, her hand on her hip.

"You are very certain of yourself. How can a mere girl, even one as determined and intelligent as yourself come to any such conclusions?"

"I am not certain of myself at all, Aunt, only perhaps desperate to know the truth."

She wiped her hands on her skirt and crossed to the dry sink.

"It is your father's death you wish to know about, not the death of this poor Cornish lass."

"That is true. But what if there is a connection?"

Her lips twitched. "I do not like to think there is a connection."

We made tea, and when we had seated ourselves and sliced some bread, I asked Winifred about the business of my father importing Cornish crafts from the village.

"Is it true that Arthur Wycke took care of sending the goods that the villagers made?"

She nodded hesitantly. "I believe that was the arrangement. Why do you ask?"

"Father mentioned it," I fibbed. "Of course then I did not know any of the Wyckes. And something Elwynd said today made me think of it."

"And what did Elwynd say?"

"Just that he remembered my father. And he knew about the goods being sent from here to America."

Again she nodded, though I noticed that her right hand was now busy fiddling with the spoon that lay on the table by her place.

"I suppose he would know of it. Yes, I believe he might even have sent some of his own carvings."

I nodded, sipping my tea slowly and observing my aunt. Her cheeks were tinged with pink, and though she gave me her demure little smile, her lids fell over her eyes. The blood was flowing quickly to my brain now, and I believed I was on the trail of something, though I was not sure what.

"I do not know what to think of Elwynd," I said. "I can never tell what he is thinking. But you must know him well. What was he like as a boy, growing up here?"

She cocked her head to one side, again fingering her spoon. "He was a good child and grew up to be a reliable enough worker. Always did what needed being done. I cannot fault him, for he takes care to look after things, as

149

you have seen."

Something about her guarded words gave me to believe that she was not speaking her mind. It made me curious. I watched her carefully, but we spoke no more of it, and I knew that I would have to get her to tell me what was on her mind another time.

That night when I retired to bed, I did not shut my door tight, but left it ajar where I could see the length of the main room. To my surprise, I saw Winifred rummaging in the drawers of the desk. I held my breath watching, hoping Rufus would not give me away.

To my surprise, she took a miniature portrait from the back of a drawer. Then she crossed the room and sat down in her rocker, placing the portrait next to a hurricane lamp on the table beside her. I could not see the face from where I was.

The rocker creaked its rhythm as she rocked back and forth, staring at the portrait. And I was determined to find out who it was she gazed at so pensively.

Chapter 11

The next morning when Winifred went to the barn to milk Heather, I wasted no time, but went to look for the picture. It was no longer by the rocker, so I opened the top drawer of the desk. At first I did not see it, but after rummaging through some old receipts, I found the photograph bound in a small leather frame.

I lifted it out and carried it nearer the window to get the best light. It was a picture of a young man, ruggedly built. I frowned in concentration. He wore fine clothes and a top hat. There was something familiar about him, though I was sure I'd never seen him before.

With trembling fingers, I slipped the photograph from its frame. But disappointment was my only reward. There was no inscription or even a date to tell me who it was. From his style of dress, I vaguely guessed that this was a man my aunt knew in her younger days, but how many years ago I was not exactly sure.

Now the dilemma faced me whether to ask Winifred about it or not. I carefully replaced the photograph in the drawer, trying to leave everything as I had found it. Still I felt guilty. Would not Winifred know that someone had been rummaging in the drawer? Such signs of invasion of privacy were hard to disguise.

Another anonymous gift arrived for me that day, and I was truly curious as to who was sending these things. At first I thought the gift might be from Lord Rhyweth, but when I opened the package, I discovered a plain wooden box. It was a small silver cross on a chain. A note in a scrawled handwriting I did not recognize urged me to wear the cross on my person at all times.

I wondered if this could be from Hannelore. She was the first one to warn me that I was facing some powerful evil that was stronger than me and perhaps not quite human. Perhaps she had sent the book and now had sent the cross, thinking I would wear it as protection.

I fingered the cross. Whoever sent it thought it would protect me against whatever evil was rampant in the village. I told myself that I was not superstitious. I believed the cross to be merely a religious symbol, not some sort of talisman against evil. As I folded the brown paper wrapping, I stared at the glittering silver necklace. Then I put it on.

When Elwynd appeared to take me riding again the next day, I had mixed feelings. I considered him a friend and I appreciated the way he seemed to go out of his way to please me. I did hope he meant nothing but friendship by it, and since he had obvious designs on Gwynneth, I thought perhaps he entertained me out of respect for Winifred.

I wanted to question Elwynd some more, and Blackie needed exercising. I reasoned it was better not to go riding alone, so we took to the highlands.

We spoke little during the first hour, but when we reached the plateau, we got down. I felt exhilarated up there where the wind was so strong you could lean on it. And there was so much open space, I felt as if I left my body and flew out over the high moorlands that stretched around us.

Amidst the scrub and gorse stood two great slabs of granite, weather-pitted and worn, with another huge slab atop them, forming a roof, the burial place of a priest,

4 FREE BOOKS

TO GET YOUR 4 FREE BOOKS WORTH $18.00 —MAIL IN THE FREE BOOK CERTIFICATE T O D A Y

Fill in the Free Book Certificate below, and we'll send your FREE BOOKS to you as soon as we receive it.

If the certificate is missing below, write to: Zebra Home Subscription Service, Inc., P.O. Box 5214, 120 Brighton Road, Clifton, New Jersey 07015-5214.

FREE BOOK CERTIFICATE

4 FREE BOOKS

ZEBRA HOME SUBSCRIPTION SERVICE, INC.

YES! Please start my subscription to Zebra Historical Romances and send me my first 4 books absolutely FREE. I understand that each month I may preview four new Zebra Historical Romances free for 10 days. If I'm not satisfied with them, I may return the four books within 10 days and owe nothing. Otherwise, I will pay the low preferred subscriber's price of just $3.75 each; a total of $15.00, *a savings off the publisher's price of $3.00.* I may return any shipment and I may cancel this subscription at any time. There is no obligation to buy any shipment and there are no shipping, handling or other hidden charges. Regardless of what I decide, the four free books are mine to keep.

NAME

ADDRESS _____ APT _____

CITY _____ STATE _____ ZIP _____

TELEPHONE ( )

SIGNATURE _____ (if under 18, parent or guardian must sign)

Terms, offer and prices subject to change without notice. Subscription subject to acceptance by Zebra Books. Zebra Books reserves the right to reject any order or cancel any subscription. ZBMS02

perhaps a queen, the treasures once contained therein long ago rifled by barbarians.

Elwynd tied the horses to a low scrubby tree limb, and we sat on a large flat rock.

Sitting here next to the ancient burial chamber, I felt removed from time. I could almost picture the gathering preparing the chieftain, priest, or queen who lay there for the passage to the underworld. Like my father, they believed in immortality. This was man's answer then, from the beginning of history, to death's challenge. Near to the tomb was a ring of standing stones.

"What are they?" I asked, pointing to the circle of stones.

He shook his head. "No one knows. Left here by the ancients long ago. Some folks used to say that these leanin' stones were people frozen for dancing on Sunday, but I never believed it."

I looked at him. "Didn't you? But you believe in other signs, don't you?"

"What do you mean?"

"That evil exists here, and that there are certain precautions that must be taken against it."

His eyes darted to me. "I wouldn't know what you're talking about. If evil walks, there's not much can be done about it except to stay out of its way."

I was baiting him, for I wondered if he knew something about the garlic flowers and the cross, but he did not seem forthcoming. So I tried another tack.

"And why do you stay here, Elwynd? If there is evil to be feared and you know its source, why not leave? Surely a man of your youth and ability could find work elsewhere."

He gave me a look I could not quite interpret then picked up a rock and fingered it. Finally he looked at me again. "I was born here," he said.

I could not answer. For was not part of what held me there the fact that my father was born in Cornwall, too?

153

What was it that tied a person to his roots so? It seemed only a sentiment, and yet I understood something of what Elwynd was saying.

"I am a Cornishman," he went on.

Of course. Most Cornishmen did not even consider that Cornwall was part of England. How could he find peace anywhere but there?

Then he cocked his head in that way he had when he was turning thoughts over. I waited for him to speak, wanting him to know I did understand.

"You cannot run away from evil," he said. "Not if you're marked for it. You might travel east to another village or one of the towns, but if you're fated to be a victim, it will seek you out no matter where you are."

But then he surprised me after all, for he said, "Aye, perhaps I will leave someday."

"I suppose most Cornishmen never leave their homeland."

He shook his head, tossing the rock aside. "Aye, them that's got no plans." He gazed moodily across the moor as if seeing his own future there. "But a man like me deserves better. I was not born to be gamekeeper and no more."

His words made me curious. "It must be difficult not knowing what you were born to. I mean not knowing what or who your parents were."

He looked at me sharply. "I've thought some about that lately. Your aunt and the herb woman always told me I was the son of a village woman and a fisherman. That my father abandoned my mother and she had to give me up."

He picked up a long stick and began to turn it in his hands. "I don't think it's true, though."

"Why is that?"

He shrugged. "Just because. I got more wits than a fisherman, and some folks've seen that."

"Certainly you have a responsible job. Being game-keeper is quite a big position, I'd imagine."

He shrugged. "It ain't that much. But wait and see. I'll get what I want someday. There's ways."

I shivered slightly. I did not like the tone in which he spoke his last words.

"Enough talk," he said. "We'd best be moving on. Can you race?"

I untied Blackie and took my reins, and now Elwynd gave me a leg up to my sidesaddle. "Of course I can race," I said. "But you'll have to point out which way we're to go. That boulder field would kill a horse. I wouldn't want to take Blackie there."

"Nay, that way."

He pointed to a flat stretch of moor, and from what I could see, no holes waited to twist an ankle. Blackie heard the word *race*, for he snorted and pulled on his bit. He wanted his head, and I was as eager for the run as he was.

Elwynd mounted. His horse was frisking about too, and he finally whirled and shouted. "To the tor yonder."

And we were off. I leaned over Blackie, my knee wrapped tightly around the pommel as we flew over the flat ground. There was something wild and free about racing across the moor, and in that moment I felt nothing but rejoicing, wishing Blackie could run forever, and I would finally discover what lay just beyond the next rise of ground and within the next vale at the rim of the moor.

The huge outcropping of moorstone loomed nearer. We were neck in neck, but now Elwynd dropped back and I caught only a glimpse of his eyes set on the goal as he kicked his horse harder.

It might have happened in that second when my attention lapsed, or it might have happened anyway, but from behind a bush a hare leapt into our path, frightening Blackie. He plunged to one side, and I struggled to keep my seat. Panic swept over me as I sensed his gallop change.

Now he broke away from our path and raced headlong

155

across rough ground. I shouted and hauled hard on the reins, which only served to break his gait.

Then he reared and kicked, still spooked. I felt myself falling, and kicked my foot free of the stirrup. But there was nothing I could do about the hard ground that was coming toward me. I landed on my back.

The world spun above me. I was painfully aware that I could not get my breath. My lungs seemed to have collapsed, and I could not breathe.

I lay there, dazed, while Blackie dashed off. Then I heard hoofbeats behind me, and in a moment, Elwynd was off his horse and running up to me. He glanced about me before he knelt, a stricken look on his face.

My breath was coming back now, and I grabbed quick, shallow breaths. Seeing that I was having trouble getting my breath, Elwynd reached for my collar to undo it, to try to give me more air.

His fingers fumbled with the buttons, and once he had them undone at the collar, he struggled to open my blouse. I felt his fingers on my throat and gazed at him through blurry vision, fighting back the darkness that threatened. Then he seemed to draw back, his own face growing pale as he stared at me.

"Elwynd," I gasped. "Help me."

His eyes narrowed, and some dark emotion crossed his face. Pain mingled with thought as I struggled for clarity. And when my vision cleared, his earlier expression was replaced by concern as he helped me sit up.

"Are you all right, Rhionna?" he said.

"I think so," I gasped, still straining to fill my lungs. "I . . . I don't think I've broken anything." I gingerly tested my arms and then moved my feet.

"I just need to rest . . . for . . . for a few minutes."

I felt pain at the back of my head, and wondered if I'd hurt myself again where I'd been injured the night of the shipwreck.

156

Elwynd rose to one knee, looking for Blackie. After a few minutes, he turned back to me.

"Can you stand?"

I nodded, and leaning on him, I got up. It was only a few steps to his horse, and he helped me into his saddle, which I had to straddle. Blackie was nowhere in sight, and I gazed dizzily across the moor in concern.

"I wonder where Blackie's gone," I said. "Supposing he twists an ankle out there."

"Don't worry about him," Elwynd said. "He knows the way home. He'll turn up. But we must get you back."

"Oh, what will Winifred say? It seems I can't go anywhere without some trouble. She'll send me home now for sure."

It was odd that when one was near ruin, trivial matters seemed to take on great importance.

"No, not the cottage. To the castle."

"The castle?" I asked shakily.

"It's much nearer than the cottage. You'll want to rest."

He walked by the horse as we picked our way back. I felt dizzy, and though we were only going at a walk, it was all I could do to keep my seat. I may have even dozed, for I felt slightly unconscious for a time. I hadn't the slightest notion of where we were, and as the sun began to set, I lost my sense of direction as well.

But at length I could smell the sea again, and when I looked up I could see the castle looming. My strength was nearly gone, and it seemed a great length of time before we finally crossed the bridge and entered the courtyard. Elwynd helped me down, and I leaned on his arm as we climbed the steps to the door, which Godreven opened.

To my surprise, Morwenna came rushing down the spiral stairs, her skirts flying behind her and her arms outstretched.

"Rhionna," she said. "What has happened? Blackie came back alone, and we were so afraid—" her words

157

stopped abruptly.

"I'm all right now," I said. "I had a fall, nothing more.

But she seemed to read my face, and her own eyes held none of the distance I had seen there before. Instead, she took my other arm and began to guide me toward the stairs.

"Thank you, Elwynd," she said. "I'll see that she rests. A fall can be quite bad. We must have the doctor look at you.

"No, really," I tried to plead, though I was feeling poorly in truth. "I'm sure the doctor has better things to do than look at me. I've only suffered a few bruises at the worst.

We climbed the stairs, and indeed my joints seemed quite stiff. I had to admit I looked forward to the castle bedchamber. After sleeping on my aunt's sticky straw mattress on a few hard slats, the luxury the castle offered seemed more and more appealing.

Then I felt ashamed. Perhaps being in Castle Rhyweth had contaminated my mind with luxury if not with evil. But I was still in no condition to think, and I let Morwenna do the leading.

We entered the room that was becoming so familiar to me and she sent a servant scurrying for Olga. I still did not know what to make of all this solicitousness. Morwenna was a puzzling creature, often cold and distant, but now seeming to want someone to fuss over.

Olga came and helped me out of my riding habit and after a quick examination for bruises, tucked me into the familiar bed. I sank gratefully against the pillows, my words slightly incoherent.

"I suppose I could do with a rest. You will tell my aunt," I mumbled.

"Of course we will. Now don't you worry."

"And you'll see that Rufus gets fed?"

Morwenna tilted her head in puzzlement until Olga whispered a few words in her ear.

"Oh," said Morwenna. Then to me. "Rufus isn't here,

158

darling. He is safe at home with your aunt. Now you rest."

They left me alone, and I closed my eyes, thinking that the old wound on my head must have been injured again. Surely I shouldn't be so tired.

I slept for a little while, and then woke. It took a moment or so to remember what I was doing here, but the aches in my limbs helped remind me. I shook off the haze of sleep and sat up to find Gwynneth seated at the far end of the room by the fireplace mending my riding habit where it had been torn.

"Hello, Gwynneth," I said.

"Oh, miss. You're awake."

She put down her sewing and came over to the bed where I sat up against the pillows. "Are you feeling all right? They said you had a spill."

"Yes. My horse was frightened by a hare and he threw me. We were riding on the moors."

She frowned. "That's a dangerous place to ride, I'd think. You wouldn't catch me out there. Even if Elwynd does seem to know his way around there."

"Elwynd?"

I had forgotten that there was a potential romance here and didn't want her to think I was interfering.

"He only wanted to show me the old burial cists," I said. "And Blackie needed the exercise."

Her blonde brow lifted disapprovingly. "Foolish thing to do. Besides the evil spirits haunt those places. You shouldn't go near 'em."

"Oh, evil spirits. Is that all you think about in Cornwall? I do believe I've had enough of them."

I couldn't help my irritation. I was tired and still a bit worse for wear, and I found that my patience was wearing thin.

She shrugged defensively. "Better to be safe than sorry."

"Yes, yes. I suppose. Well, I shall get up. I'm feeling better now."

159

"Mistress Wycke says to call her when you're awake. If you're up to it, she hopes you'll dine with her in her sitting room."

This was a surprise. "Oh, well, that would be very nice. But really I'm quite recovered. I can go home now, for I don't want to be any more trouble."

"Mistress says you're no trouble." Then her tone of voice became intimate. "If you ask me, she wants the company. Be good for her if you stayed, miss. She don't get that many folks to talk to."

I leaned back against the pillows again. "Oh, I see. Well, of course I would enjoy it. You may tell her I'll stay."

We found something fitting for me to wear, and at the appointed time I went along to Morwenna's rooms in an adjoining wing. I found her reading a book, which she put down when I entered.

"Oh there you are, Rhionna," she said, rising from her sofa. "I hope you're quite all right now. I wanted to send for the doctor, but I didn't want you to be angry with me."

I was amused at the slight bewilderment on her face. Now she was playing the role of little girl afraid to lose a friend. But it struck an emotion within me, and I realized I was right about Morwenna. She hadn't many friends, and perhaps that was why she did not respond well to people.

A table was set before a cozy fire, and Morwenna led me to it. "I thought you would prefer to dine here where we can have a quiet conversation rather than a formal dinner downstairs."

"That was thoughtful of you." It was on the tip of my tongue to ask where her brother would dine, but I did not have to.

"My brother often dines alone," she volunteered. She smiled. "We so rarely have reason to dress for formal dinners downstairs. I rather dislike them."

In her own surroundings, Morwenna seemed much

more relaxed than I'd seen her before, and her comfort helped put me at ease. We dined and chatted like girls. I told her a great deal about life in New York, which led quite naturally to the questions I had determined to ask her about the people I had met since I'd been here.

"It seems that your father knew mine," I told her. "My father mentioned him several times." This was not true, but it served my purpose.

"Did he?" She searched her memory. "I'm afraid I don't remember my father mentioning anyone by the name of Fowley."

"His first name was Leslie."

She shook her head. "I'm sorry, but then my father was often very preoccupied. I wouldn't know if they were acquainted."

Still I pressed her. "I believe they had some business together. My father imported goods from Pendeen. Some of the handmade crafts that came from the villagers."

"How interesting. What sort of crafts?"

"Wool, lace, handmade carvings. Things like that."

She cocked her head with interest. "It was good then for the villagers. It's been very bad here since some of the mines closed."

I let out a long breath of air. Why was I so insistent that there was something to be learned here about my father's death? Was it simply my own inability to accept what was probably an accident? Since I had come to Cornwall, I was led to believe that evil doings were afoot, but there seemed to be no connection between them and the reasons I had left New York. If there was a thread that bound these events together, I was missing it.

I did not see Geoffrey that night, and I knew I ought to be glad. We stayed talking quite late in her rooms, and Morwenna offered to walk back with me along the dark corridors to my room.

As we left her room, I heard the music, distant

and haunting.

"Your brother plays the organ tonight."

"Every night."

"I am curious about the organ. He said he had it installed."

"Yes, a few years ago."

"I should like to see it sometime."

She raised a speculative brow at me. "I never like to go into the organ chamber. It is in a horrid place. It occupies part of the old dungeons."

I shivered, thinking how odd it must be to play music in such a place every night.

We stopped near my door.

"Good night, my dear," said Morwenna. "You must stay with us a few days. Surely your aunt can do without you for a brief spell."

I was about to refuse, when I remembered what Gwynneth had said. "Well, I suppose I could stay for awhile."

"Good, then it's decided."

I missed Rufus and Winifred that night, but again I gave in to the comforts of life in the castle. The music drifted upward as I began to relax, and I found that I was quite accustomed to it now. When he stopped playing, I came out of my doze. But then he began again, and the music soothed me, and I drifted off to sleep.

Chapter 12

The next day I sat with Morwenna in an upstairs parlor watching her do needlework. This part of the castle had been the solar, or women's quarters, in medieval times. The room which was large and now decorated with contemporary furnishings still had that feeling of domesticity about it, and was done in softer colors than the formal parlor downstairs.

There was a sewing corner, a reading corner, a music corner with a spinet, and a round table in the center of the room with a cut-glass oil lamp on it.

The sun was shining, for once, and I was feeling quite relaxed. I had slept undisturbed the night before, and I believed this was the first day that I felt anything like peace since I had arrived in Cornwall.

I should have realized that part of my good mood came from the sense of anticipation within me. When the door opened and Geoffrey came in, I felt my spirits lighten even further. He seemed in good spirits as well, and I wondered what the night had done to refresh him. And I could not help but notice his eyes lit with pleasure when he saw me. I examined every detail of his face and satisfied myself that he seemed well rested and less worried than the last time I had seen him.

"I heard we had a guest last night," he said, coming to me and lifting my hand with his. "It seems you cannot keep that pretty head of yours out of trouble. A fall from a horse this time, was it? And my own horse, too."

"Elwynd had her up on the moor," said Morwenna.

Brother and sister exchanged glances, but I made an effort to ease their concerns. "It was broad daylight, and Elwynd has pointed out to me the places to avoid riding. I am sorry if I endangered your horse. I suppose we should not have raced like that."

Geoffrey laughed out loud. "Not only must she explore the countryside, much of which the native villagers would not dare to set foot in, but she races across the moors as well. Such spirit."

I blushed. "I suppose it was foolish, though it did not seem so at the time."

"Yes, we could all say that about ourselves at one time or other."

However, the mirth in his eyes told me he was only teasing me, and in spite of myself I was relieved that he was not displeased. Luckily Blackie had returned to his stable unharmed.

Then Geoffrey's voice took on a more intimate tone, and just before he let go of my hand, his fingers brushed across the back of it. "You look well enough today," he said. "I am glad."

Then he lifted his hand to my cheek and touched my face with his fingers.

We smiled at one another until I began to feel embarrassed. Then he fingered the silver cross I had around my neck, looking at me quizzically.

"I have not seen this before," he said.

"I—my aunt gave it to me," I lied.

His look queried me as he turned it over in his palm. "A fine piece of workmanship."

"Yes, isn't it?"

He turned and strode over to inspect his sister's work then, eyeing the embroidery critically.

"And what have we here? I did not know you fancied such handiwork, dear sister. What has brought about this spate

164

of domesticity?"

She pulled her lips back in impatience as if she were very used to her brother's unwelcome teasing.

"I do not sew and stitch as many women do," she said, tossing her head. "Because there are no other women to talk to while doing it. Nothing is so dreadful as sticking your fingers with a needle all day, crossing your eyes at tiny stitches, the muscles in your shoulders tightening, and no one with whom to share an hour's gossip. Thankfully, Rhionna has consented to give me a few hours of her companionship. Besides, what need have I to do needlework? Your mending is done well enough by Olga."

"True enough. Olga is very accomplished at such matters. But I think that perhaps you are practicing in case you find yourself in another home someday with women enough to satisfy your desire for gossip and a man who wants his wife to do his sewing, not his housekeeper."

She frowned, her high cheekbones taking on a tinge of pink. "I cannot think what you mean, dear brother. No one has asked for my hand, and you very well know it. You perhaps will be burdened with a spinster sister all your life."

"I don't doubt that no one has proposed because no one can stand that biting tongue of yours. Somehow I do not see you in the role of submissive wife."

His teasing roused her defenses and with blood flushing her face, she seized the embroidery she was working on and hauled it back as if to throw it at him but he stayed her arm, thus avoiding the pins and needles.

"Now, now, dear sister. You know I was only teasing. I think it is a very good thing that you sew." He cast a smile at me across the room. "Rhionna is a double blessing if she encourages you in this enterprise."

He chuckled at his own humor, but from his remarks, I wondered about Morwenna's prospects for marriage. I had thought that Lord Stratton's visit to the castle was brought on by more than his friendship for Geoffrey, but perhaps I was wrong. Though the couple had disappeared the night we had all dined together, it did not necessarily mean that Stratton was courting her.

Then Geoffrey turned his eyes on me again, compelling eyes that made my pulse quicken. At that moment, it seemed entirely incongruous that he might have an evil bone in his long, lithe body, for his eyes sent me a ray of warmth, and I felt the slow throbbing in my veins. Even without touching me, my body responded to his, as if I took energy from him. We gazed at each other for some seconds, then he spoke.

"The reason I sought you ladies out is to remind my sister of the Easter ball and to inform Miss Fowley of it. Though this castle may be a cold and dreary place for most of the year, the coming of spring has traditionally been celebrated here with a grand ball. If your mourning will allow it, Rhionna, I hope you and your aunt will attend."

I could not help but return his sly smile, my responses coming alive to him. "My father did not believe in a long period of mourning. I am sure he would want me to attend."

"I can see your father was a man of wisdom as well as untraditional habits."

"That he was." It seemed quite natural to go on. "But then of course your father knew him."

"Did he? I was not aware of it."

My hopes fell. If I could not get information out of Morwenna, I had hoped I might learn something from her brother. But it seemed I was to be disappointed here as well.

"That is too bad. There were certain business matters of my father's I was thinking of looking into. I had hoped you might be able to help me with them."

I was treading on dangerous ground, for I hadn't thought out what I would say if he pressed me, but as was my foolish habit, I forged ahead.

Geoffrey cocked his head. "I would be intrigued by this business you speak of, however I do not know of it."

His expression was sincere, and I believed he was telling the truth. Now it was my turn to appear puzzled. For I truly was growing more curious about Arthur Wycke's with my father. If there was no business, what then? Or was there business, but of a secret nature? But Winifred knew of it.

"For heavens' sake, how can you talk about balls and business in the same breath?" said Morwenna. "If we are to give the ball, it will be a great deal of work. You will help me make the plans, won't you, Rhionna? Geoffrey is absolutely no help on the matter."

Geoffrey winked at me. "Do not listen to Morwenna's complaints. She does it to mask her own enthusiasm. For with the ball come many eligible men of her station. It is just possible, if she does not put on too sour a face that night, that one of them might deign to pay her court."

I thought Morwenna was about to throw the pincushion at Geoffrey, so I quickly intervened. "Of course I'll be what help I can. But I wouldn't know where to begin in planning such a large affair."

"There's nothing to it," said Geoffrey with a wave of the hand. "We've done it so often, we hardly need to issue orders. The servants know what to do. And of course they have their own party late on the same night."

"That is nice. Then everyone has something to look forward to."

"That is so. And now I will leave you ladies to whatever mischief you have planned for today."

"Hardly mischief," said Morwenna. "I thought Rhionna deserved a rest. She works so very hard at her aunt's cottage, and she is not used to it."

"I have always worked very hard," I said in defense of myself, for I did not know if Morwenna were ridiculing my inability to do hard work or the necessity for it. "But it is true I am not used to all the outdoor work my aunt does. She is a strong woman for doing such hard work. I only hope I have

167

half her strength."

"You have great strength," said Geoffrey, coming to bow over my hand, which he brushed with a kiss. "But do not ruin these," he said, reaching for my other hand. The look he gave me caused me to miss a breath, but I pulled my hands away.

If I could not control my feelings around this man, then I was in as great a danger as if he were the evil they all said he was. I was no innocent. I knew where such feelings led, and I was afraid Geoffrey Wycke was only toying with mine.

He stood. "I look forward to seeing you both at supper this evening."

He left the room and I struggled to turn my attention back to Morwenna. We made light conversation, and she asked my advice on her needlework. When I could again concentrate, I saw that Morwenna did quite fine work, and I thought she did not deserve her brother's teasing.

An hour before supper, I went to my room to put on a suitable gown, and to my surprise Gwynneth was there with Rufus, who leapt up to greet me.

"For heaven's sake," I said, accepting his doggy kisses. "Where did you come from?"

Gwynneth and I laughed as Rufus bounded between us.

"I went to the village today," Gwynneth explained. "Your aunt was there with Rufus, and she asked me to bring him here to you, seeing as how you were staying on."

"How thoughtful of her." I was surprised that Winifred would not keep Rufus at home, but Gwynneth's expression explained it.

Her smiles were replaced by a look of concern. "I think she was worried about you."

"Well," I said, petting Rufus. "There's nothing to worry about. I hope you reassured her."

"Oh yes, miss, I did." Then she gave a funny little grin. "But your dog needed a change of scene."

I laughed at her humor, as she continued, "I accompanied your aunt to her cottage, and I brought you this."

Laid out on the bed was one of the gowns I had bought in St. Ives, a lavender crepe de Chine and purple velvet. Gwynneth dressed my hair, commenting as I finished dressing on my silver cross.

"It was a gift from my aunt," I fibbed.

"Quite pretty it is," she said. "Goes with the dress quite nicely."

I tried to tell myself I was not superstitious and only wore the cross because it was a lovely piece of silver jewelry. But I knew that was not entirely true.

At supper, I sensed that Geoffrey was preoccupied, and I wondered what had happened between midday and now to change his mood. Neither was Morwenna particularly talkative, so we ate the stargazy pie filled with stuffed herrings almost in silence. Then we took our coffee in the formal parlor.

"Perhaps we can have some music," I said. "Morwenna, do you play?"

She made a face. "Not very well. Mother made sure I learned, but I'm afraid all the talent went to Geoffrey."

"Now, Morwenna dear sister, that is not true," he said modestly. "But we have not given our guest an opportunity to entertain us herself if she so desires."

"I'm afraid I am not very good on the piano either," I said. Though I too had learned to play a little, the thought of demonstrating my poor keyboard skills in front of Geoffrey filled me with dread.

"I do sing a little," I said.

His eyes lit with interest, and he rose and went to the harpsichord. "In that case, I believe I can accompany you."

He took a music book from a shelf by the harpsichord and handed it to me. "Perhaps you can find something in there."

I nodded, turning the pages. I was unfamiliar with most

169

of these English songs, but my eye fell on *'O mio babbino caro,'* the beautiful Italian aria by Puccini, wherein Lauretta begs her devilishly clever father, Gianni Schicci, to help her lover's family recover their fortune. I had studied it, and I handed it to Geoffrey.

He smiled. "A most appropriate choice."

As he began the introduction, I realized the risk I had undertaken in singing for him. Though I had sung for friends before, now butterflies seized my stomach and I had to lean on the harpsichord for support. But Geoffrey raised his eyes to me and I began.

I sang the aria slowly and lovingly, and he followed me easily, anticipating where I would take a breath. I began to relax, swept up in the romantic music. Indeed the acoustics of the room made my voice reverberate and echo, giving me confidence as well. I hung onto the high notes just a trace, and Geoffrey's accompaniment enhanced the sound. My eyes met his on the last phrase and together we brought the aria to a close.

The notes died away and then after a moment during which the music seemed suspended in the air, both Geoffrey and Morwenna applauded.

"That was very good, Rhionna," said Morwenna. She stifled a yawn. "However, I shall not be able to stay for more music. My brother may prowl about the castle at night, however I do not. I need my beauty rest. It is my habit to retire early. I rise before the sun. I'm sure you do not mind my leaving you alone."

I bid her good-night and after thanking me again for my company, she left us.

"Perhaps I should go up too," I said, feeling suddenly uncomfortable, but Geoffrey raised a hand.

"Not so soon, I hope? I was looking forward to your company for a little while yet. Perhaps you would not mind if I played something."

"Of course not."

170

He nodded and turned back to the harpsichord, and I settled more deeply into a plush ladies' chair. He played a sonata by Scarlatti, and as usual, even though he was not playing music of his own composing, I was put under his spell.

The piece abounded with brilliant scale passages, cross-hand sections and rapid repeated notes as well as the rhythms and harmonies of the composer's adopted country, Spain. Out of Geoffrey's long, elegant fingers came the gay rhythms of a Spanish guitar. I felt as if the music lifted me out of my body and we danced together on an altogether different plane of existence.

Then he stopped playing, and when he looked at me his eyes were the embers of a dark smouldering fire that set my feelings ablaze. I thought when he finally rose and came to me, that he would take me in his arms as he had the last time, but he did not. Instead, as I rose to my feet, he gently laid his fingers on my cheek, brushing my forehead with the softest of kisses.

"My dear Rhionna," he said softly. "What a pleasure you are to me. You have brought beauty back into my life."

"But surely you have beauty in your music," I said, afraid I would sway against him from the dizziness I felt.

He pulled the corner of his mouth back in irony. "My music has been sad, shut off from the rest of the world. And I have not played for others, until now."

"Then I am greatly honored. But you should play your music for others, for you are very good."

He shrugged. "The world is not ready for my music. They listen to music by Mendelssohn, Handel, Bach, and the new composers, John Stainer, Hubert Parry, and Charles Stanford. Of them all I am influenced slightly perhaps by Mendelssohn. Except for that, I do not follow a traditional path."

Thinking of the snatches of organ music I had heard late at night, I thought perhaps he was right. It was strange

171

music, and perhaps not suited to the concert hall, certainly not for a church.

"I would like to watch you play the organ. Might I see it sometime?"

His eyes immediately shaded and his jaw seemed to tense. "That would not be possible. I allow no one in the organ chamber."

"But why?" The words were out of my mouth before I could stop them. He played the harpsichord for me here. I did not see why he would not play the organ for me as well.

His eyes flashed with a dark inscrutable look. "I compose in the organ chamber. I never take anyone there. It would be bad luck."

"Oh I see."

I didn't see, but I could hardly question it. Surely he was not that superstitious. My frustrations rose, and I struggled to push them aside, remembering that he too was Cornish.

"Come, I will see you to your room."

He led me from the parlor and we walked along the dark corridors. I felt as though I was becoming used to the darkness of the castle at night, relieved only by the flickering of the candles in their sconces. I sensed that we were being watched, and as we turned to climb the stone steps, I saw Jonas' familiar hunched figure with his long extinguisher.

Our footsteps echoed as we climbed to the floor above, and then we made our way to the door of my bedchamber. Geoffrey's arm went around me and I looked up. I saw the passion in his eyes then, but also restraint, as if he had a reason to withhold himself tonight.

"Rest well, dear Rhionna," he said, his lips coming down for a kiss.

My own arms slid around his neck, and he drew me to him, his kiss deepening. I rejoiced at the feel of his hard body next to mine and felt disappointment when he pulled away. I could not see his face for the shadows, but his voice was low and full of intensity.

"Do not be disturbed if you hear sounds in the castle. I shall be working as usual tonight."

"Goodnight, Geoffrey. It was a lovely dinner."

I slipped into the room to find the bed turned down and a fire in the fireplace. Gwynneth sleepily helped me out of my dress, and then I crawled into the bed, pleasure and a feeling of wanting more mingling in me as I drifted off to sleep.

I was awakened some time later by Rufus' whining, and I turned over in the bed.

"Rufus, what is it? Come here."

I unconsciously patted the bed, forgetting that he wasn't allowed on the bed in the castle. But he didn't jump up. Instead, he paced back and forth, continuing to whine and give gruff little barks. I wondered if Gwynneth had forgotten to take him out before bedtime, and coming more fully awake, I sat up.

"Now where is my dressing gown?" I muttered to myself. "Just a minute, Rufus. I'll take you downstairs if that is what you want."

The fire had gone out, so I lit the lamp beside my bed. Then finding my slippers and tying the dressing gown tightly around me, I picked up the lamp and went to the door. It creaked as it opened, and cold air rushed in. I shivered, looking down at Rufus, who looked up at me with pleading eyes.

"Are you sure you have to go?" I said. If it was this cold in the corridor, I could imagine how cold it would be outside.

The few sputtering lights remaining lit in the corridor cast long shadows, and I had to gather courage even to walk as far as the main staircase. I had never walked these halls alone, and the prospect was more terrifying than I had imagined it would be. From every corner I felt as if a pair of eyes lurked, or that something from the shadows might jump out at me like the bat that had attacked me in the vale

173

near the cottage.

We met with no one, but my knees were shaking by the time we came to the main staircase. The stone bannister was cold and rough to the touch and I found myself crouching against it. Rufus stayed at my heels as if he too did not want to venture out of the light thrown by my small lamp.

We turned the corner onto the landing above the entry hall, and then I stopped in surprise. For standing at the foot of the stairs was Morwenna in a black velvet dressing gown. She seemed to be talking to someone out of sight, behind the heavy oak doors that led to the courtyard outside. I stared, open-mouthed.

Morwenna had said she was going to retire early, yet here she was. She had not noticed me, but was speaking in a low tone, her gestures agitated. Something did not seem right, but it took me a moment to figure it out. Finally I realized what it was.

Opposite her stood the full-length gilded mirror that I had passed in the main hall dozens of times. Although a dim flicker of light bounced off the gilded frame, no reflection of Morwenna came from the mirror as there ought to be, even though she stood directly opposite the glass. My mind registered the connection with something I had read in the horrid little book about vampires, but before I could react, Rufus barked loudly and bounded down the stairs.

Morwenna looked up, her eyes wide in surprise, and she grimaced and recoiled at the approach of my dog. The main doors stood open, and Rufus growled, his claws scrabbling across the stone floor as he chased whoever had gone out.

"Rufus, come back," I yelled, scurrying down the rest of the steps. I hurried after him and Morwenna followed me. He had slipped through the door before it closed. I hauled at the heavy oak door and went out, racing down the steps. I found Rufus standing in the courtyard, barking in the direction of the gatehouse.

"Rufus, what is the matter?" I knelt and gripped his collar. "Whoever were you chasing, you bad dog?"

Morwenna stared at Rufus and then in the direction he was barking. I looked up at her. "Who was it?"

"Only Elwynd," she said.

I blinked, the strange occurrence unnerving me. "What was he doing here at this hour?"

I had Rufus under control now, and he sat obediently next to me.

"One of the village women is expecting a child, and the husband went to Elwynd, asking if Dr. Pearce was about the castle, for he had been summoned here earlier to tend one of the servants who was ill."

"But why did he run?" I asked. "I didn't know he was afraid of Rufus."

Morwenna eyed me speculatively. "The barking must have startled him."

We turned to go in and made our way upstairs. I felt extremely nervous. Morwenna bid me good-night at my door, and I was too frightened to try to make sense of her explanation. Rufus had settled down now, but back in my room I still could not sleep.

Then the incident of not seeing Morwenna's reflection in the mirror came back to me. It had slipped my mind while I was trying to calm Rufus and get him back upstairs, but now my thoughts returned to it. Feeling troubled, I rose and put on my dressing gown and went to poke up the fire again. There were things not right at Castle Rhyweth, but I could not seem to put my finger on them. The strange little book I had read said vampires have no reflection. I tried to remember if I had ever seen Geoffrey's reflection in a glass.

When I thought on it, I realized that except for the mirror downstairs there were no others in the castle. In this room, Gwyenneth always brought me a hand mirror. I shuddered. The rational part of my mind tried to reason that there was an explanation for all of this. But in the shadows of the night, I listened to the fear that grew within me, until I was completely at its mercy. The reactive part of my mind had me in its grip, issuing commands of self-preservation, whether they were rational or not.

I rose. I must leave the castle at once, I thought. While I did not believe that Geoffrey would harm me, the pounding of my heart and the fear coursing through my veins told me I was in great danger. And I had never been quite comfortable with Morwenna. She was a strange woman.

I looked down at Rufus. "We must leave now," I whispered, "before it is too late."

I was shaking as I dressed in the riding habit Gwynneth had mended for me, and found a cloak to wrap over me.

"We must be very quiet," I told Rufus.

I felt unsteady, but I had decided on a course and had to pursue it. I had been foolish not to heed earlier warnings, but now I was in fear of my life. I did not understand these Cornish and their superstitions, and if evil lurked in the castle, I could not be certain of its source. But one thing had imprinted itself on my mind. If there was danger here, I still had a chance to escape its net.

I opened my bedroom door slowly, afraid that I might be caught. But no one lurked in the corridor. We moved stealthily along, my eyes now used to the darkness, for only one lamp flickered nearby. We came to an alcove just before the main staircase, and I slipped into it, knowing that from there I could not be seen, but I could see. I had thought there was a shadow moving up the stairs, and I waited, my heart pounding in my ears as the shadow moved up the circular wall.

Jonas finally emerged on the top step. I shrank further back against the cold stone, praying that Rufus would not give us away. But Rufus held still, and Jonas went on. I counted to a hundred, then deciding it was safe to continue, I stepped out of my hiding place. Another thought struck me, and I paused long enough to consider it.

I did not hear the organ music now, so perhaps Geoffrey had gone to bed. It was said that vampires sleep in coffins. If I saw Morwenna and Geoffrey alseep in their beds, would it not put my mind at ease?

Even before I had decided to do so, my footsteps took me down the corridor in the direction I knew Geoffrey's bed-chamber to be. There was still no one about, although I had no way of knowing if Jonas would come back my way.

I came to the door I knew led to Geoffrey's room and with heart pounding, I reached out my hand for the door handle. I did not know what I would say if caught, but something drove me on. I turned the handle carefully, afraid it would squeak. Then I pushed the door open a crack. All was dark in his sitting room, and I could see only a sliver of light coming from what must be his bedchamber.

I stepped into the room and closed the door behind me, realizing that at any moment I could be compromised. But the need to know the truth drove me forward, and I tiptoed across the room. Placing my hand on the door to his bed-chamber, I pushed it inward. Then I could see the predawn light spilling in through the open window, dimly illuminat-ing the empty bed. A folded nightshirt lay across the foot.

I tried to swallow, but my throat was dry. If he was not in bed, where was he? Terror filled me, and I quickly crossed the room again, then opened the door to peer out into the corridor. It would be dawn soon, which brought me some relief. At least I would not have to travel the distance through the woods in complete darkness, for that prospect horrified me as much as staying in the castle.

I fled down the corridor to the main stairs and de-scended. Then I turned and ran in the direction of the kitchens. If I could get to the stable, perhaps I could find Blackie, saddle him, and get away. But somehow in the twists and turns of intersecting corridors, I became con-fused. I ran up against sets of stairs I had not seen before. Thinking I had gone too far, I turned and ran back the other way. The corridors seemed narrower here, and the gargoyles set into the walls to hold candles seemed to grimace at my confusion. I felt tears spring to my eyes. Was I trapped here then, never to get out?

"Oh, Rufus," I finally cried, shrinking down to sit on the bottom of a set of spiral stairs that went I knew not where. "We're lost. Help me, help me," I sobbed to no one in particular, muffling my cries in Rufus' fur.

Then to my horror, I heard the echo of evil laughter coming from somewhere above me. It began softly, no more than a whisper as if carried on the wind, then built to a half-human, half-unnatural sound. It must be directed at me, but who was it, and where did it come from?

I looked up to see dawn's rays coming through some high windows, but no one was there. Still, the laughter echoed, bouncing off the stone walls until it seemed like a chorus of monsters mocked me.

"Stop," I screamed, standing up and holding my ears. My tears blinded me, but I fled, not caring in which direction, wanting only to escape the horrid, evil laughter. I ran up a short flight of steps and down another corridor, the laughter following me. Finally, it seemed to stop, but I ran on, the tears streaming down my face and Rufus at my heels, until I finally turned another corner. Long arms reached for me.

"Rhionna," a deep voice said.

But I struggled. "Let go of me," I cried. But the arms seemed to entrap me in an iron grasp.

"Rhionna." Now I recognized the voice and looked up in horror at Geoffrey's face.

Then I threw back my head and screamed a long, piercing scream.

Chapter 13

"Rhionna, what is the matter?" Geoffrey's voice finally penetrated my hysteria. He shook me hard, bringing me to my senses.

I still choked on my screams, but after some moments fought to gain control of myself. I didn't know what I expected to happen, but nothing horrible befell me except that as I stood shaking and sobbing, Geoffrey picked me up and carried me along the corridor.

"Hush now," he said. "You've had a fright. And what are you doing about the castle at this hour fully clothed?"

"I—" I tried to give an answer but could not. More light was coming in through the windows, and as the shadows withdrew, I was more able to speak coherently.

"There was laughter, evil laughter, coming from somewhere."

I felt limp and confused. Someone had threatened me. Had it been Geoffrey? But now he looked down at me with concern in his eyes, his grip on me sure and strong.

"We'll speak more of this later," he said, drawing his mouth into a grim line. Then he repeated his other question. "But where were you going so early?"

"I . . . I," I struggled to get my breath. "I was leaving."

We reached my bed chamber and Geoffrey kicked open the door. Then he strode in and laid me on the bed. I was more in control of myself now, however, and sat up.

"I did not know you rose so early," he said with a half smile. "Of course, I am usually abed at this hour, and so am not familiar with your morning habits. But surely you were not going without saying good-bye."

He unbuttoned my cloak and let it fall back from me, his hand resting on my shoulder. I was still trembling and hardly knew how to answer him.

He lifted my chin with his fingers and forced me to look into his eyes. When I did so, I felt my resistance weaken. "You said you had a fright," he said. "Tell me about it."

I pulled away slightly, but I answered his question. "I was going to the kitchens to get Rufus something to eat," I lied. "And I missed my turn. I became confused and wandered into the wrong part of the castle."

"So that explains what you were doing in the . . . there," he said, changing his wording at the last moment.

"But someone was watching me," I said, my voice tightening. "I felt it. Then I heard laughing. It was an awful sound. I was so frightened."

I could not help myself and placed my hands over my eyes as if to blot out the horror.

"Come now," he said, gathering me into his arms. "It's over now."

He rocked me gently, and though I was still rigid, the motion did something to soothe me. Still, he had not denied that someone had tried to frighten me.

At length, he said, "And where were you when this laughter frightened you?"

I shook my head. "I don't know. There were some high windows, and I could see the dawn. Then I ran and came to the short flight of stairs. I don't know, I don't know."

My head was against his shoulder, and I craved the comfort and warmth it offered, but part of me was still fearful. Geoffrey himself had been somewhere other than in his bed. Could it not have been he who had watched as I raced the maze of corridors? My heart was troubled, and I knew not where to turn. I wanted to give in to his masculine strength, let him bear my dilemmas on his strong shoulders, but that was not possible.

"Well," he said, "you must rest. You are hysterical. I can hardly let you leave in this state."

"I am not hysterical." His condescending tone angered me, and I pulled away and sat up. "I do not need any rest."

Indeed this was not true, for it was still very early, and the sleepless night I had spent was telling on me.

His eyes took on that teasing look that previously had charmed me, and he ran the back of his fingers across my cheek.

"A little rest only, I think. For your eyelids look very heavy to me." He laid me back on the pillows.

"Come, Rhionna, let me kiss you to sleep." And he lowered his lips to mine.

I resisted his kiss at first, but the warmth of his body over me drained the last of my determination. Instead I moaned softly as he raised his mouth to softly kiss my cheeks, my ears, my throat. "Do not fear, beautiful Rhionna. I will not let anything hurt you, if there is indeed something trying to do so. You can rely on that."

I swallowed and looked into his somber, serious eyes. Then I felt my mouth respond to taste of him again. This time his arms went around me and he pressed me to him. I felt the blood rising within me, and when his hands slid down my side to caress the length of hip and thigh, I did not resist, though I knew I should. I had dressed so quickly I had not bothered with a corset, and his hands on the curves of my body were now discovering this fact. I was embarrassed by the pleasure on his face, and I lowered my eyes.

"Rhionna, you tempt me so. Perhaps I should send you away just as you wish to go. For I am not sure I can control myself around you."

He kissed me again, his words interspersed between caresses. "You have already seen how powerless I am to remain the gentleman around you."

181

He held me tightly again, and I think that it was only the confines of our clothing that kept us apart then, giving Geoffrey time to come to his senses. Finally, he pulled back.

"However, I will let you rest. I will see that you have no interruptions. If you have determined to leave us today, so be it. I will have the carriage made ready."

He left me, and I tried to gather my wits. Realizing that I did need the rest, I lay back and closed my eyes. Though I was still determined to go home today, I felt safer now that it was daylight. My irrational thoughts were tucked safely away now in some dark chamber of my mind.

I must have slept, for when I awoke, I felt hungry. I put myself together, striving not to look like I'd had such a horrible night. Then I left the room and made my way downstairs. I had no idea what time it was, but when I entered the dining room, I saw that silver dishes and a large coffee urn were still on the sideboard. Godreven stood by in his usual formal dress.

"Good morning," he said. "Would you care for breakfast?"

"Thank you, I would."

I seated myself and he served me, then quietly withdrew. I began my breakfast alone, the clock at one end of the room marking the minutes. Then, the door opened. I looked up, expecting to see Geoffrey or Morwenna enter, but to my surprise, Lord Stratton came in, dressed in riding attire.

I was so surprised to see him, I failed to speak.

"Ah, good morning, Miss Fowley," he said, dropping his riding crop on the end of the table. "May I call you Rhionna? It is such an enchanting name."

"I—that is, of course." I sat up straighter, regaining some composure.

He nodded in my direction as he crossed to the buffet and lifted up one of the silver corners to inspect the food.

"And please call me Enys. The title is a bit cumbersome for all but the most formal occasions."

"Very well," I said.

"Just got back from a most pleasant ride," he said.

With that sixth sense that well-trained servants have, Godreven entered the dining room. "May I serve you, sir?" he asked Lord Stratton.

"Yes, a bit of ham, a scone, and clotted cream."

He pulled back a chair and took a seat across from me. "Didn't know you were here," he said.

"Nor I you."

"I got here quite late last night," he explained after he took a sip of the coffee that Godreven brought. "Knew old Geoffrey would be composing. Didn't want to disturb him. Just had Olga fix me a room."

"I see. And what brings you to Castle Rhyweth this time?"

My mind was racing. Had Morwenna known of his arrival? Could it have been he that she was talking to downstairs last night rather than Elwynd as she said? But if so, why the subterfuge? Worse still, could it have been he who had been prowling the castle and making that horrible evil laughter?

Looking at him now with his blond hair falling across one brow, as he put away a plate heaped full of food, it was difficult to fathom. He looked at me with a twinkle in his eye.

"Any excuse to escape London for a bit. Parliament can be so dreary."

"Indeed," I said. "But is Castle Rhyweth so much more tempting than your own home in Devon?"

"You have not seen that monstrous place. I wander its halls with little to do." Then he gave me a wink. "And besides, my mother is there. Rules like a tyrant. There's no need for me to manage the estate. She sees to every penny."

183

"I see." I finished my meal then said, "I must be going now. My aunt will be expecting me."

He stood as Godreven cleared my plate. "It seems that we only meet when you are departing. Perhaps it will be otherwise some time."

"Perhaps. Good morning, sir."

He bowed "Good morning, Rhionna."

I left the dining room and went to get Rufus, who I had left in my room, and then came back downstairs. I spoke to Godreven, telling him that Lord Rhyweth had said he would have the carriage ready, and he went to see about it.

While I was waiting I strolled into the picture gallery, finding the dark oils in daylight quite different than they had been at night. Motes of sun danced across the long gallery, and the portraits seemed oddly less alive than they had by lamplight. I heard a footstep behind me and gave a start. Geoffrey walked in, the dark circles under his eyes making him look more tired than usual.

"Good morning," he said. "I see you are ready to leave."

"Yes," I said. "Godreven has gone to get the carriage."

He gave me a distant smile, and I felt relief that he did not ask me to delay my departure. "Having another look at the ancestors, I see?" he asked.

But I hardly heard him, for my eye had fallen on a portrait near the end of the row. Of course I had seen the painting of the tall man with broad shoulders and silver hair highlighted about his temples before. I stared at the man. Yes, I thought, the features were the same, though in the miniature of my aunt's he looked much younger.

"This painting," I said. "It is one of your father isn't it?"

"Yes," said Geoffrey. "My father, Arthur Wycke. I thought I had pointed him out the night I showed you the gallery. But of course I was rather distracted that night."

I heard the reminiscent tone in his voice, but I did not respond to it. Rather, I stared as if not seeing him. The realization struck me so suddenly and with so much force,

184

I felt myself sway on my feet. My aunt had been in love with Geoffrey's father. I choked on my silent questions. Did he know? How did she get the miniature portrait? Did Arthur return her love? If so, was it platonic love only, or more?

It stunned me to imagine that my aunt had perhaps not been so circumspect in her maiden life as I had been led to believe. But now I was aware that Geoffrey was gazing at me speculatively.

"Something seems to have startled you. I have never known my father's portrait to create quite such an effect."

As usual, Geoffrey's sensuous tone mixed with wry humor completely disconcerted me. I struggled to form an answer.

"It's just that I thought I saw this picture somewhere else." Then not wanting to explain where, I said, "I was only trying to assess which features your father shared with you."

Geoffrey glanced critically at the picture. "It is perhaps difficult to judge from this painting. However there is one of my father in his younger years hanging in the library. I will show it to you sometime and let you judge for yourself."

"Yes, that would be very nice, some other time. I must go now. The carriage will be waiting."

"Yes, of course." He held the door for me.

Somehow my limbs moved and I went out with Geoffrey and down the steps to the waiting carriage. As we approached the shiny black brougham, I tried to think. Just before I reached it, I turned to Geoffrey.

"Thank you," he said to Malcolm. "I will see that Miss Fowley is settled in the carriage."

Malcolm bowed and climbed onto the driver's seat.

"Well," said Geoffrey, the light returning to his eyes as he stood near me next to the carriage. "Have you now recovered enough to say good-bye?"

185

Flushing at my own temerity, I knew I had to ask him a question before I left. "I was just wondering, after looking at the picture inside . . ."

He leaned one hand against the carriage above my shoulder. "Yes? What were you wondering?"

I took a deep breath and plunged ahead. "Were your parents happily married?"

A cloud seemed to replace the fiery interest in his eyes from a moment before, and his forehead puckered slightly as he straightened. "Such a question deserves a serious answer," he replied. "Not one I can give in two sentences."

I pressed my lips together. "I'm sorry. I suppose I have no right to ask.

"And I wonder why you ask."

But I could not find words to answer.

He shook his head. "I don't know why I should be telling you this, and I dare not flatter myself that you will tell me your reasons for asking. But since you are so curious, no." His look perceptibly darkened. "I'm afraid my parents' marriage was not happy."

I stared into his face, but my mind was reeling. I gratefully took the hand he offered to steady me as I stepped up and then seated myself on the plush seat of the carriage. He closed the door, and I gave him one last glance through the glass as he told Malcolm to drive on. Then the horse's hooves were clattering over the cobblestones.

We picked up speed and rushed over the bridge, then onto the road. As we topped the rise and took the Cliff Road, I saw the waves break and rush to shore far below. Now only a few remnants of the ship that brought me here remained. Much of the wreck had been dismantled and used for firewood.

I had almost decided to leave Cornwall. The twists and turns I had followed seemed to have little to do with my father's death and everything to do with strange goings on here, events that were no business of mine. But now I had been presented with something on which I could not turn my back. And I hardly knew how to put my discovery to my aunt.

By the time we left the Cliff Road behind and passed through the woods, I decided that I would need to find the right moment to put the question to Winifred. I could hardly blame her for not telling me of her long ago love. She had been a village girl; Arthur was a great lord. And just as there had been rumors about Geoffrey's liasons, could it have not been the same with his father? Certainly I was curious, but I did not want to invade Winifred's privacy without good reason.

I would wait until circumstance permitted, and then surely if I asked the right question she would tell me.

Chapter 14

My aunt seemed glad to have me back, and I could see
she had been anxious about me. I assured her that the fall
from my horse had been nothing but my own stupidity, and
that the best thing to do when you fell from a horse was to
ride again, which I knew I would do before long.

I needed to see if my money had been wired to the bank,
and so I suggested that I take Nedda and go to St. Ives.
Winifred balked at my traveling the distance by myself. She
was deciding if she could leave her chores until tomorrow so
that she might accompany me, when it turned out the
matter was settled by Lord Stratton, who drove up in his
very elegant carriage. I heard the jingle of harness bells and
the rumbling of wheels and went to look.

I was awestruck by the arrival of the shiny red and gold
carriage with coat of arms on the polished door and brass
lamps on either side of the box. The liveried driver pulled
the perfectly matched grays to a stop and the footman got
down to open the door. The sight seemed quite anomalous
in this humble setting.

"It's Lord Stratton, the earl from Devon," I said as the
carriage door opened, and the lord himself emerged.

"What could he possibly want here?" I asked the air.

He came through the gate and up our flagstone walk,
and I went out to meet him.

"Good morning again," said Lord Stratton.

"Good day," I said. "This is again a surprise."

He smiled rather sheepishly. "I did say I would be here a

few days. You see, my mother is arriving. I—" Then he stopped and sighed. "May I come in?"

"Oh, yes, um, do come in. Oh, Aunt Winifred, this is Enys Northcote, Earl of Stratton. My aunt, Miss Winifred Fowley."

I had never introduced a lord before and had no idea if my etiquette was correct.

"My lord," said Winifred.

He bowed. "Pardon my intrusion, madam, but I have come to ask a favor."

I gestured to our humble abode.

"After you," he said, and I led the way inside.

When we had gotten inside, I glanced around quickly. There seemed no place fitting to offer him a chair, so we remained standing, but he did not seem to notice.

"What can we do for you, my lord?" I asked. When he answered, he addressed my aunt.

"Well, you see, it is rather complicated. My mother has decided to descend on Castle Rhyweth. I just got her letter, which arrived only half a day ahead of her. But I've just had word, I must go up to London sooner than I'd thought. I will be able to meet her in St. Ives, but I cannot take the time to escort her back, for I must go on. I thought perhaps you could spare your niece for the day, if she would be willing to act as companion to my mother on the return trip."

"I?" The notion completely took me aback. Why should Lord Stratton's mother want to travel with me? And what would I say to her?

"Well yes. I know it is an awful imposition. I would of course be anxious to make it up to you at some future opportunity. I am simply desperate, you see."

I still stared at him blankly, but he continued.

"I had asked Morwenna if she would like to come, but she refused."

"Morwenna?" Then light began to dawn. Was he bringing his mother to meet his bride to be?

"I see. Well," I still hesitated, looking questioningly at Winifred.

Finally, she spoke. "Well, it does seem to solve our dilemma. Rhionna has an errand of her own in St. Ives and I did not want her to travel there and back alone."

He turned hopeful eyes on me. "Then will you accept?"

"I suppose so. I would be pleased to meet Lady Stratton. I am sure she is a fine woman."

A smile turned up the corners of his lips. "She is frightful, but that is no matter."

It only took me a few minutes to get ready. I said goodbye to Winifred, and Lord Stratton led me out to his carriage where the footman held the door for us. I had to stifle a giggle as I fell into the plush seat and Lord Stratton took a seat opposite me. When I came to Cornwall, I'd no idea at all I would be spending so much of my time in elegant carriages. Then the driver turned the vehicle around and we set off.

"You cannot know how much I appreciate this, Rhionna. It relieves me of so great a burden."

"It is nothing," I said. "And as my aunt said, I have to go to St. Ives in any case. I must go to the bank there."

"I will see to it that you take care of your business and I assure you I will be of any assistance that I can be."

"How long do you plan to stay in Cornwall?" he asked after I had given him my own brief history.

"I don't know," I said, hearing the uncertainty in my own voice. I smiled at him. "My father's business is in the hands of a capable manager, but I should like to oversee it myself when I return to New York."

"Ah, then you are a woman of means."

I could not help but respond to his teasing, for I did not take his remarks as an invasion of privacy.

"Not great means, but yes I am fortunate to have something to return to. And my father left me a home in a part of

190

New York called Chelsea."

We fell silent as we gazed out the glass windows. We followed the Cliff Road north of the castle for a distance. The sky was a bright azure that met the sea far distant, and I could see two sailing ships along the horizon.

"Will you be attending the Easter ball?" I asked him, trying to make conversation.

He turned back from gazing out. "Yes, most assuredly. I would not miss it. You will be in attendance, I hope."

"It appears so."

"It is always a grand affair for these parts."

"Then I shall look forward to it." I was afraid my voice did not carry the enthusiasm of my words. Then I asked, "What does your mother plan to do while she is here?"

"Do? Why nothing. That is, except pass judgment on everyone and everything and make trouble."

I could not suppress a grin. "Is she truly so difficult?"

"My dear, you do not know the meaning of the word until you have met the Countess of Stratton."

I remembered that he had said he spent little time at his manor house because of her, and I wondered what she would be like. We spent the rest of the ride amicably, Lord Stratton entertaining me with anecdotes about London, which I took a fancy to seeing one day. The hours passed and soon we were rumbling over the streets of St. Ives, with all its hustle and bustle.

We stopped first at the bank, where I checked on my account. The money had come and I drew some out. Then I accompanied Lord Stratton to a prosperous-looking inn. We passed through an arched entry to a large courtyard, and there stood another coach, much like the one we had arrived in, with the same coat of arms identifying it.

"Well, the old battle-axe has arrived."

I was shocked but amused at his language and hurried after him as we made our way into the inn. It was a busy place. The innkeeper was busy serving his patrons, while in

191

the corner sat a woman in a gray traveling suit and feathered hat. Lord Stratton strode purposely toward her, and I trailed behind.

"Ah, dear Mother. How nice to see you," he said when he reached her table.

"There you are at last, Enys," said the woman, and she lifted her cheek, which he bent to peck. "I was beginning to fear I would have to eat something in this dreadful place. Lunch was horrid."

"I am sorry for the delay, Mother, but the road was quite rough and Morely could not run the horses. However we came as swiftly as we could. I would like you to meet your traveling companion. This is Miss Rhionna Fowley, from America. Miss Fowley, my mother, Mary, Countess of Stratton."

"My lady." I smiled and dipped in a small curtsy, but she merely glared in my direction.

"What do I need a traveling companion for?"

He sighed with great melancholy. "I fear I cannot accompany you to Castle Rhyweth. I am due in London."

"Poppycock. You're always due in London, but you seldom stay there for long."

"Mother, really. I am involved in influencing the laws of Parliament. You make it sound as if those with a seat there do nothing."

"Most of them don't."

"But you see, Mother, I have a conscience. It is my great responsibility to see that the people of this great land are looked after. If I am to have the opportunity to formulate laws, I do not want them being passed without my consent."

"Hmmph." She turned slate gray eyes on me. "And where have you dug this young woman up?" Her expression was immediately suspicious, making me color. But Lord Stratton hastened to explain.

"She is a friend of the Wyckes. I knew you would be disappointed that I would not be returning to the castle and

192

thought you might be fond of a little conversation."

She lifted a brow, but I stood firm, my chin lifted. I thought her expression softened just a trace. "Well, it has been a dreary ride, with nothing to look at but rocks and water."

I suppressed a smile. In spite of her "battle-axe" qualities, I did not dislike her. Then an even more humorous thought struck me. If it were true that she had come to meet Morwenna, I almost looked forward to seeing whose stubbornness would outdo the other.

"Very well," Lady Stratton finally said. "Let us get on with it. I should like to arrive in time for a decent supper."

We went outside and said good-bye to Lord Stratton who said he would return in good time for the Easter ball. "Take care of my mother, Rhionna," he finally said. "And don't let her scare you."

"Be off with you, Enys. We will get along quite nicely."

We settled into her coach and as we took to the road, I waited for the countess to speak first.

"Come from America, have you? What for?"

I swallowed. "My father recently passed away, and I wished to visit my aunt who farms here."

"I see. Farms here, does she? On Lord Rhyweth's lands?"

"Yes, my lady. She raises some sheep." It felt foolish making conversation about Winifred's sheep, but I could think of little else to say.

But I needn't have worried, for Lady Stratton lead the conversation where it suited her fancy, confronting me directly as if challenging any contradiction to her opinions, of which I gave none. But when she finally asked me about my knowledge of the Wyckes, it was with a narrowed gaze.

"How did you come to meet Lord Rhyweth and his sister, Morwenna?"

"Rather by accident, really. You see the ship I was on was bound for St. Ives, but she was lured off her course, and we shipwrecked on the rocks below the castle."

"Shipwrecked?"

"Yes, my lady, it was quite frightening. Lord Rhyweth was on the beach directing the rescue."

"So you were saved."

"Yes, and taken to the castle to recover. I was there several days."

"And then?"

"When I was well enough, I went to my aunt's cottage."

"Hmmm."

I felt as if she were passing judgment, though I could think of no reason she should. But as her son had said, this seemed to be a habit of hers.

We rode in silence for a time, then she asked, "How long do you plan to stay in Cornwall?"

"I am not sure. I inherited my father's import business in New York, which is being run by his manager. However, I have always had an interest in it and so may return to see to it."

I did not know her opinion of American women in business, but her opinion on the future of young women like myself was clear. She said, "Have you any plans for marriage?"

"None," I said briskly.

She clucked her tongue. "A girl your age should get married."

I held my head even higher. "No one has asked me."

Her eyes rounded slightly. Then she said, "I see."

It was not quite true that no one had asked. For there had been several young men who had called at our house in New York. However, I had discouraged them from calling a second time.

Then her thoughts seemed to turn to her own situation. She narrowed her gaze, looking out the windows. "What do they say of the Wyckes in this part of Cornwall?"

"Um, well, my aunt has a great deal of respect for them. The Wyckes have always been good landlords, she says."

"Have they now?" She seemed to reflect on her thoughts. "And what of this Morwenna?"

I was surprised that so noble a lady was seeking my opinions. Perhaps she assumed that what I said did not matter, for someone of my station could not possibly have the ear of Lord Rhyweth and his sister. And I did not tell her that she was mistaken.

"Morwenna seems a very capable girl."

"Capable is she? I wonder. Hmmph. Something's afoot between my son and her. I've come to find out what. I don't trust his judgment one whit."

I could not help but smile. How apt had Lord Stratton's description been of his mother. But she was going on.

"I met Lord Rhyweth once." She looked at me. "Strange fellow if you ask me. Not at all like Enys. One wonders what they have in common."

I said nothing, hoping my face did not show any reaction. But she spared me from any conversation about Geoffrey.

We gave up conversation for the last hour except for an idle comment here and there. At last the Cliff Road rounded the castle and took the bridge over the chasm. We pulled to a stop in the courtyard, and Lady Stratton gathered herself together to descend.

"Well, my girl," she said as her footman came round to open the door. "We've got here at last." And she got down.

I followed, but she was already bustling up the steps to where Godreven stood at attention by the oak doors. I was relieved of my burden, though it had not been as unpleasant as Lord Stratton might have feared.

The footman still held the carriage door. "Pardon me, Miss, but Lord Stratton instructed us to deliver you back to your cottage."

I turned. "Oh, thank you, but I would prefer to walk. I have a need for some fresh air."

"As you wish."

It was true. I had been couped up in the carriage all day so that my legs needed stretching. There was still plenty of light, and a nice long walk would feel good. The weather was a bit brisk, but with my light cloak I would be fine.

I set off at a good pace, the wind coming up once I got to the Cliff Road. It made me dizzy to look down the jagged cut of rocks below me at the dizzying tide, so I stayed far to the left of the road and kept my eyes on the level scenery above.

When I reached the woods, the sun was lowering, but still long fingers of light poked through the trees. I paused beside the marker that pointed the way to St. Melan's glen. All around me was silent, and then a bird called, a long, lonely sound and the trees began to rustle. I shivered, for I did not like that place, and hurried on. I must make sure to get to the hollow before the bats came out, I thought to myself. I had the odd sense that someone was watching me, but I was sure that was only my imagination and the memory of the bad experience I had had when I had hiked to the hermit's glen.

I had success this time, for when I left the woods there was still a rosy glow over the land. The promise of rain, and the fresh air invigorated me.

When I reached home, all was well, and I spent the evening entertaining Winifred about Mary, Countess of Stratton.

Chapter 15

For the next week we saw no one from Castle Rhyweth. At first, my gaze kept turning that way as I imagined what the inhabitants might be doing. It was with great effort that I pulled my imagination back from such fantasies, for I had to turn my mind toward practical matters. There was plenty of work here to keep me busy. Elwynd stopped by twice. He politely inquired if I had recovered from my fall, and I made no mention of my memory of his strange reaction that day.

We had just finished our breakfast of milk and bread on a fair Friday morning when I heard a horse on the road outside. Going to the window, I saw the rider dressed in forest green riding habit, her long dark hair tucked under her hat.

"Morwenna," I exclaimed.

Winifred came to stand by me and watched Geoffrey's sister trot her horse up the road. What was more surprising, she lead Blackie, who was following behind her own horse. She rode into our barnyard, reining in by the stepping block, which she used to dismount.

I unconsciously wiped my hands on my apron and tried to tuck stray wisps of hair into my snood, but when I opened the door, the expression on my face still must have been one of complete surprise.

"Morwenna," I said. "What brings you here?"

"Good morning," she said. "You should not be so surprised to see me. Though I seldom come this way, I try to

197

ride often. It used to be said that I had a good seat."

From the way she held herself and her horse, there was no doubt of this. "I can see that you do have a good seat," I said, still mystified by her calling on me at the humble cottage. Then I remembered my manners. "Would you like to come in?"

"Thank you."

She stepped in and gazed at the surroundings, which must have seemed extremely humble compared to hers, but then she had lived here all her life and had no doubt seen the inside of a villager's cottage before.

"Would you care for some refreshment, Miss Wycke?" asked Winifred, who stood very straight, appearing not at all humbled by the mistress of the castle.

"Thank you, not just now. I am on an errand I have decided to call on Hannelore Treleaven, and I wondered if Rhionna would be good enough to accompany me."

"Me?"

"Yes. The herb woman has some remedies I wish to learn about since I am often called on to help nurse the sick at the castle. It has been many years since I have ridden to Hannelore's cottage in the highlands, though I used to go there as a child. I should appreciate the company."

"I am honored that you should ask me, Morwenna," I said. "But I have only returned from the castle yesterday. I fear my aunt needs me today."

From the look in Winifred's eye I could see that she did not approve of my riding off with Morwenna, but neither would she refuse Morwenna's wishes.

"I will have help from Elwynd today, child," she said to me. "But remember what happened the last time you rode on the moor. You must promise me you will not race again."

Morwenna smiled. "I can promise you that, dear lady. Though it is said I have a good seat, I do not race or jump. She will be safe with me, and I thought she might appreciate the opportunity to convince herself that she is still a good rider, even though she had a spill. I brought Blackie with me."

"I had been telling my aunt the best thing to do when you fall from a horse is to ride again."

"Well then."

I sighed. It seemed the decision had been made. "My aunt will pour you a cup of tea then while I change for riding."

"Thank you."

I donned the habit I had bought in St. Ives, and in a quarter of an hour we were off.

"It is early yet," said Morwenna as we left the farm and took a path that led upward. "But if we stay to tea, then we must skirt the moor on our homeward track and jog home by the High Road."

I followed her lead as we left the fields behind and made the high plateau. Again I wondered at Morwenna's unpredictable behavior. She made no mention of Enys Northcote, and I did not ask about him. Whatever was between them was none of my business, though in another sense everything and everyone that crossed my path in Cornwall was my business as long as I was playing the role of investigator. I wondered if Morwenna had chosen today to visit Hannelore in order to escape Lady Stratton, but I kept my speculations to myself.

Morwenna led me farther east than I had been before, and in half a mile, the moor swallowed us up. When I turned to look back I could see no sign of habitation. The castle was not visible from here either, nothing but the bare, brown highlands as far as the eye could reach, rising to craggy rocks that did little to shield the wind that howled in clefts and crannies even though moments before on the lowlands the day had been still. Our horses picked their way around the moorland scrub.

Morwenna did not make conversation, so I kept silent. An hour at least had passed, but it seemed to me we were no nearer our destination.

"There are more boulders here than I remember," said Morwenna.

The track we were on descended to a slippery path. We twisted and turned. Then, the path brought us to a battered wooden gate, green with lichen, swinging on squeaky hinges, giving access to a swollen stream. The day, which up to that point had been comparatively bright now darkened, and a cloud that had been following us brought a sheet of rain, which began to pour down on our heads. If I had felt disheartened before, I now felt desolate. The stream swelled to a torrent, rushing by with greater swiftness.

"We must get to higher ground," said Morwenna.

Our heads bent low in the saddles, we forced our horses up a steep incline. Then ahead, I saw what appeared to be a dilapidated cottage.

"Is that it?" I shouted.

"No," shouted Morwenna, "but it'll keep us dry."

We rode toward the refuge, dismounted, and led the horses to the rear. Disappointment befell me. The cottage was empty, but what was worse, it was partly fallen in, the rain driving through the empty windows and noisily cascading onto the tin roof. But we led the horses in and huddled against the fungoid walls, brooding that we were truly lost.

No longer did Morwenna look the regal lady. The rain had plastered her clothing to her, and her hair hung in strings over her face. I imagined that I did not look much better, and I thought I had never known greater despondency.

"Where are we?" I asked, trying to keep the panic from rising.

"I wish I was certain. We're east of the High Road, but how far east, can't tell anymore."

It rained for another hour, then turned to an icy drizzle,

and then a dank fog, making our world murky. To make things worse, we had lost all sense of direction. It seemed useless to challenge Morwenna about country she had grown up in, for she was equally nonplussed.

"It was years ago I came this way," she said. "I did not realize the landscape could change so. I must have missed the track that leads to Hannelore's."

We emerged from our ruin and looked about us, examining our horses.

"There's nothing for it," she finally said, "but to let them lead us home. We'll leave the reins loose about their necks. They'll know the way."

I was doubtful, but had no better suggestions, and so we mounted once again, the rain still pattering on the roof. I did as Morwenna instructed, leaving the reins loose.

The horses seemed sure-footed even among dead heather and loose stones, and they plodded forward. I felt better anyway, being away from the abandoned cottage and in the open, even though we were soaked. We soon gained higher ground and discovered a disused railway track, which our horses stumbled along. I could not imagine where this railroad had once led. Or perhaps it was never finished.

"It's a line for trolleys to a stone quarry," said Morwenna. "We can't let the horses take us there, they'll break their legs. We'd better dismount."

We led the horses from the railway track, and then using a large boulder as a stepping stone, dismounted again. Once away from the track, the horses seemed surer, and headed straight across the moor, in the direction of the menacing crags we had seen earlier.

The day lengthened. We had no idea of the time, and it was too dark to see anything now. I had not even brought matches in my pocket and doubted if Morwenna had. I would meet my death here not knowing why danger haunted me at every turn. Perhaps Morwenna planned to leave me here to die. Irrational images began to fill my mind. I wanted to ask Morwenna why I had to die. Why here?

But my horse nearly collided with my companion's, for she had drawn up and was pointing. "They've done it. Look."

Unbelievably, torches blazed ahead.

"Who can it be?" I said in relief. They must have missed us and had sent out a search party, the torches lit to guide us back.

"I told you they could do it," said Morwenna, pulling herself up straighter. "Horses travel by instinct."

Now I could see figures with waving lanterns wandering to and fro upon the road ahead. We made the road and proceeded forward. I shook my head at my earlier fears. In an instant all was safe. We were found, and I could allow myself to think of food and scalding tea. It seemed we had not been so very far after all, and it dismayed me that one could wander off the beaten path so easily. We had gone nowhere but in a circle.

There they are," a voice shouted.

A dark figure approached on horseback, a long black cloak flowing behind him. Even before I could see his face, I knew it was Geoffrey. The lantern bearers stood to the side of the road, holding the lanterns so we could see.

"Where in God's name have the two of you been?" The anger in Geoffrey's voice made me shrink further into my saddle.

"We went to visit Hannelore Treleaven," said Morwenna when he had drawn up beside us and wheeled his horse to the same direction as we were going. "Only I missed the track. I'm afraid it's my fault. We lost the way."

"Lost the way. My sister? I can hardly believe that. We used to fear that you were half animal, for it seemed you preferred living on the moor to living in the castle. You ought to know it like the back of your hand."

Like the back of her hand. Exactly what Stratton had said earlier.

"That may be, but it was a long time ago. Anyway, nothing looked the same today. I cannot help it."

Her voice broke and I thought the wetness on her cheeks was not just rain. I couldn't help wanting to defend her against Geoffrey's anger.

"I'm sure it's quite easy to get lost out there." I said. "The moorland plays tricks on you."

But he ignored my comment, still casting aspersions at his sister.

"You might at least apologize to Rhionna for getting her soaked to the bone. I begin to fear whether she will live through her visit to Cornwall, or if these experiences will drive her to leave us sooner than we would like."

I did not tell him I had begun to fear the same, but we plodded on until we came to the Cliff Road, where I stopped.

"I shall be going to my aunt's cottage," I said.

"Nonsense," said Geoffrey. "You are soaked. She would not forgive us. You must come and change into something dry first."

But I held firm this time. "No. I can dry off in front of the fire in Winifred's cottage just as well as in the castle. I would rather go home."

The horses danced, impatient to be in their stables, their noses in their fodder.

"Oh, very well," said Geoffrey. "If you insist, I will ride with you to see that you get home safely."

"That is very kind but it is not necesssary."

He turned to Morwenna. "I shall go with Rhionna," he said. Then he shouted to the others, "Ride on."

The search party turned, their torches hazy in the mist. Then he clucked to his horse and led the way toward the Cliff Road. I followed, wishing I was already in front of the fire at my aunt's. However, I sat rigidly in the saddle, trying

203

to stay alert to any possible mishap.

Below us the surf crashed on the rocks, and I was glad when we left the cliffs behind and our horses trotted into the forest, though here the darkness prevented me from seeing anything but tall, crooked shapes. Only the sound of the horses and the squeak of leather told me I was not alone. I felt little safer with Geoffrey than I might have by myself, and resentfully appreciated his offer of escort. My throat was tight with fear and every sense was alive to the slightest movement and sound, anticipating possible danger.

Owls hooted, and the wind rustled through the leaves. It seemed the forest was alive with sound. I do not think I breathed until we were out of the woods and trotting through the hollow where bats had attacked me. If they waited in the branches, they did not make themselves known, and finally we were on the road that ran between the fields, and in a short while I could see a light in the cottage window and felt blessed relief.

We reached the cottage, and Geoffrey dismounted then helped me down, his arms giving me strength in spite of my resistance. He pounded on the cottage door, and Winifred opened it, a frightened expression on her face.

"It's me, Aunt Winifred. I'm sorry if I've worried you. Morwenna and I got lost. But the horses brought us home."

"Thank heavens, child. Get inside and dry off." She stepped back.

I turned to thank Geoffrey, but he had followed me inside, his eyes quickly taking in the small cottage and the blazing fire in the hearth.

"Thank you for bringing her home, Lord Rhyweth," said Winifred. Then to me, "Now go and change. I'll put on some tea."

I went into the bedroom and, closing the door, took dry clothing out of my trunk. It took me some time to peel everything off. Then I rubbed myself dry with a rough linen towel. My skin was reddened and clammy, but I felt much better. When I had put on a clean cotton gown dry stockings, and slippers, I went out.

I thought Geoffrey would be gone, but instead he had removed his cloak and was seated in the rocking chair by the hearth, sipping a cup of tea. He looked as comfortable in our humble abode as he did in his grand quarters. He and Winifred were speaking in low voices.

But it was their expressions that took me aback. Geoffrey was charming her with a half smile, as if they had just shared some private joke. Winifred was leaning forward slightly in her seat, drawn into their intimate conversation.

Geoffrey caught my eye and rose. Now the charm he had been pouring on my aunt flowed over me.

"I must apologize for my sister," he said. "She did not tell me she planned to lead you astray."

"I do not think she meant it to end that way."

If indeed it had been her intention to insure that I had yet another bad experience in Cornwall, she succeeded. But if so, she had certainly suffered for it herself. However, I put my cynicism aside and moved to pour the tea that my aunt had left steeping.

"Would you like another cup?" I asked Geoffrey, half hoping he would refuse and leave. But of course he did not.

"Thank you. I would." He handed me his cup.

I needed to rest and gather my thoughts. And besides I wanted to talk to Winifred about perhaps going home. Except for my wild uncontrollable feelings about a man who was above me in this classed society, there was little for me here. I did not want to abandon my aunt nor my mission, but I was feeling irritable. Those who had tried to impress upon me that I didn't belong here had succeeded. I had come with nothing but questions, I would leave with the same.

I refilled Geoffrey's and Winifred's cups, and as I handed Geoffrey his, my fingers brushed against his hand. Our eyes met, and the flame leapt between us. I hastily lowered my eyes and served my aunt her cup. Then I pulled up a straight-backed chair, and we sipped in silence. I glanced at my aunt out of the corner of my eyes. I noticed with irony how she seemed to take on elegant airs whenever we had a visit from the nobility. It was as if she put herself on their level, and I would have found it amusing if I weren't feeling so wretched.

"Lord Rhyweth and I were just speaking of the upcoming Easter ball," said Winifred. "He says he has told you of it."

I glanced at her sharply. "He has."

"He had kindly invited us both."

I took another sip, both my hands cupped around the warm mug. Was that anticipation I heard in her voice? She who had been so averse to our going to the castle in the first place? I had noticed that since her first reservations, she had been reluctant to place the blame for all the ill deeds of late on Geoffrey Wycke. Now she and I seemed to have reversed roles. She had been swayed by his charm, or by memories of . . . what? But now I was not so sure. I glanced at Geoffrey and felt a pang of hurt deep in my heart. The look in his eyes was full of interest, kindness. And yet he had been wandering around the castle in the wee hours of morning the night I had been so frightened.

I tried to keep my expression noncommittal. Geoffrey and Winifred went on to speak of former Easter balls, thus relieving me of the burden of conversation. It was as if the two of them were on some distant plane, leaving me alone with my own thoughts, of which I had many.

I was ready to admit defeat, and yet . . . perhaps someone was hoping I would do just that. Someone was trying to lead me away from finding out what I had come for. Who? I tried to study Geoffrey without being too obvious. Certainly I could not be sure. My heart told me one thing, my head another.

Morwenna? Was that why she had suggested the ride

across the moors? To discourage me further, to perhaps reinforce a decision to leave Cornwall she had hoped I had already made?

The hints of their vampiric blood had frightened me. And yet, when I was in a more reasonable frame of mind, the thing seemed fantastic. Here I was sitting two feet from Geoffrey and I could attest to his all too human qualities, could I not?

But if neither he nor Morwenna were truly vampires, then who was responsible for the death of the girl only two weeks ago? It was not my business, but it made me curious. And someone might be leading me away from clues to my father's death. If that were so, then would it not be best to stay and persist in finding them? But would I live to do so?

Geoffrey and Winifred were both looking at me and I realized they had spoken.

"I'm sorry," I said. "I'm afraid my mind was wandering."

Winifred gave me an understanding smile. "That's all right, child. We were just speaking of the ball. Lord Rhyweth insists that we be his honored guests."

"We? I, um, hadn't thought about it."

"You will have time. It is weeks away."

She rose and Geoffrey also. "Thank you for the invitation, Lord Rhyweth," said Winifred. "We would be honored."

I simply stared at him, open mouthed. I shut my mouth when he turned his gaze on me in amusement.

"And thank you for seeing my niece home safely," she continued.

"My pleasure."

He strode to the door, took his cloak from the peg where it hung and flung it across his shoulders. His look became more serious as he met Winifred's gaze. "You need not fear," he said. "While Rhionna is here, she will be under my protection."

The sparkle in Winifred's eyes was replaced by a more

sober look as if she too were now replacing nostalgia with reality.

"Thank you, my lord," she said.

He took my hand, and though it trembled in his, I would not meet his gaze.

"Good night, my dear," he said. "Let us hope there shall soon be an end to the unpleasantness you have experienced while here."

I looked up, startled at his words. "Then do you believe you know the source of it?" I challenged.

He narrowed his eyes. "Perhaps. But I must be sure. Until then, it might be best if you stayed close by your aunt's side."

I glanced at her and caught her slight nod of understanding. Was this what they had been speaking of while I was dressing?

I saw him go, then shut the door on the gusty night.

"Winifred," I said. "What did he mean? Do you not believe that Geoff . . . that is, Lord Rhyweth himself could be the source of evil in this land? I thought you did not fully trust him."

She had seated herself again by the smoky fire and gazed at it as if looking into the past. "I was not sure at first," she said. "But I was foolish to listen to old wives tales and superstition."

"I can see that the garlic plants are gone," I said with a touch of sarcasm.

She shrugged. "Those were only to please Hannelore. She is a wise woman in many ways. But in this I believe she has erred."

I sat on the chair across from her. "Then if not Geoffrey, who? You cannot tell me that girl was killed by a wolf." I hated to tell her of my fright in the castle for fear of upsetting her.

"I do not know who or what is causing all the trouble," she said. "But I believe the evil that lurks here will find it has a

208

very formidable enemy."

I remembered Geoffrey's words about my being in his protection. But how could he protect me from as far away as the castle?

"Yes," she said, rocking dreamily. "We shall see."

Chapter 16

I supposed we must go to the ball. Why was it that just as I had decided I could make the break with Cornwall, indeed that for my own good I must leave, that events conspired to keep me there? For with the knowledge that I would accompany Winifred to the Rhyweth Easter ball, came the unwanted sensations that accompanied thoughts of Geoffrey. Indeed I believed that perhaps he had cast some sort of spell over me, and that soon it would be too late to save myself from him.

The day before the affair, a large package arrived from the castle. I took it from Jonas, then waited as he turned back to the wagon in which he had come.

Closing the door, I placed the large box on the table, and Winifred came to help me open it. We cut the heavy twine that bound it, and then lifting the top. I gasped.

Red satin blazed at me. "It is a gown," said Winifred. "Lift it out carefully."

I did so, holding it up against my form as Winifred looked at me appraisingly. The rich material was gathered in a train in back, while the long apron front fell over a darker plush underskirt laid in pleats. The sleeves were gracefully caught up inside the arm.

"Quite an extravagant dress," said Winifred. "Try it on, my dear. We must see that it fits."

"But Aunt Winifred. I cannot possibly wear so bright a color. I am supposed to be in mourning. Even if I do not wear black, I have been keeping to the more subdued colors."

"Nonsense. You know very well that your father did not believe in the usual traditions."

She moved closer and arranged one of my curls on my shoulder against the brocaded satin, nodding to herself. "Very flattering," she said. "That red makes your hair look a shade darker. It is striking. Go on, let us see the fit."

Already feeling my resolve weakening both about attending the ball and about wearing so rich a dress, I went into the tiny bedroom to try it on. It fit as if it were made for me, and as Winifred did me up, I looked down to see that the square neck of the basque made my bosom appear more abundant than it did in my more modest dresses. Surely I could not expose myself like this, even though it was an evening dress. Besides, my chest would freeze.

We returned to the front room and I turned around until Winifred was satisfied that the dress needed no altering. As I moved the satin whispered against itself. I thought immediately of my satin slippers. They would go perfectly.

"Look here is a note," said Winifred lifting a folded piece of paper from the box and handing it to me. I opened it nervously and read the scrawl.

Please accept this gift as an atonement for my sister's hasty act of leading you out on the moors and into inclement weather. I took the liberty of guessing your size from the gowns you wore while you were our guest. I hope you will allow me the pleasure of seeing you in it tomorrow night. Yours, Geoffrey Wycke.

My heartbeat quickened as I gazed at the scrawl, which had been written by the hands that had caressed me. I involuntarily raised my hand to my chest, trying to stifle the excitement that was building within me. I thought that by keeping my distance from the castle for the last weeks I could put Geoffrey out of my mind, but it was not so.

"It's from Geoffrey." I was too overcome even to use the more formal title I usually did when speaking of him to others.

I did not miss the look of interest that came into my aunt's eyes, and in that instant I realized that my aunt had the same streak of the romantic as I did. A hopeless empathy filled me.

"Oh, Aunt," I said, collapsing on the chair and reaching to clasp her hands. "Are we both lost to the power of Geoffrey Wycke? Has he charmed you as much as he has charmed me? How can I have the willpower to stay away from a man who may be dangerous to me if my own chaperone is as taken with him as I?"

Our eyes met, and hers misted over. "It is not quite as you think, my girl, though you are right I have not been strict enough with you. I should have sent you packing the moment you arrived here, but my own feelings have not allowed me to do so." Her lip trembled, and she sat down.

"I have spent many a night dreading the consequences," she said. "But my convictions do not seem to follow me into the light of day."

"You do not fear Geoffrey then? You do not think he is as guilty as everyone says he is?"

She shook her head slowly. "I do not fear him. But I fear something." She shuddered. "Something I cannot name."

I frowned. "Then do you think it is as he says, that he protects us?"

She shook her head. "I do not know. I believe he would protect you if he could."

"And you?

"I am not in danger."

Her words made me feel a prickle at the back of my neck. "How can you be so sure?"

"Because," she said slowly. "It is young women who are the victims here."

Her gaze held steady, but mine wavered. "I'd best take off the dress now."

I walked back to the bedroom where Winifred helped me out of the gown. Then we folded it gently in a clean sheet to keep it for tomorrow night.

The next day I tried to put Winifred's words out of my mind as I went about the usual chores. But in the afternoon she bid me stop and rest, for the evening, which she still looked forward to, would be long.

Winifred dressed my hair, piling it on my head, leaving ringlets at the back of my neck and smaller curls around my forehead. I was surprised at her skill at hair dressing. As I held a small hand mirror and watched her work I thought again that there were things about Winifred that belied her upbringing as a peasant. She had something of the lady in her, and I sincerely regretted that she had not been born into a higher class, or married into it. For it seemed a woman with her intellect and grace deserved more than she had. But she never complained, and I wondered at her humility.

"There," she finally said. "Now let us have the dress."

She lifted it over my head, and after I had wriggled into it, she fastened me up. My corset seemed to push my bosom even further up and out, making me feel embarrassed.

"Aunt," I said "Don't you think I am exposed too much. Surely I need a shawl to cover myself."

She eyed me critically, and the corner of her lip pulled back in a bit of humor. "Certainly you will have no want of dancing partners looking that way, but I will give you a black lace shawl for your modesty."

She found the shawl for me and draped it about my shoulders, making me feel more comfortable.

"Now," she said. "You'll need some jewelry."

213

"I have my silver cross," I said.

"No, no," she said. "That will not do. But I believe I have just the thing."

She went to her nightstand and reached in the drawer for a small wooden box. From it she extracted a cameo, strung on a velvet ribbon.

"That is very lovely," I said. "And the black ribbon goes with the shawl."

I held the cameo to my breast, and she was about to tie it behind my neck when there came a knock at the door.

"Who can that be?" It was too early for the carriage Geoffrey said he would send.

Winifred went to get it, and from the bedroom I saw that Jonas stood in the doorway. They exchanged a few words, then he handed her a small package and turned to go. She shut the door and brought the package to me. This time there was a note on the outside. I tore open the envelope, not surprised that this too was from Geoffrey, and the tone more personal.

Dearest Rhionna, The dress was a gift of atonement to make up for my sister's deed. This one comes from my heart. The necklace belonged to my mother, and she would wish you to wear it on this night. Geoffrey

My hands shook as I tore open the brown paper and then opened the velvet box. The fiery ruby pendant that lay on white silk shot its rays into my widened eyes. I lifted the gold chain from which the red jewel dropped, too stunned to speak.

"Aunt Winifred," was all I could say.

She appeared much calmer, coming to finger the necklace. "I see that Lord Rhyweth thinks very highly of you, my dear. Put it on."

She fastened the clasp of the necklace, the pendant lying just at the top of my cleavage, its coolness making my skin tingle.

214

"I'm not sure I should wear this," I said. "What can he mean by it?"

I knew perhaps even then what I hoped he meant, but I could not, did not, dare allow myself to voice my thought.

But Winifred looked pleased. "You will be the loveliest young woman there," she said, looking at the overall effect. "You cannot help but be so."

"You look quite handsome yourself," I said, admiring the black mozambique and lace dress she wore. "I did not know Mrs. Tucker was so talented," I said, speaking of the village dressmaker.

"Oh, Ellie Tucker did not make this," she told me. "It was given to me some years ago by a dear friend as a sign of great esteem." She did not elaborate on her benefactor.

We were ready when the carriage came, its lamps flickering in the darkness and swaying as the horses turned the carriage about. We settled ourselves and headed back toward the castle. As we rumbled over the rough road, my excitement built, and I was glad my aunt had decided we should attend the ball after all.

As we rolled over the bridge and into the courtyard, I pulled aside the curtains to look out the carriage window. The courtyard was ablaze with torchlight, and liveried footmen were helping guests alight. When it was our turn, we pulled in front of the stone steps, and a servant opened our door and lowered the step so we could get out. My cloak pulled around me against the chilly night, I descended then waited for my aunt to follow. We followed the other guests in and turned our wraps over to waiting servants, tonight wearing white brocaded livery instead of their usual black.

We climbed to the second floor where the anteroom to the ballroom was abuzz with conversation as one by one the guests were announced. As we neared the double doors I could see beyond to the blazing chandeliers that shone on the ladies' fancy ball gowns and the handsome evening costumes of the gentlemen. My eyebrows raised at the titles that were announced ahead of us.

"Lord and Lady Anthony Durnham," Godreven's refined voice enunciated. The middle-aged couple entered the great room and descended the few steps leading to the ballroom.

"The Earl of Stratton and Mary, Countess of Stratton."

Lord Stratton came forward, leading his mother decked out in violet feathers and lace, and a draping gown ending in beaded fringe of crimped silk. As I caught his glance I gave a smile, which he returned. They nodded regally to people on either side, and he led his mother in.

Then it was our turn. I stepped nervously forward, but not before Winifred gave me a once over and separated the black lace shawl that I had wrapped around me practically up to my neck.

"Now is not the time to be modest," she said, pushing the shawl down around my shoulders.

"Misses Winifred and Rhionna Fowley," said Godreven. I swallowed and stepped forward, lifting my skirt with one hand, desperately hoping I would not trip.

A hush and then whispers followed me as we passed through the double doors and descended the steps to a red carpet that led down the center of the ballroom. I was quite unused to these formal proceedings and my cheeks burned in embarrassment as everyone's gaze turned upon me. I heard someone on my right give a gasp and I glanced quickly in that direction. A woman was staring at my throat, her face pale. My hand moved to my throat, thinking she was looking at the necklace. But I felt my aunt's fingers nudge me at the waist and we walked on.

216

But there was another intake of breath, this time on my left side, and I saw clearly a woman stare and her partner frown. I stared straight ahead, my jaw rigid.

Why were they staring? Was there something wrong? Was the ruby necklace causing such a reaction? Surely not, judging from the glittering assembly here. My quick glance told me there must be twice the worth of my necklace on almost every female arm, throat, and ear.

At the end of the eerie procession I was glad to come up to Morwenna, who stood at the foot of the room, her dark looks accentuated in lush green satin and velvet. She held out her hand as we approached.

"Good evening, Rhionna. I'm so glad you came."

"Thank you," I managed.

"And Miss Fowley," she greeted my aunt. "I am pleased to see you within these walls."

Winifred seemed to stretch an inch taller. "It is a pleasure to be here. Thank you for inviting me."

I was aware before I saw Geoffrey that he had approached on my right. He bowed first before Winifred, and it slightly annoyed me that she was so taken in by his elegant manners. Then he turned to me, his eyes praising my looks and lingering on the brilliant ruby resting above my bosom.

"Ah," he said. "The necklace looks stunning on you, as I thought it would."

"It is a very generous gift, Lord Rhyweth. I was hesitant to accept it, but I could not offend you by not wearing it."

"I am glad you did not."

"The dress too," I said. "I assure you, it was not necessary to make amends in that way."

A strange light came into his eye. "I see you protest my gifts. Would you then deny me the pleasure of seeing so lovely a young lady attired as she ought to be when it is in my power to decorate that beauty?"

I was hard put to reply and so merely lowered my eyes. There was a rustle in the room behind us, and the musicians began tuning their instruments. Geoffrey lifted my hand.

"Will you do me the honor of accompanying me on the Grand March?"

"I —" but when I looked into his eyes, I felt that my answer was of no consequence. Already I was overcome by his handsome looks, his graceful figure ready to lead me onto the dance floor. But most of all it was his eyes that swayed me, for every time I looked into them I felt as if I saw deeply into his soul and became one with it.

My petticoats rustled as we moved to take our places in the line. The music began, and Lord Stratton lead his mother at the head of the line, they being the highest ranking couple present. We began the march, proceeding from the bottom to the top of the room. I glanced quickly about me, and my knees turned to jelly as the looks I read in the faces we passed ranged from curiosity to something that bordered on horror. Again, I had the sensation that something was horribly wrong, but my firm hold on Geoffrey's arm, and the certainty in his features when I glanced at him, gave me the strength to move slowly with him to the ceremonious music.

When Enys and his mother reached the top of the room, Enys turned left, and Lady Stratton went to the right. The gentlemen followed Enys single file, and I realized that in a moment I would have to let go of Geoffrey's arm and follow the ladies. I felt myself waver but then took a deep breath and when the moment came, I managed to keep my balance. I kept my eyes straight ahead so as to avoid the strange glances I felt must await me. My expression must have been chiseled as in stone.

The leaders reached the bottom of the room and

passed to the left of each other, the gentlemen moving around the outside, the ladies to the inside of the room. Somehow my feet kept to the rhythm. At last Enys met his mother again. He turned and joined her and the other couples followed, all now marching around the room to the right. With great relief, I saw Geoffrey approach and reached out my left hand to take his right arm, my limbs feeling wooden.

When the circle was completed, the Grand March ended. There was polite applause, and the musicians launched into the next dance, a waltz. Geoffrey did not hesitate, but placed his right hand on my waist and led me out.

It was not difficult to follow his steps, for my body simply followed his direction. He led me in small steps at first, and then as we began to move and sway easily together he became more daring, sweeping me around the room, my feet gaining certainty from his. The music was like wine, and soon I was part of the dance, hoping it would never end. Out of the corner of my eye I dared to read the expressions of those watching us, and I guessed how my red dress and his black cutaway must have flashed across the floor, the light from the chandeliers above reflecting the fire from the ruby I wore.

My head spun and I began to relax, giddy with the intoxicating music. For though I did not know what it was that had caused the assembly to stare at me when I made my entrance, I now saw a few looks of curiosity mixed with admiration and in some cases envy. Yes, I thought to myself. How many other women would trade places with me right now? How many others would like to be the chosen one? The one decked out in Lord Rhyweth's generous gifts and spinning in his strong arms.

Throughout the dance, his eyes never left my face, and as the piece came to a close, he slowed, lowering me in a slight dip on the last chord. There was a pause, and then the orchestra began another tune and everyone changed partners.

I felt breathless as Geoffrey lifted me up, his eyes still pinned to me. I was flushed, vulnerable, the way I always was when he looked at me like that, as if we stood alone on the solitary moor rather than in a crowded room full of people all talking and some gazing at us still.

"Thank you," he said, his lips pulling up at the corners in a pleased expression. "You dance very well."

I felt the heat in my face and thought my skin must have turned a color to match my hair and the dress. "It was you who led the dance," I said in an attempt at modesty.

He was about to continue the repartee when we were interrupted. Lord Stratton came up and slapped Geoffrey on the back.

"Well, Geoffrey, old chap. You've done yourself proud leading this charming lady in the Grand March."

"Hell, Enys. I see you are being your cheeky self as usual," Geoffrey said.

Lord Stratton bowed to me gracefully. "You look lovely, Rhionna. If I had not had my mother on my arm, I would not have let this scoundrel get away with having the first dance with you."

Geoffrey seemed unperturbed, and I was relieved to see that here at least was one friend who did little to defer to Geoffrey, perhaps because of his rank or his long association with the family. I liked Enys Northcote more and more and judged that his teasing of Geoffrey was done out of affection.

I was also perhaps still under the effects of the dance, swept away by the glittering society of which I so suddenly found myself a part, and quite easily carried away by Lord Stratton's flattery.

"I suppose you will insist on dancing with Rhionna," said Geoffrey.

"If she will do me that honor."

Before he surrendered me, Geoffrey squeezed my hand. "Do not believe a word of what this man tells you, nor allow him to get you alone. He is my best friend, and I do not trust him for a minute."

I grinned at Geoffrey's mock seriousness and assured him I could take care of myself. Then I rained a smile on Lord Stratton, who returned my expression with easy flirtation. The warmth in his blue eyes made me smile even wider, and then he led me onto the dance floor.

At that moment I caught a glimpse of Morwenna watching us from the corner of the room. Her eyes narrowed, and I feared she was going to be in one of her bad tempers. Surely she was not jealous of Lord Stratton's attentions to me. I considered him a friend, but nothing more. He was every bit as graceful as Geoffrey and quite schooled with his movements, and as he led me in the stately polonaise, I slid along with him like a swan. And as soon as we were used to each other's movements, we began to chat.

"How long have you known Lord Rhyweth?" I asked him.

"Since we were boys, though I did not get to come this way as often as I wished. My father and his were friends in Parliament. Couldn't get Geoffrey up to London much though."

"Oh?"

"He detests the place."

"And you," he asked, after a pause. "Do you still have designs on seeing London while you are here?"

"I don't know. I had thought I might leave very soon."

He raised a blond brow, his look turning slightly more serious. "Come now, this does not sit well. Then you are not so enamoured with the legends of Cornwall that you feel you cannot leave it?"

"No." I refrained from remarking that indeed some of the legends of Cornwall were driving me to leave rather sooner than I had planned.

I do not know what made me decide to confide in Lord Stratton, perhaps it was his easy manner and open empathetic expression, but I found myself telling him rather more than I might normally have spoken to a person I hardly knew.

"I have not told you the real reason I came here in the first place," I said. "There were mysterious circumstances surrounding my father's death. I am not convinced it was an accident."

He raised a blond eyebrow, his look penetrating mine. "Oh? Do let us get some refreshment and then you must tell me the rest. I love a mystery."

We left the dance floor and proceeded to the refreshment room where two long tables were laid with a variety of food. I declined any wine, but accepted a plate of cheese, fruit, and scones. He led me to a linen-covered table where a single candle burned, and we refreshed ourselves with the food. Then I proceeded to air my thoughts, and Lord Stratton proved an avid listener, giving me his entire attention. Some instinct told me I could trust him, and besides, he was obviously not involved in my family background in any way. I found myself pouring forth all my concerns, including my suspicions and the mysterious events that had occurred since I had arrived in Cornwall, even my concerns about the accusations the villagers were making about Geoffrey.

"Of course I try not to listen to them." I said.

Lord Stratton's expression turned very grave, and when I had finished, he said, "I did not know any of these things. I am not in this part of the country very often. Of course I was here that dreadful night the

222

young girl's body was found in the field. I did not know there had been others missing before." Dazzling blue eyes probed mine.

"And you? You do not consider the danger you have found yourself in sufficient to drive you from this place? What do you mean to accomplish by staying?"

I stared at my hands. "I know, it's foolish perhaps. I was thinking of leaving. I had been so convinced that someone here in Pendeen was responsible for my father's death. The sheets from the letter I read made me think it. But then when I got here, I lost the letter and my questions seemed to lead nowhere. I am beginning to wonder if I was wrong."

He was thoughtful, weighing my words. "You say you lost the letter."

"Yes. It must have been the night I nearly drowned. I had carried some papers on my person, but Geoffrey said the satchel they were in contained only two letters from my aunt."

Lord Stratton frowned, the gaiety completely gone now from his usual expression. He voiced what I had thought. "You say you were quite dazed. Could not whoever undressed you have taken the letters?"

My heart beat in trepidation as I told him what I had suspected. "Gwynneth undressed me. But then I lost consciousness. Olga and the doctor came then too. Geoffrey told me that Olga brought him the letters from my aunt so they could discover my identity. But he said there was no letter to my father."

I pressed my lips together then said, "I do not think Geoffrey believes there ever was such a letter."

"Has he said he does not believe you?"

I shook my head. "He says he believes me, but I can see in his eyes he does not."

Lord Stratton drummed his long fingers on the table. "Perhaps the housekeeper, the maid, or the doctor took the letter before they delivered the remaining ones to Geoffrey. Perhaps one of them has a reason to deceive you."

"I have tried to reason it out, but I cannot see what any of them would have to gain by it. Gwynneth is not from this district and had never even heard of my father. And Dr. Pearce does not seem to have any reason to meddle in my affairs."

"And Olga?"

I met his gaze. "I do not know. She has been at the castle a very long time. She came here with Geoffrey's mother. She must know a great deal about what has occurred in these parts."

His blue eyes flashed. "And what is still occurring, perhaps?"

Chapter 17

I thought of the close-lipped, secretive housekeeper and wondered for the hundredth time if she had stolen my letter, but if she had, why? Then Enys broke our pensive mood by looking around and rising.

"Come," he said. "You have given me much to puzzle over. However, decorum requires that you circulate among the guests. Besides, from the look in Geoffrey's eyes I would not be able to get away with dominating your company for the entire evening. I'm afraid there are other gentlemen who would like to dance with you."

Then he leaned closer to me and whispered in my ear. "But I will not forget what you have told me. I am honored that you have considered me a confidante."

I blushed, already worrying that I had been too open with him. But I had no more time to contemplate my possible mistake, for Lord Stratton surrendered me to an elderly gentleman who he introduced as Sir Morris Cresswell. I tried to smile as I followed the portly gentleman onto the dance floor, but I felt stiff, my expression frozen on my face.

I had several partners after that. I danced with a short man who held me at arm's length and whose steps were rather more like walking than dancing. Then I had an energetic partner who strode about knocking me against the other dancers in the schottische and a large man who trod on my toes during the polka and finally a dignified gentleman who led me in forbidding silence. All of them held me at arm's distance, and after a quick glance at my necklace, averted their eyes from my face.

I began to wonder again if there were something about the necklace that aroused this strange reaction. Perhaps it was an heirloom and they recognized it as having belong to one of the Wyckes, possibly Geoffrey's late wife.

Only Lord Stratton seemed completely relaxed with me when he came to partner me in the quadrille, though this time I noticed that his eyes strayed more than once to Morwenna, dancing in another square, whose brilliant smile with her white teeth and her flashing eyes seemed to dazzle everyone around her, though she did not look our way.

I did not see Geoffrey dance with anyone though several times I caught a glimpse of him in conversation with those at the sides of the room. It was very late when Lord Stratton gave me once again to his friend.

Geoffrey took my hand, which had so lately been held in Lord Stratton's. "I told you not to trust this devil," said Geoffrey, his eyes half joking, but half serious.

I immediately felt my blood rising, for had I not done exactly that? But I covered my thoughts with frippery. "You are quite right. He has flattered me to death. No man with such a silver tongue can possibly be sincere."

Our voices mingled with laughter, then I felt Geoffrey's arm slip around my waist as he whispered into my ear. "And now it is my turn."

Lord Stratton left us and I touched the gold chain about my throat. "This necklace," I said. "Is it an heirloom?"

"Why no," he said. "That is, the stone itself has been in the family for a very long time, but the setting is new.

226

At the advent of this affair I had the ruby reset in this newly made necklace only for you. I hope you do not mind."

"No, of course not. It is just that all my partners seem to gaze at it as if they recognized it. That is the only reason I ask."

"Do they indeed? Well, perhaps they are envious that their host has bestowed such a gift on one so lovely. I hope you are not uncomfortable being the center of attention, for you are so tonight."

He smiled to himself and glanced at the noisy crowd. "I do not mind saying it was the effect I was striving for."

I swallowed, not quite knowing how to tell him that being the center of attention was not what made me uncomfortable, but that several other things did indeed. We circulated for a time among the guests, and I could see that they all offered Geoffrey much deference, but it struck me that not one among them except Lord Stratton was what one might call a warm friend.

I sensed the distance between Geoffrey and the other gentry, and I felt the familiar sense of unease at what he might have done to alienate them so. Was I blinded to some evil in him that everyone else saw? Was I so blinded by the passion that his touch and glance aroused in me? No less so tonight.

When we had worked our way around the room, Geoffrey steered me toward the French doors that led to the balcony.

"Ah," he said as he shut the doors behind us. "I had a need to escape. This is much more refreshing."

The sky was clear and I looked at the starry heavens above us while below the surf pounded on the cliffs. I was entranced by the wild beauty, feeling that it brought out the wildness in my own nature. And Geoffrey's nearness heightened my feelings.

227

He took me in his arms then, his cheek resting against my hair. I felt the heavenly bliss of belonging in his arms, and realized in spite of the conflicts within me that this was where I belonged. That this was where I desired to be above all else.

Then he sought my lips, pressing his mouth against my willing one. My arms entwined around his neck, my hair falling loose from its pins and billowing over the edge of the balcony, as my heart sang for joy. I felt breathless, but I found the strength to pull myself away from him.

"What if the other guests should see us?" I asked, aware of how disheveled I had already become, my gown and my hair disarranged as a result of our desires. Even though my own emotions were quite out of control, I still had enough sense not to wish to risk embarrassment.

"Of course you are correct," he said. "You must forgive me. My only excuse is your beauty and the response it causes in me."

"Yes," I answered, meeting his gaze steadily.

I wondered if it were my imagination, but I felt that at that moment something deeper began to grow between us. He parted his lips as if about to read my thoughts but then a shadow passed over his eyes and he suddenly pressed his lips together. He seemed to withdraw into himself, turning to stare out to sea.

I did not quite understand his behavior. I flattered myself thinking that perhaps his feelings for me were growing. The moment of recognition between us was real. Left standing beside him, I felt suddenly cold and disappointed. I had been ready to reach out for him to replace all the doubts and fears I had had with a growing trust, a feeling that I was coming to know him in a deeper way. My mind raced on, searching for a reason. He had started to respond and then stopped. Why?

His first marriage had ended so unhappily that perhaps he could not bear the thought of another such bond. My thoughts and emotions raced on irrationally. How dare he take away the bliss he had given me?

The wind whipped my hair around me and the sea raged below, my thoughts driving me nearly mad. If he would not have me for his wife, would he not take me for his mistress? For I was ready to give myself to him, I realized recklessly, no matter what the consequences might be. If I was under some sort of spell then so be it. I would compromise my soul if need be, for I knew that I could not live parted from him.

I had reached out my arms to him and was about to fling myself at him with foolish words when a door rattled behind us. I cursed under my breath and turned away, crossing my arms and hugging myself. Footsteps scraped behind us, and I took deep breaths to calm my rapid breathing, hoping the brisk air would cool my flushed face.

"Ah, stealing away from your own party, are you?"

I heard Enys's teasing voice and turned to find him striding across the balcony, Morwenna on his arm.

Morwenna's startled look must have equaled my own as we stared at each other, but Geoffrey had perfect control of himself.

"You know me too well, Enys. I do my duty as host and then seek solitude."

"If you can call this solitude."

Lord Stratton leaned carefully over the edge and peered into the white spray coming from waves that beat against the walls. He pulled back.

"I'm afraid these heights quite dizzy me."

"It's something one gets used to," said Geoffrey. "Why Morwenna used to chase me along the top of this balustrade when we were little mites."

She didn't deny it, but flashed him a look with her

dark eyes.

"She's half cat then, I'll swear," said Stratton. "But Rhionna looks frozen, old man. You'd better take her in."

"Yes, we were just going."

He reached for me, and I nodded to the other couple as we passed. If Morwenna had her sights set for the handsome Devon lord, that might explain her jealous looks earlier. I hoped now that she had him to herself she would discover she had no rival in me.

"I ought to see if my aunt wants some refreshment," I said to Geoffrey when we returned inside, as much to take my attention off my earlier feelings as to appear the dutiful niece.

Geoffrey too seemed to regain his responsibilities of host. He bowed slightly. "By all means," he said. "I fear I must make myself available to my guests for at least another hour. After that I may excuse myself from them, leaving them to dance until dawn if the musicians hold out that long."

It was on the tip of my tongue to ask him where he would go when he excused himself, but I did not.

I found my aunt already in the refreshment room seated at a table with a matronly lady in lemon yellow and white faille and a tall gangly young man, who Winifred introduced as her companion's son. He bowed over my hand very seriously, and I guessed that this might be one of his first formal occasions, for he seemed hardly out of knee breeches.

"Well, Aunt," I said. "I see I was mistaken to have worried that you would find refreshments. I see by the size of your plate that you have no need of me to wait on you."

"I appreciate your concern, Rhionna," she said with a twinkle in her eye. "But the Ewegans have taken care of me. We have spent the last hour gossiping like two hens while Todd has waited on us hand and foot."

"Your lovely niece must favor her late father," said Mrs. Ewegan. "For I can see that she shares your looks, Winifred."

"Thank you."

And to me she said, "Your aunt was a handsome maid in her day. I can remember how I was afraid my husband would forget himself for looking her way."

"Now Martha, you go too far," said Winifred.

"Perhaps, but I'll leave you to your niece's company. And she, I dare say, is in dire need of resting her feet, which have no doubt been stepped on by every gentleman in the ballroom."

"My feet are quite whole," I assured her. "But I could do with a rest."

The lady and her son left us, and I accepted a glass of punch from a passing waiter before I joined my aunt at the table.

"So, Rhionna. Have you been enjoying yourself?"

"Yes, Aunt. And you?"

But I knew her answer before she put it into words, for I had never seen such a sparkle in her blue-green eyes, nor such a blush on her pale cheeks. I could see something of the beauty of which Mrs. Ewegan spoke, and for a moment I thought I was looking at a younger Winifred, a girl with hope and passion in her face.

Then the image faded and I saw before me my aunt, just as she was, but with a look of nostalgia in her gaze. I smiled.

"You are extremely spirited tonight," I said to her. "I was afraid that you might not be so."

"Yes, it is good that I came here." She gestured to the surrounding walls. "Do I not remember my youthful parties here? Granted, I was not always invited to the grand ballroom, mostly I made do at the party for the poorer folks. But they were just as gay, and Lord Rhyweth spared no expense on our refreshments. And our musicians played lively tunes. How handsome Lord Rhyweth looked then."

It took me a moment to realize that she spoke of Geoffreys father, Arthur. I glanced at her to see her lower lip trembling and a faraway look in her eye. My curiosity turned to excitement. Now seemed the time to broach the questions I had been harboring.

"You say you attended the parties given for the villagers?"

"Yes, that is so. While here, upstairs like tonight, the gentry wiled away the evening."

I watched her closely. "But at least once before tonight you were invited here instead?"

She nodded dreamily. "Yes, that—" She broke off and stole a sideways glance at me. Then she pursed her lips.

I leaned forward, lowering my voice, sensing that now was the moment to get her to tell me what I wanted to know.

"It was Arthur Wycke who brought you here, wasn't it? He entertained you at one of the balls, did he not?"

Her face paled, and she looked at me helplessly, realizing that I had guessed the truth. But I reached for her hand to reassure her.

"It's all right, Aunt. You can tell me. I had guessed it. It's his picture that you keep at the cottage, is it not?"

She nodded, withdrawing her hand and fidgeting with her napkin.

My own excitement rose as I went on. "You were in love with him, weren't you?"

She gave a little jerk of the head, indicating that the answer was yes. I pressed on. "And he returned your love."

She could not refuse me an answer.

"He did. We could not marry, of course. His marriage was arranged to a lady of his station."

"Yes, I can see it all now," I said. "You were lovers, weren't you?"

Her eyes glazed over, and she parted her lips as if to deny it, but then her shoulders sagged and she dropped her head.

"Yes," she confessed. Then she lifted her chin, her pride returning. "Yes," she said again. "We were lovers, and I've never regretted it."

I do not know what made me say it, but the words spilled out of my mouth. "Aunt Winifred, did he give you a child?"

Winifred paled dreadfully as she stared straight ahead. I was afraid I had gone too far, shocking her out of her reverie. For surely I did not mean to say anything that would hurt her, and now I was afraid she was going to faint.

But she did not faint. Her face turned several different shades before returning to its normal one, and I rose to fetch a glass of wine, which I handed her. She sipped it slowly.

"Aunt," I said into her ear. "Let us go somewhere private where we can talk."

She nodded, aware perhaps that I would not be satisfied until I knew all of the truth, and I surmised that she would not like the idea of airing her secrets where others could hear.

We rose and made our way out of the refreshment room. I had seen a small sitting room nearby and I led her there. I closed the carved oak doors behind us, ensuring privacy. She seated herself on a leather sofa in front of a glowing fire in a huge stone fireplace, and I crossed to hold my hands out over the fire, my back to her.

I was still unsure of her mental and emotional state, brought on by my questions, but I needn't have worried. For it took no more prodding to get her to speak. She stared into the fire that leapt up from thick logs, which seemed to help her focus her thoughts.

I just turned around when she began, her words slow at first and then building, her tone more confident.

"It is true; I loved Arthur Wycke. And why not? He was young and handsome, always smiling, always with a kind word to say, hoping for a better day for all Cornishmen. And he loved me too. But what was I? The daughter of a poor tenant farmer. Such a match could not be."

She shook her head. "The Wyckes' own fortune was dwindling. He needed a marriage that would refurbish the family coffers. I'll never forget the day Arthur's father told him they would be going to the continent where he would be introduced to the best of families."

A tinge of color came into her pale cheeks. "He took me with him up to the moors to tell me. I could not bear it. Then he took me in his arms. We —" she broke off.

I waited until she got herself under control. Then she continued in a strong, steady voice.

"But our time together could not last. He left for Europe. Oh, perhaps they were surprised at his choice, a Hungarian heiress from a little known family. But her fortune was sorely needed here."

She glanced once at the elegant surroundings of the room we were in, at the furniture, rugs, and paintings that Magdalena Druga had bought, perhaps. She gave a little sound at the back of her throat. I waited, afraid she would not go on. But after a moment, she continued.

"And so they married. Magdalena was much admired. So much so that rumors went about that other men's ardors were not always resisted at her bedroom door. I wanted to believe those rumors, hoping they

234

would send Arthur back to my arms."

She gave a sigh, remembering. "But they did not. Arthur was an honorable man He kept his marriage vows, though he swore he always loved me. I have many letters to attest to that fact."

And I had one as well, I suddenly realized. Everything clicked into place as Winifred talked. Why had I not seen it before? Arthur had handled the imports from Cornwall. Perhaps one of Arthur's reasons for helping my father in business was so that Winifred would indirectly be taken care of. It was because of Arthur's concern for Winifred that he assisted and encouraged my father, who I knew had sent Winifred money when he could.

She continued, a sad smile on her lips. "But he could do little about the child that was already in my womb by the time he sealed his vows with Magdalena. The child we had made with our love. When my time came, Arthur saw that I had the best midwife." Her expression became fixed again. "The child, of course, was taken from me and given a home."

I frowned. "Who was the child? Did you ever know its name?"

"No. I did not want to know." She gave a quick, guilty smile, tugging at her handkerchief.

Sympathy for my aunt's lost love flowed from me, but still I felt unsatisfied. The ending to the tale made me wonder. But Winifred looked quite drawn, and I was afraid to push her further. I knelt before her and took her hands.

"Thank you for telling me, dear Aunt. I know it must be hard for you to speak of it."

She shook her head, gazing on me with tears brimming.

"It is painful to speak of what has been so long buried, but it comes with relief, my child. In my later days

I have often thought it a mistake to hide so much in one's heart. We are a closed folk, we Cornish. We would perhaps be the healthier if we aired our innermost thoughts more frequently. Then we might not look so much on the dark side."

I nodded. "Perhaps so. In any case, I am glad you have told me. Come now, I will see you to your bedchamber and sit with you a while."

"That would be very nice."

We were staying the night at the castle as were guests who had come great distances. I was surprised that Winifred had agreed to this scheme, since it would be a simple matter to borrow Geoffrey's carriage once more to take us home. Now I thought with melancholy that perhaps it was Winifred's own nostalgia that had made her agree to stay here. At last she would have one night's stay in the noble home that had been denied her in her youth.

We climbed the stairs to the floor that had been made ready for guests and inquired of Olga as to which one was to be Winifred's bedchamber. The housekeeper showed us the way. She did not meet my gaze, but kept her eyes lowered. Just before she left us, she gave me a quick sharp glance, then turned away, leaving me feeling uneasy. I still had questions about Olga's behavior around me, but no matter, tonight my attention must be on my aunt.

I helped Winifred into her dressing gown and then folded back the covers for her. She got into bed and I sat beside her for a while.

"It was a lovely party," she said, her eyelids drooping. "You must return. The dancing is not yet over."

I remembered that the dancing was to go on all night, but that Geoffrey would have left the guests by now.

"Yes, I will return for a little while, though I too am

236

tired," I said.

"Like the old days . . ." Her eyes closed.

Before she drifted off to sleep, she mumbled a name. At least I thought it sounded like a name. I bent closer, to see if she would repeat it. She stirred. I frowned in concentration, for she mumbled something else. But the syllables were unintelligible.

Chapter 18

I saw no more of Geoffrey that night and wondered if he had slipped away to work on his music. Lady Stratton intercepted me on her return from the refreshment room, swooping down on me, her feathers waving as she moved.

"There you are, Miss Fowley," she said. "I see you have become quite the center of attention this evening."

I sensed the disappointment in her voice and thought perhaps I could get her to tell me why I was being gazed at so strangely.

"My lady, perhaps you can help me. I am not at all used to such attention. From the way everyone has been staring at me, I feel as if I have done something to offend."

I lowered my eyes with what I considered the proper amount of modesty. "Perhaps it is the bold color of my gown."

"It is not that," she said. Then she let out an exasperated breath. "It is nothing you have done. Come, let us sit in a quiet corner where we can talk."

We seated ourselves in two high-backed chairs where there was no one to bother us. She scanned the crowd with her eyes as if satisfying herself first that everyone was accounted for. Then she turned to me and spoke.

"You seem a sensible girl," she began. "It is only

238

because of that that I confide in you."

"Thank you, my lady."

She frowned very seriously. "I don't mind telling you the true mission of my visit here. Although Enys and Geoffrey Wycke have been friends for some years, I lately have become concerned with the amount of time my son is spending here. It is as I suspected. He is infatuated with Morwenna Wycke."

"I see." Of course that was obvious, but I let her continue in her own way.

"Having the Wyckes as friends is one thing, but marrying into the family is quite another."

"Oh?"

"Yes. I have been disturbed by certain rumors I have heard even as far away as Devon about the activities of Lord Rhyweth."

It was as I suspected then, even the evil rumors surrounding Geoffrey had reached Lady Stratton's ears.

"I understand there have been several young women missing from the environs, and quite frankly the finger is pointed at Lord Rhyweth. I have noticed that he has paid you rather a lot of attention. It chills me to say it, but I am afraid for your health."

I lifted my chin. "I am aware of what you speak, Lady Stratton. Others have warned me."

"And you have not taken heed?"

"I have not taken heed of ridiculous accusations. I hope to find proof that there is no link between Lord Rhyweth and the missing girls. However, I appreciate your concern for me, and I will take care."

Her mouth turned into a hard line. "You can see the reasons for my double concern for Enys. Whatever bad blood may be in the Wycke family, no good can come of his courting Morwenna. I have determined to put a stop to it."

"But Lady Stratton. Why not wait until there is proof of what is afoot here. If Morwenna or Geoffrey are guilty then you have every right to see that your son does not keep company with them. But what if they are innocent?"

"If they are innocent, he can do what he likes. Until then . . . Well, I have decided to have a talk with him."

I nodded. Somehow I did not think that her talking to Enys would change his behavior one whit, but that was a family matter between them.

When we finished our conversation, I left Lady Stratton, dancing once or twice with older gentlemen. I soon excused myself, though, to go to bed. I saw Morwenna dancing with Lord Stratton and from the satisfied look on her face I decided that she must be making a conquest.

I needed to speak to Geoffrey, but I would have to wait until morning to do that. I left the festivities behind, making my way upstairs. Here the corridors were darkened as guests repaired to bed. In my own chamber I got out of my gown alone. I did not want to send for Olga, and all the other servants were at their own party.

I slipped into bed, many thoughts crowding my mind. If the organ played that night, I did not hear it.

I finally drowsed off to sleep to the sound of carriages rolling out of the courtyard. A number of guests had remained, however, for at breakfast the next day the dining room was quite full. As was their practice, neither Geoffrey nor Morwenna were present, but as I entered the dining room, Lord Stratton saw me and came in my direction.

"Ah, good morning, Rhionna," he said. "Did you rest well?"

"Yes, and you?"

240

I saw the glimmer in his eye as he answered, "Quite. But come now, you must sit with me. What will you have to eat?"

I asked for scones and clotted cream.

"Will you be staying at the castle or do you return to Devon?" I asked him.

He gave me a devilish grin. "Duty calls, but I have decided to put off duty for once. I promised Morwenna I would remain a few days."

"That is good. I'm sure Lord Rhyweth and Morwenna will enjoy your company."

He set down his coffee cup and gazed thoughtfully at his plate of eggs. "One hopes so," he said. Then in a lighter tone, "If you have no plans for the day, perhaps you will consider riding out with Morwenna and myself later today."

"Oh, I would not want to intrude."

"Nonsense. It will be no intrusion at all."

We spoke no more of my concerns from the night before, but it was hard to concentrate on frivolous conversation. I decided to take a stroll in the picture gallery after breakfast, and it was there, as I sat in the window seat gazing out at the ocean, muted through the closed windows, that Geoffrey found me.

His step was so light that he startled me when I looked up to see him only a few feet away. He looked rested, a smile playing about his lips.

"There you are," he said. "Musing thoughtfully, I see."

"I was waiting to see you," I said.

His eyes flickered with interest, but my own look must have turned more serious as I thought of my mission, and he sat beside me, waiting for me to speak.

"I spoke to my aunt last night," I said. "She told me something surprising. That is, it is something I wonder if you know."

"What is that?" he asked.

I cleared my throat. Now that I had him here, I was not sure how to put my question since I was unsure if he knew of the affair between my aunt and his father.

"It has to do with your parents," I began. "My aunt apparently was infatuated with your father. She and your father . . ." I cleared my throat. I could not look at Geoffrey's penetrating eyes. "I believe they had an affair."

He was silent for a moment and I looked up, trying to read his expression. He gazed at me meditatively, absorbing what I said.

"Is that what Winifred told you?"

"Yes. And I believe her."

"I do not doubt her word." He smiled gently. "Fascinating is it not? The attraction the Fowley women seem to have for the Wycke men."

I blushed. "That is not the reason I have brought it up."

"I am sorry. Pray continue."

I struggled with my words. "I first suspected it when I saw a picture of your father in our cottage. I saw her gazing at it one night. When I saw the portrait of your father later here, I realized it was the same."

He nodded thoughtfully.

"Yes. It could be so. My father never confided his personal affairs to me, of course. But I remember the kindness he seemed to show your aunt. He took special care to see that her farm had what she needed and more. And perhaps he never pressed her for rent." He shrugged.

"I have already told you that my mother was a high-spirited woman with a temperament that she sometimes vented on my father as well as on poor Olga. When my mother was in a fit of rage, I would not blame my father if he turned elsewhere for comfort. Mother had many admirers as well. I have told you it was a marriage of convenience. Such things do happen."

I looked down. "Winifred said your father kept his marriage vows, that he was her lover before the marriage to your mother but not after."

He turned to me lifting my hand. "But why has your aunt told you this now? Perhaps to warn you against me? Perhaps she fears that her fate will become yours?"

That this was very likely was not the present issue. "There is more," I said, forcing myself to look into his dark, inviting eyes. "It seems they had a child."

He lifted his eyebrows and stared at me unblinking for a moment. Then he lowered my hand slowly. "This I did not know."

"I do not think she planned to tell me. But I guessed it. I was watching her face in a moment of nostalgia, and when I guessed her secret, she could not hide the truth from me. I am sure of it."

"And who is this child?"

I shook my head. "The child could be dead by now for all I know. Winifred said she does not know, that the child was taken from her at birth and taken she knows not where. But I think she is lying."

Geoffrey stared into space. "If I knew who this bastard child was, I would see that something was done for him or for her, if need be."

He stood, leaned a hand on the window frame and looked out. "This child," he said, "would be near my own age. Perhaps a year or two older."

We did not speak for some moments, then Geoffrey turned and lifted me off my seat. "You have given me much to think on," he said.

It was not my meaning to weigh Geoffrey with this

243

burden, only I had hoped he could help me uncover more of the secret. I supposed I had hoped that Geoffrey knew all about my aunt's affair and could tell me who the child was, and I said as much.

He smiled down at me ironically. "But what could you gain by this knowledge?"

I shrugged. "I am not sure. There seems to be a great many unanswered questions about my family that I am just becoming aware of. I cannot rest until I know the answers."

We had strolled halfway down the gallery and stopped, gazing at each other. He lifted a finger and ran it along my cheek.

"And what will you do with these answers? Perhaps the questions are better left buried. The truth is not always pleasant."

I wrinkled my brow. "It may not be pleasant, but the truth sets us free, does it not?"

He moved his head from side to side, doubting me. "And this freedom, is it so important?"

As if to put an end to words, he lowered his lips to kiss me. It was a gentle warm kiss, with a promise of more. But there were guests about the castle, and anyone could interrupt us. Knowing this, he drew away.

"I have business in St. Ives today. But I hope I may find you here on my return later this evening. I would like to keep you here one more night."

I wavered, knowing my aunt would want to go home today. But I did not really want to leave yet.

"I have promised Lord Stratton to ride out with Morwenna and him later this morning," I said.

"Very well. Perhaps with Enys as chaperone, Morwenna will not get you lost this time. I will instruct him to keep you safe."

He lifted my hand and kissed it. "I do not like to see

you worried. I will do what I can to set your mind at ease. I trust you with Stratton. I would not like to think of your being alone until some of these matters are resolved. I too am searching for the truth, though I am not sure it is the same truth as yours." His gaze was quizzical "Time will tell."

He left me, and after watching him go, I went upstairs to dress for riding.

I thought I might feel awkward accompanying Lord Stratton and Morwenna on their ride, but Enys was so entertaining and Morwenna in one of her more companionable moods, that I enjoyed myself heartily. We rode back the way Morwenna and I had gotten lost just to see how we had fallen off the track. In the light of day with no storm brooding, we were able to keep our bearings better. We pointed out to Enys the small cottage where we had taken shelter, and even then I shivered looking at it. I never wanted to be that cold and drenched again.

Refreshed from the ride, we gave our mounts to Andrew, then I returned to my room. As soon as I closed the door behind me, a small folded piece of paper caught my attention. It was tucked under the glass lamp by my bed, a corner sticking out. It did not have my name on it, but I sensed it was for me.

I approached the bed, picked up the piece of paper and unfolded it. My pulse quickened as I read it. It was printed in a block hand in an attempt at disguising the handwriting.

If you value your life, go back to Amerika.

I stared at the misspelling. Had the author of the note not known how to spell America? Or had it been spelled that way in an attempt to further hide the writer's identity, perhaps to throw suspicion on Olga.

Someone wanted me out of the way, but why? I had done nothing to earn anyone's enmity. Unless I was

beginning to turn up things about the past that someone wanted to keep buried. Could that be it? Did
someone want to stop me from digging up the truth?
Was there some secret that I had not yet brought to
light that someone feared I would?

If this were the case, whose secret had I come close
to revealing? On whose hidden motive was I trespass-
ing? While the uneasiness alarmed me for the hundredth time, I knew immediately what I would do. It
would be best to act as if I had found nothing. Whoever had left the note hoped to frighten me into leaving. Instead, I would try to get the culprit to reveal
who he or she was.

My thoughts were brave even though my knees
were shaking. I folded the note and tucked it in my
bosom. Then I dressed for dinner.

Geoffrey did not appear at dinner that evening
when Morwenna, Enys, Lady Stratton, and I met to
dine. It was a rather stiff affair with the countess continually raising her eyebrows and sending disapproving looks at her son, who completely ignored her and
kept us entertained.

When I mentioned that Geoffrey's business must
have kept him in St. Ives longer than he expected,
Enys shrugged.

"It's no use trying to account for Geoffrey's actions.
Haven't you noticed by now he keeps strange hours?
He would most likely forget to eat altogether if his
cook didn't prepare meals on a regular basis just to
keep herself employed. No doubt he'll turn up."

"No doubt."

I felt restless after dinner and after leaving Enys and
Morwenna together in the formal parlor, I went into
the library to get something to read. Winifred had
gone home today, but I was keeping my promise to
Geoffrey to stay one more night at the castle. It

annoyed me that he had asked me to stay and yet did not appear. After the warning note I had had, I did not feel easy being there, but I felt closer to the answers now, and a need to pursue them even at the risk to my own safety.

I selected a volume of Jane Austen's, and leafed through the book. As I left the library, I was still looking at the novel and when I glanced up I saw I had taken a wrong direction.

I suppose I should have turned around, but suddenly I heard the organ music, and it seemed to come from the end of the passage. It was much louder there than upstairs. Curiosity won out and I moved farther along the corridor thinking that that way might lead to the music chamber. I was in a part of the castle I had not explored before, and I wanted to see for myself what Geoffrey did when he played the organ, for I did not understand why such secrecy surrounded his music.

I wanted to believe that he had good reasons not to allow anyone in the organ chamber, but until I saw for myself what he did when he worked at night, how could I be sure that he was not up to something more secretive? Conflict tore at me. I was falling in love with him, and I wanted to trust him. But even yet the doubts planted by his naysayers lurked in a dark corner of my mind, driving me on my mission of exploration.

The music had stopped as I came to a set of stairs that lead downward. With my hand against the stone wall for support, I descended. When I reached the landing and glanced ahead, a door opened and a figure passed through. That end of the corridor was in shadow, but I thought it was Geoffrey.

"Geoffrey?" I called after him.

But the heavy door closed. My heart beat rapidly as

I went forward. There was no need to feel as if I were sneaking about, I tried to tell myself. I had every right to want to speak to Geoffrey. But for all my brave thoughts, I paused with my hand on the door when I reached it.

Then the scrape of a sole behind me made me nearly leap out of my skin and I turned, stifling a shriek. Jonas stood glowering at me.

"What would you be wanting, miss?" he asked.

My hand fluttered to my chest as if to keep my heart within my rib cage.

"I—I thought I saw Lord Rhyweth go this way. I wanted to speak to him."

"Master Rhyweth be working now."

"Yes, I suppose he is."

He shuffled aside, waiting for me to pass, but once over my fright and hoping that Jonas would not harm me, I was not so ready to give up.

"Tell me," I said. "Does this way lead to the organ chamber? Master Rhyweth said he might show it to me one night."

"The way to the organ chamber does not lie that way. Master Rhyweth will show you the organ chamber another night."

I hesitated, not knowing what to say next for Jonas' sudden appearance in the dark passage unsettled me. "Well, I suppose I can speak to him another time."

If the way to the organ chamber did not lie this way, where was Geoffrey going? For who else could it be but he? But I could tell from Jonas' harsh expression that he would not give me the answers.

Seeing no other alternative, I made my way back along the passage until I turned the corner and could no longer feel Jonas' stare. Then I shivered. Had I continued without being caught, what would I have found? Did Jonas inadvertently save me from some horrible danger?

I began to breathe easier as I came to the main staircase and climbed upward to the main hall. There I came to the mirror in which I had seen no reflection of Morwenna when she had stood beside it the night Rufus woke me. I could see my own reflection in it plain enough now. I remembered the little volume about the undead said that those cursed with vampire blood had no reflections.

As I stepped closer to touch the mirror, running my fingers over the smooth glass, a dark irregular shape behind it caught my eye. I leaned over and peered behind the mirror, cautious at first.

The dark mass did not move, so I reached out to touch it, discovering that it was a bunch of material stuffed hastily in the corner. I knelt and pulled it out. Now I saw that it was plain black damask, and when I stretched it to its length, I judged it to be a little longer than the mirror.

Someone must have hung the material over the mirror that night, revealing only the frame in an effort to prevent the mirror from reflecting. I knew now that someone wanted to frighten me into believing that Morwenna and Geoffrey were vampiric. But who and why?

Chapter 19

"Oh, miss, it's dreadful news."

I was scarcely awake when Gwynneth came to open my windows and stoke up the fire to take the chill out. I struggled to drag my mind back from the weird images that had filled my dreams.

"Nan Goosmoor is missing and what with all that's happened recently I'm dreadfully worried."

The word missing registered in my fuzzy mind and brought me sharply awake. I sat up against the pillows.

"Who is missing, Gwynneth?"

She wrung her hands together. "Nan Goosmoor. She's my good friend. One of the only ones who's treated me decent and not like an outsider if you know what I mean. But she ain't been seen since the night of the big party. We was all in the big room downstairs while you folks was upstairs. There and in the kitchen we was, I mean. But after midnight, no one's seen her."

I was fully alert now and threw back the covers, reaching for my dressing gown. The news itself was frightening enough, but I did not like the added coincidences that came with it.

"Are you quite sure? How is it that she was seen up until midnight but not after?"

"Andrew was dancin' with her. Then she and I had a bit of a chat. Nan took some mulled wine with

250

Elwynd and me. I saw her go to the kitchens with Cook, then Elwynd wanted to dance with me again. But I was pretty tired. I'm not used to stayin' up late since I have to start workin' at six in the morning, carrying the coal and seein' to all the fires in the upstairs rooms."

I frowned. "And so you went to bed?"

"I was near dead on my feet. Elwynd took me to my room, but I didn't let him stay. He was a bit put out by that, but I was afraid of bein' caught. Anyway, that's all I knew. No one really said anything yesterday, but then Ellie Tucker from the village said Nan'd been gone from her bed two nights in a row."

My heart sank like a leaden weight. "This is serious," I said.

I did not want to believe that Geoffrey had anything to do with this, yet desperation and grief clawed at me. Seeing Gwynneth with such worry in her eyes, I knew I had to say something to try to give her hope.

"I'll see what I can find out," I said. "If you hear any developments, come to me directly. Let us hope there is no tragedy in this."

She nodded, but I could see from her pinched look that she was not optimistic. Neither was I, and I felt relieved when she left me alone and I could give vent to my emotions.

A large sob escaped me. "Please Geoffrey," I whispered, sinking down on the bed and grabbing a pillow to hug against my waist. "Please let it not be so."

And yet I had seen him with my own eyes going down a mysterious passage I knew not where. And Jonas had been trying to cover his master's whereabouts. Jonas. I could ask him.

No sooner had the thought crossed my mind than

251

I discarded it. He would never tell me what I wanted to know. But there were other ways. I half hated myself for betraying Geoffrey with that part of me that still did not trust him. Part of me was so certain that he was basically good. And yet the reactive part of my mind swarmed with a multitude of questions I could not answer.

I dressed, hastened downstairs, and took breakfast, waiting impatiently for Morwenna to appear, which she eventually did. I did my best to appear that I was lingering over my coffee. At last Morwenna motioned for Godreven to pour her a cup, then she dismissed him and joined me at the table. I wasted no time, crossing my fingers that Morwenna was not going to be in a temperamental mood today, for I needed straight answers.

"Morwenna, I accidently discovered a strange passage in the lower northwest wing of the castle last night. I was wondering where it led."

She frowned, the sleep not yet quite gone from her eyes. "A passage, you say? There are plenty of those in this place."

"Yes, I know." I tried to be patient. "I took a wrong turn last night, then I heard Geoffrey's music. I followed it, thinking I would come to the organ chamber, but instead I came to a set of stairs that led downward, then a door. Jonas was there. If I had my directions right, it seemed that way would only lead to the cliffs. Do you know of it?"

She took a few sips of coffee, which seemed to brighten her wits.

"Oh. You must mean the old escape route. All castles are built with escape routes, you know. The one on the north was for escape by sea in Henry Tudor's day. It leads to Penhallow Cove."

She tossed her mane of dark hair back and took a

bite of scone. "I explored it as a girl, but of course I wasn't supposed to."

Then she stopped mid-bite and stared at me. "But how could you have found it? It was closed off years ago."

My spine tingled, but I said, "Perhaps I saw another passage than that."

But she shook her head. "There aren't any other passages but that one on the north side. Of course there is the way to the dungeons on the west wing, and that is where Geoffrey works. But that has been converted, and you would have known if you were on that side. You can't hear the sea from there when the windows are open."

I toyed with my coffee cup, trying to get her to continue talking. "Was the north passage ever used for anything else?"

She shrugged, intent on her eggs now. "The servants will all tell you that it was used for smuggling in the days when England was at war with France, but I hardly know the truth to that."

"Smuggling?"

"Yes, this coast was famous for it, though not so famous I suppose as the southern coast. Still, we had our smugglers."

Something began to click in my mind as she continued. "But as I said, my father had the passage closed," Morwenna continued. "I am surprised you saw Jonas there. What was he doing?"

I took a breath and said, "Doing his master's bidding, I suppose. Evidently Geoffrey had preceded him there."

She lowered her fork and looked at me strangely, and I could not judge from her reaction whether she suddenly realized that she had said too much, or whether she was also guessing at what he might have

253

been doing. But she ate no more, only sipped her coffee.

Finally she said, "I really haven't the vaguest notion what he might have been doing there. Perhaps he intends to open it up again, though what for I cannot imagine. We are not in danger of being beseiged by French pirates."

"No, I suppose not."

Was it guilt I read in her eyes? Or suspicion. I had no way to judge, only that my words had struck her. It seemed too suggestive to bring up the latest news about the missing village girl, and I did not know if she knew of it. But I sensed that now was not the time to ask.

She left me to go about her business. She must have known I was leaving that day, but she made no special farewell, leaving the dining room as if preoccupied.

As I was waiting for Andrew to saddle Blackie, I wandered into the picture gallery. I passed down the row of portraits coming to stop in front of the painting of Geoffrey's late wife Elizabeth. I looked into her pale blue eyes, admiring her creamy complexion. From the way she leaned for support on the back of the chair in front of her, I could see the delicacy of her constitution. Yet there was the look of intelligence about her.

If only the picture could talk, I felt that the woman there could help me piece things together. What did she really die of? The allusions that Geoffrey was something not quite human or perhaps had inherited blood from some legendary source were too fantastic to be taken seriously, and yet there were moments when the idea had chilled me. Elwynd had told me that the specialists did not agree upon what ailed Elizabeth. And what had happened to the maidens

254

who were suddenly missed from the vicinity?

The image of Geoffrey disappearing through the large heavy door going down some strange passage did not sit well with me. And he had not appeared this morning for me to ask him about it. I wondered again that if I had proceeded down that passage would some ill fate have befallen me?

Images warred in my mind. There was the warm, sensuous Geoffrey that held me in his grasp, and then there was the strange distant Geoffrey who I did not understand.

And now there was this new revelation that my aunt and Geoffrey's father were lovers and had had a child. There was also the fact that Elwynd had known my father and had done business with him. Both my father and Elwynd had warned me against being here, yet I was headstrong enough to remain in Cornwall in spite of the warnings. And something about the warnings and the dangers surrounding me did not jibe. I had had the same sense when Morwenna mentioned smuggling at breakfast. Yet I still could make no sense of it all.

There was something else too. I remembered the look on Elwynd's face the day I fell from my horse. It was the same look on the guests' faces when I had appeared at the ball. Could they all see something in me that I could not see? It was frightening, as if an apparition followed me and I could not perceive it.

I stared at the late Lady Rhyweth, feeling more muddled than when I had come in. If I stayed here as long as she had, would her fate befall me?

"I understand you wish to see the organ chamber."

Geoffrey's words frightened me almost out of my skin, so deep had I been in thought. I blinked and met his dark, inquiring gaze. My heart hammered in my chest and words stuck in my throat, as my

255

emotions tumbled helter-skelter after the thoughts which had preceded them.

"Yes," I finally managed. "I have always been curious about it, and last night —" I did not know how to finish.

"Yes. I understand you were wandering along the lower passages. I will show you the right way to get there."

His hand touched my shoulder and then drifted down my back as he escorted me along the corridor to the main entry hall. Then he led me down a narrow curving staircase until we were in the bowels of the castle.

I felt too intimidated to ask him where he had been going if not to the organ chamber, but followed meekly along. At least I was being shown the lower part of the castle at last. An opportunity would arise to ask about the passage used for smuggling.

We approached a heavy oak door with wrought-iron plates. He lifted down a large key ring from the stone wall and inserted a skeleton key in the keyhole then replaced the key ring on the wall. As he opened the door, it scraped on its hinges, and we went through.

"This part of the castle was used to keep prisoners in the days when the dungeons were used. I have not brought you here because I did not want to alarm you. Some people do not find it pleasant to be here."

We passed through a room which had been cleared mostly of its former contents. But iron plates inserted into the wall were left with a single link of chain. I swallowed. Even though I could tell that Geoffrey had done a good job of renovation, the place was still dreadful. I shivered as we passed through, for I could clearly imagine prisoners crouched in their chains. I forced my gaze straight ahead as I followed Geoffrey.

We passed through another door into a semicircular chamber that sloped down in tiers from where we stood. Red velvet seats lined each landing as in a small theater, except that the front row contained only benches, also upholstered in red velvet, but with no backs.

The organ was installed at the bottom, the tops of the organ pipes hidden in the shadows thrown by the one flickering oil lamp mounted on the wall. Geoffrey went ahead of me.

"Now you are here," he said. "This is where I work."

"It's magnificent," I said, following him down the aisle between the velvet seats.

I envisioned him upon the seat, his hands on the manuals, playing the music I had heard late at night, the sound coming from pipes that ranged in size from that of a pencil to others that looked large enough for a man to crawl through. What I had heard had been only dim snatches, but in this small chamber, the music would be very loud indeed.

"Jonas pumps the bellows there for the wind supply. I have experimented with a steam system, but I have not perfected it yet."

He pointed to a chamber behind the organ, and I shook my head. So the faithful Jonas had to work at night as well, whenever Geoffrey played.

"The action is mechanical, opening the valves under the keys to let wind into the pipes."

His words were still describing the workings of the organ, but his eyes had taken on that quality I had seen when we had been alone before. His words seemed far away, and some other more basic need was taking over. I felt it too as he walked toward me where I stood in the center of the floor.

The blood seemed to pump to my extremities, and

I was keenly aware of the flush in my face, the way my ears tingled, the spring unwinding within me. The formal shield I always sensed about Geoffrey when he was in the presence of others lowered, and with it went the weight of his position, his responsibilities, whatever curse held him so distant from people.

I could sense why he cloistered himself away here. This was his private sanctum where he could give vent to the hidden darkness of his soul. And yet I was no longer intimidated by him. For all I had tried to do to keep my distance, to heed the sensible reasons I knew I should hesitate, it was too late. I had somehow become a part of him.

I think it was because I saw past the darkness in his eyes. I also saw something in him that seemed like part of me. There was an unexplainable link between us. It was that link that I clung to as he took me in his arms. It was what united us as his mouth probed mine, as his embrace tightened, as our bodies sought each other's.

We were alone in another place and time. The rest of the world, the rest of our lives were on the other side of the heavy door. Here in Geoffrey's chamber, what was done was very private and I was filled with the same sense of intimacy I had felt the first night I had been alone with him, that all my rational decisions no longer mattered.

Clothing became disarrayed as hands sought to touch, lips to probe and kiss. He set my innocent body on fire so that I answered his caresses with those of my own. We reclined on the velvet bench, Geoffrey's movements becoming more demanding, my mind numbing with pleasure. I was inexperienced, unaware of what to do to please him, and yet I knew that with my heart and soul I desperately wanted to please him. I wanted to fulfill his needs, to answer his desires. I closed my eyes, letting the oneness I felt with him be my guide, as flesh met flesh, his pleasure evident from the release in his voice as he whispered to me, his urgency mounting.

Something bloomed between us, the seed of love that had been so long buried in him sought fulfillment in me. Then in the most private gesture, he ignited the flame that carried me to another plane, an explosion bursting in my ears just as his thrusts pressed into me, my soul encompassing his.

The stars in my mind showered over us, his heart throbbed against mine and still he pressed me against him, his face lowering to lay upon my breasts, his hand still holding me against him intimately, the heat intense, but gently receding as we clung to each other until the lamp went out.

I trotted Blackie out of the courtyard and onto the road leading to my aunt's cottage. We rode through the woods swiftly, and after what had happened only an hour before, I felt great relief at returning to the cottage. Rufus bounded out to greet me. I put Blackie in the barn then went in to find my aunt sitting and sewing with Hannelore Treleaven.

"There you are, my dear," Winifred said. "I had thought the Wyckes might have persuaded you to stay longer."

"I'm afraid I haven't the patience for visits." I said.

"Oh?" She glanced up from her work but evidently did not attach any special meaning to my words.

Hannelore's keen eye settled on my expression, however, and her gaze narrowed, making her long sharp nose seem all the sharper. I felt my face flush, and wondered if her special abilities extended to

259

mind reading.

"I should be going along," said Hannelore. "You'll be wanting to speak to your niece."

"Please don't leave on my account, Hannelore."

"I've work to do. Emily Toombs is having a difficult pregnancy and I have a remedy for her. The powder of calumba mixed with powdered ginger, each one-half ounce, and one drachm of senna makes a remedy that allays the vomiting. It can be used with good effect both before and after the confinement."

The herb woman gathered her things and bid my aunt good-bye. At the door she gave me one last glance, her expression sending a chill down my spine.

I changed into a dress for working around the farm and then laid my plans, for despite my personal dilemma, I had to remember my role as sleuth. In one way, the release of pent up passion between Geoffrey and myself had cleared my mind, making it feel razor keen for what I needed to do.

The passage in the bowels of the castle had given me a hunch. There was one person I was very anxious to speak with now that the facts were beginning to gel in my mind, and he would be arriving soon.

Later that day Elwynd came to repair some thatching on the barn roof. After speaking to Winifred about what needed to be done, he placed the ladder by the barn and climbed up. Midmorning Winifred brewed some tea. Seeing my opportunity to speak with Elwynd out of earshot from anyone else, I decided to take him some tea. I poured a mug and went outside, approaching the ladder. With one hand

I climbed up the ladder to hand the mug to him.

"You do skillful work," I said to him as he stopped to rest and sip the tea. "Can you show me how it's done?"

"Aye, I can show you. It's not as easy as it looks."

He helped me clamber up the roof until I was perched beside him on the peak of the roof, both sides sloping away toward the ground. He had laid a bundle of straw beside him and drove in a hazel spar to hold the new thatch. He lent me his gloves and showed me how to place the straw and drive it in. I tried, but I finally shook my head, giving up.

"I think it would be some time before I could develop such a skill," I said.

He was obviously pleased at the admiration. "Most thatchers like to leave their trademark," he said. "I'll work a circle and cross there." He pointed to the side facing the cottage and the road. "Then there'll be the trimming of the eaves. You have to cut it properly."

He picked up a scythe blade, the edge of which appeared quite sharp. I had admired the straight, clean-cut eaves on thatched cottages I had seen and wondered how such precise work could be done with such an unwieldy tool.

I looked out from my perch. From here we had a splendid view of the land sloping down to the ocean.

"It's quite a view," I said.

"Yes," he said, picking up the mug, evidently not yet anxious to continue his work.

"I just returned from the castle today," I said. "I stayed there an extra night after the ball."

A shadow passed over his eyes, but he nodded noncommittally. I carried on in a conversational tone. "Morwenna and I were discussing my father's business. I am thinking of returning to America soon, and I told her that I planned to continue the practice of importing handmade crafts from the local villagers just as my father did."

He nodded, glancing at me sidelong. "That would be very good."

"I imagine I could get some very good woven materials just as my father used to. You will help me, won't you?"

He paused. Then said, "I might do so."

My heart hammered, but I knew Elwynd had no idea of what I was leading up to. I was careful that my expression was ingenuous.

"I admired the handiwork from Pendeen long before I knew it was Cornish. We sewed with the woolens and lace in our house." I took a breath, but continued. "And then there was the gold, the jewels, the stolen art?"

Elwynd looked straight ahead. His grip on the mug tightened. The wind had picked up slightly and I clutched the thatch with both hands, my knees pressing in to help me keep my balance. I thought I had been acting my part very well, but I lost my courage in the face of the angry look he now gave me. Out of the corner of my eye I saw him change his grip on the mug and move his other hand nearer to the scythe.

"So you know about the smuggling, do you?" he said. "What of it? Fair traders we were. We used our wits to better our luck and fill our bellies."

I only stared at him, pressing myself deeper into the thatch, not knowing what to say next.

"Your father is dead now," he went on. "What does it matter?"

I tried to gather my wits. I never expected such a blatant confession. I had expected him to give me some telltale sign if I were on the right track. Though it was hard to believe that my father had done anything illegal, I had finally begun to wonder if that was the reason he did not want me to come to Cornwall, that he had something to hide and that I might find out about it.

"So it is true," I heard myself say.

He clamped his mouth shut, peering at me. I realized that he was as startled as I, but now that the surprise was past, I would be hard pressed to get him to tell me more. I could see him relax a little about the jaws, and he lowered the mug by his side.

He shrugged. "That was all many years ago," he said. "Harmless really. There were some stolen goods passed into your father's hands. Some wrecks with valuable cargo fell into our hands. It was best to send the stuff away without the customs agents knowing. Your father was leaving Cornwall anyway, why not send the goods with him? It was a good arrangement."

"Wrecks," I said. "I see. Wrecks that happened of their own accord or wrecks that were lured to that cove like the ship I was on?"

His fist tightened again. "Would you be making accusations, now?"

"Does it matter? It is your word against mine."

I was still having difficulty believing that my father's business was not entirely legitimate.

"Like I said, that was a long time ago. No reason to dredge up old events to ponder in the present. What good will it do?"

"Then tell me just for my own satisfaction, how long did it go on? Did you send my father other stolen goods later? Were there other wrecks?"

He shrugged and looked away. "We'd no need to send the goods to America for long. In truth the business stopped soon after he left." He looked back at me. "He was a legitimate businessman by that

263

time. Said he had no need of the pickings of wrecks. Had a family by then. Said he wanted to live an honest and straight life."

I sighed in relief. Such a thing might be true. These Cornish seemed to think that the wrecks were sent for their benefit, to even up the score that geography and economics had tallied up against them. But if my father had gotten a foothold in America and saw he could make an honest living, he must have realized that he wanted a decent life, not one dependent on the misfortunes of others. He had crossed the ocean and had seen life from another point of view.

Elwynd was watching me closely, working his lower lip. There was still a trace of malice in his eye, and I glanced down from my precarious position. Supposing Elwynd decided I would not keep my silence, that his explanations did not satisfy. How simple it would be for me to have an accident and no one be the wiser.

The ground below suddenly looked quite far away, and it was some distance to the ladder. I swallowed. I had to say something to reassure him.

"I believe what you say is true, Elwynd. Knowing my father, I can believe it was just as you tell it. As you say, it would do no good to raise the issue now. There is no one to blame. I suppose many people were involved and who would care? It is all in the past."

He slowly let the air out between his lips.

"I am curious though," I said. "How did you come to know so much of this since it was so long ago? You could scarcely have been more than a lad."

His eyes were shaded as he spoke. "As you said, there were others involved. I was sworn to secrecy."

He seemed to work one or two thoughts in his

mind, turning them over. Then he stared at me.

"How did you come to know of this yourself?"

I saw no good in bluffing, and I wanted him to believe I was being honest with him. "There is a passage in the castle," I said. "I happened on it and Morwenna told me it was used for smuggling. But that was more than a century ago. It occurred to me that if it was used for smuggling then, why not more recently?"

He studied me until he was satisfied. Very carefully I started to inch my way toward the ladder, still afraid that at any moment he would shoot out a foot and send me flying over the edge. The wheat straw stuck into me through my clothing and I scraped my knees, my hands shaking when I finally grasped the ladder. I tried to steady it before lowering my foot on the top rung, trying not to look down, for I still felt dizzy.

But Elwynd did not move, and I felt thankful that we were on the side of the house toward the cottage with Aunt Winifred most likely watching out the window.

Slowly I lowered my feet, rung by rung until I reached the last one. I was never so glad to be on solid ground. Rufus came around the barn to meet me, and as I gazed up at Elwynd I saw the challenge in his eyes. Trembling, I reached for Rufus' collar and led him away with me.

That evening as I sat with my aunt in front of the sweet turf fire, I told her of my discovery of the strange passage at the castle and then I recounted what Elwynd had said to me, leaving out the threat I had sensed from him.

Winifred observed me with that somewhat distant look of wisdom tinged with the irony that she always seemed to see in life. Her hands were busy carding wool, and she glanced first at me and then at it.

"There are many things about the people of Cornwall one comes to understand if one lives here long enough." She rocked back in forth, the creak of the wooden rocker accompanying her words.

"Yes, there was smuggling. Fair trading, as we call it, has always been the natural thing to do, either when booty was washed up on our shores, or when our boats slipped out of these coves at earlier times. It's our legacy from the Hundred Years' War when Cornish ports supplied ships to carry Plantagenet armies across the Channel. How easy it was for our ancestors to attack and board a French vessel. With the end of the war, the taste still remained.

"A hundred years later our target was the Spanish ship not the French. Privateering was permitted by the government. And so it has continued in one form or other down to our own times. It's a way of insuring ourselves against losses in trade that's a gamble of fortune in the best of times. Even Hannelore obtained some of her most useful herbs and roots from ships from the Indies that happened our way. Fair trading has always been considered harmless, and the wealth was shared by all."

"By all? How do you mean?"

"It is true what Elwynd said. The goods were sent to America for a time. My brother Leslie, your father, saw to the distribution from his warehouse on that end. But it is also true that after he married and settled down, he no longer dealt in stolen goods. Had no reason to. He wanted to make a fresh start, and his legitimate business was on its feet by then. Of course he still imported the woolens and other things the villagers made. Sold many a skein of wool spun on that spinning wheel."

I sat thinking. "If the wrecks took place in the

rocky cove like the wreck I was in, the castle must have been involved. That is what the passage was used for then, to haul the contraband into the castle for hiding and to load it onto a ship for my father later?"

She nodded. "That is how it worked."

"Then," I said, leaning forward. "Those within the castle were involved. Who was it led them down the passage?"

Her mouth twitched and she looked over the rims of her spectacles at me, shaking her head from side to side. "You really are too inquisitive for your own good, Rhionna."

"But I am right, am I not? Someone there had to have helped them."

"Yes. Arthur Wycke helped them."

"Arthur."

"Yes."

I sat back in my chair. I immediately made the connection. "Then it must have been Arthur who told Elwynd about it. Elwynd must have helped them unload the goods into the castle. And then Arthur made Elwynd promise not to tell anyone."

A strange look came into Winifred's eyes. Her lips were drawn tighter as she said, "It was a very long time ago. I suppose it happened that way."

I was afraid I was losing her, for I could tell when she was not saying everything. I pressed on quickly. "You say my father was not involved after he had a family, but surely the wrecking did not stop. Surely that continued. Did Arthur turn the business over to someone before he died? To Geoffrey or even to Elwynd since he was involved since the beginning? I cannot believe they gave it up. As you said, fair trading is a way of life here."

Winifred gave a little jerk of the chin. "I did not

always follow their goings on. Sometimes it is best not to remember who one saw in the dead of night in the shadows of the moon."

I waited, staring at the crackling fire, hoping she would say more. I sensed I had opened the door on a subject she had had much time to think about over the years. If it involved Arthur it could not help but touch Winifred. I was right, for at length she began to speak of it again, each word a weight that seemed to be lifted from her.

"It was harmless enough at first. But Leslie was right to quit when he did. I do not think it led to any good after all."

"How do you mean?"

"I do not think it was good for Elwynd. It taught him to want too much." Her hands worked faster and her mouth tightened. "He became the victim of his own greed."

I nodded, remembering that Elwynd told me he deserved more, and that one day he would have it. Had he been carrying on illicit activities since then, putting his ill-gotten gains away somewhere to be drawn upon when they were very fat?

"Then you do not know if the smuggling continues?" I asked.

She gave a sigh. "I have not wished to know. Perhaps that was wrong."

She turned pensive, and I could tell she would say no more. I put away our tea things, then I prepared myself for bed.

Winifred put on her dressing gown then rummaged in the desk and got out Arthur's picture. She came back to sit before the dying fire, which she sat staring at as she rocked herself to sleep.

Chapter 20

The next day was Sunday and I accompanied my aunt to chapel. The cold stone building with its thin, bent preacher did nothing to inspire me. I felt very much the hypocrite attending chapel only to help keep up appearances, since I had a faith that was more like the ancients, but sitting on the hard pew, observing the stone sober faces around me gave me a chance to think.

I heard not a word of the sermon and my limbs were stiff from sitting, so I was thankful when the time came to arise.

Outside we greeted many of the villagers. Gwynneth came up to me, the worried look still on her face, for nothing had been heard about her friend.

"Oh miss, I'm at my wit's end," she said. "I don't know what to do. Poor Nan. There's still no sign of her."

I squeezed her hand. "Everything possible is being done," I assured her. "Even now the constables are searching the neighborhood. Lord Rhyweth assured me personally that he would not rest until she is found."

I was not sure how much my words assured her, but she thanked me. I saw that Elwynd was waiting for her and watched out of the corner of my eye as she went to him. Winifred and I stood about exchanging a few words with our neighbors, and finally left the crowd to untie Nedda where we'd left her hitched to the wagon.

We passed not far from where Gwynneth stood close to Elwynd, and with a shift in the wind, I caught his words, ". . . come tonight."

I stiffened. She glanced up at him then turned away, the pink tinging her cheeks. She had agreed to a tryst with him. My aunt had the reins in her hands and had clucked to Nedda. I turned sideways, watching Gwynneth as the wagon jerked forward. I wanted to warn Gwynneth not to go. But what could I say? It was not that I was so disapproving, for did I not know myself how reckless one became when the seeds of passion were sown? The heart will do foolish things.

But lately I did not trust Elwynd. We took the track and I turned back once to see Gwynneth walking in the opposite direction toward the castle. Elwynd was nowhere in sight.

We came to the woods and as we began to bump through them, Rufus began to whine and pace about in the back of the wagon.

"Sit down, Rufus," I said. "You'll fall out."

We had been this way many times and he had learned to balance himself in the middle of the wagon bed, preparing for the descent into the hollow that I always dreaded, even in the light of day.

But now he was whimpering, stretching his nose ahead. I held onto my seat with one hand and to Rufus' collar with the other. We passed through the woods and just as we came out and plunged into the hollow, I could smell it too.

"Smoke," I said. Rufus was trying to warn us.

Panic set in, for we did not yet know where the smoke was coming from. Nedda whinnied and jerked her head.

270

"Gidap," Winifred yelled as she balked at the top of the hollow. But we came out and passed the clump of trees. Then we could see across the fields to flames that crackled and a black cloud of smoke that poured over the land.

"The cottage," I yelled, half standing up in my seat. "It's on fire."

Winifred slapped the reins, finally making Nedda go. She galloped along the road, but balked again near the gate to our fields. But we were close enough now. I jumped down and started to run toward the cottage. One corner of the roof had caught, and when I came nearer I could see the wall of flames through the window.

I knelt before Rufus, who had followed at my heels. "Rufus, go get help. Get help!"

My intention was strong, and he sensed the danger. I pointed in the direction of the road where we had come and he jumped up once, understanding my command and then with a bark set off at a run down the road, barking as he ran.

"The barn," said Winifred coming up beside me. "We've got to get the animals out."

The thatched cottage roof was going up like tinder, and if the wind changed the sparks would leap to the barn. We ran toward it, throwing open the doors. I grabbed Heather's halter and pulled. She mooed loudly and seemed as if she would stand her ground. But then she must have smelled the smoke, and after I gave her a great smack on the rump, she came with me.

Winifred had the gate on Blackie's stall open and I whistled to the horse. He trotted out, but at the barn door whinnied and reared. Already the smoke was so thick the animals were panicking. I would have to tie something over his eyes.

I tore off my shawl and used it as a blindfold, struggling with the nervous horse.

"Come on, Blackie, we've got to get out of here." In a moment of desperation, I climbed on the nearby railing and flung myself onto his back, straddling him and using the shawl as reins.

"Go on," I shouted desperately, kicking him as hard as I could in the ribs. Flames were eating their way across the barnyard, and I saw Winifred carrying the hens in their cages a safe distance away. She had let the sheep out, and they were running, bleating in all directions.

Finally Blackie reared and leapt forward. Miraculously I kept my seat, and we were out. But now I couldn't stop him as he fled blindly toward the field. I hung on desperately, seeing out of the corner of my eye that more people were coming at a run, some on horseback, to help.

The gelding plunged onward, leaving the field behind. As we ascended toward the uncultivated highlands suddenly I saw a horse and rider coming down from my left. The shawl slipped down from Blackie's eyes, and he shook it off. I let it go before it tangled in his feet and clung to the horse's neck.

I saw that it was Geoffrey who circled to come up on my left and then leaned out of his saddle to grab Blackie's mane.

"Whoa there," he said. "Whoa."

I was breathless when we stopped. "Geoffrey, there's been a fire."

"I saw," he said. "Get on in front of me."

He dismounted and helped me down. Then he gave me a leg up on his mount and climbed up behind me.

He held me tightly against him then we turned and raced back toward the conflagration. A bucket

272

brigade had been formed from the well to the cottage, and some of the men were digging trenches around the cottage and barn, throwing the dirt onto the fire as well. I got down and took my place in line between the well and the fire, desolation overcoming me that the effort was so slow. I knew we could not save the cottage and little else. There was more hope for the barn, for the villagers had thrown enough water on the corner that had caught to put it out. The stone walls of the cottage would remain standing, but everything within would be ruined.

I worked until my back ached. The only reward was that at last we got the fire under control. But we could do nothing except stand and watch it take everything Winifred owned.

I don't know how many hours had passed when I finally found her, standing resolutely watching the last of the embers that had been her home doused with a bucket of water.

"Oh Winifred," I said. "I'm so dreadfully sorry. Whatever will we do?"

Her mouth was in a grim line, but she said, "It could have been worse. No lives were lost, and the animals are safe."

"Yes. That's true."

But the prospect of rebuilding sent me despairing. How long would it take? Even with the villagers helping, how could we afford to repay them?

I had lost all track of Geoffrey, but now I saw him striding across the barnyard, his trousers stuffed into tall black boots and his shirt sleeves rolled up. His face was blackened with smoke and grime, and I realized he had been working alongside the rest of us.

"Your barn has suffered little," he said to Winifred as he came over to us. "It will require some repair to

273

the thatch and some new timber for that corner."

"A trick of fate," she said. "The thatch was repaired only yesterday."

"Was it now?" he said

She nodded, meeting his gaze. "Elwynd was up on the roof of the barn yesterday."

He frowned. "I am sorry. However, if your neighbors will be good enough to gather the thatch, you may take it from my coppice. I can supply the timber you need myself."

"That is very kind of you," said Winifred. "But it will be some time before I am able to repay you."

"I am in no hurry for repayment. I am sure you can repay me in fleece from your sheep."

He raised his eyes to mine, and I realized what a sight we both made. However brief the moment, I saw the relief that registered in his eyes and I could not help but think he was grateful that I was safe.

"Your niece was very brave to have saved my gelding," he said to Winifred. To me he said, "It was clever to use your shawl as a blindfold. You thought quickly."

I glanced down, wiping my soiled hands on my ruined dress. "Our first concern was the animals, of course." I looked up. "Thank you for coming after me. I was afraid Blackie would step in a hole up there."

"It was lucky that I was riding on the highlands."

"Yes," I said, only then the glimmer of a new thought beginning to force its way into my tired mind.

"We shall have to see if there is any way to tell how the fire started," he said.

I looked at the gaping ruins of the cottage, blackened stone and fallen timbers. "How can anyone tell? Could it not have been an accident?"

"We may not be able to determine. But I am sure you would like to know."

My stomach felt queasy. Everyone else had been at chapel. Only Geoffrey had been riding nearby. Would it not look as if he himself started the fire? But of course there was no reason, not when he had immediately offered to replace the thatch and timber himself. Anger began to creep over me now that everything was safe and the worst part of the work done.

"Who would have done this?" I said. "For what reason?"

I turned to Geoffrey wishing irrationally that he could provide a ready answer. "They could not have meant to harm our persons, for we were not at home. What did they mean?"

His eyes were full of concern. "That is what I am wondering." Then to both of us he said, "After you have secured your animals, you must return to the castle. You cannot stay here. I will supervise the rebuilding myself, beginning tomorrow."

"You are too kind, Lord Rhyweth," said Winifred. "We seem to be continually falling on your mercy."

"It is a light burden, I assure you. And it is the least I can do under the circumstances. I'll see that some of my men stay and help you round up your sheep."

At least the sheep pen was not touched. And the barn was usable as well. It was no use trying to sift through the charred remains to see if we could salvage any of our belongings. The only things I regretted losing were the letters I had brought with me, and I had lost one of those already. If Winifred felt any sentimental loss, she did not show it. I thought about her treasured portrait of Arthur and was sorry it had been lost.

As if aware that the best thing to do in the face of a tragedy was to work, we threw ourselves into the task of rounding up the sheep. Some of them had strayed to the highlands, and the men who had stayed to help went after them. Rufus helped route the sheep out as well. Winifred and I shooed the rest into the pen, and at last they were all accounted for. It was near nightfall when we put the last of the animals in the barn, fed, and watered them. Then we turned poor Nedda, who had been left in her harness all day, toward the castle where we would find beds.

"Come Nedda," I said. "One more trip and then you'll get fed and curried."

She wickered as if in response and we climbed onto the wagon. Rufus leapt up behind, proud of his part in summoning the villagers and in helping with the sheep.

We rumbled over the road, our hearts heavy. I was numb with exhaustion and could think of little else at that moment except badly needed rest. We finally rode through the gatehouse and onto the courtyard. I thought how odd it was that fate kept returning me to this castle, where I had been warned so often not to set foot. While I gave some credit to the warnings, the question of their source had until now eluded me.

We dragged ourselves up the steps. Godreven met us, informing us that we were expected. He sent Rufus with one of the servants to the kitchens, though I surmised that by now the dog probably knew the way.

Olga settled us into our rooms, and I was so fatigued from fighting the fire that I could barely move. The housekeeper drew me a bath, which helped remove some of the grime. Then I donned a dressing gown and bid my aunt good-night. Returnng to my room, I went to the window to look out at the moon before climbing into bed. I saw a figure scurrying across the courtyard from the kitchens, and then the hood fell back and I recognized Gwynneth's blonde curls.

Gwynneth, I wanted to call out but did not. I remembered her meeting with Elwynd. I clenched my hands on the window ledge, wanting to stop her, and yet what would I say? That Elwynd had looked at me strangely on more than one occasion and that I did not trust him? That he had been involved in my father's smuggling and she should not meet such a man. Nothing I could say would seem like anything but interference in her affairs. Part of me wanted to throw caution to the wind and act on instinct. The other part of me was too dependent on reasoning everything out.

I watched her cross the bridge and take the path toward the village. If they were meeting there, she ought to be safe enough. I paced about my room for some time worrying. Yet I could not bring myself to follow her. I would look foolish going into the ale house to find them there or even some more private spot of assignation.

In spite of my anxiety, my limbs ached and my own emotions were exhausted from the fire. I fell into bed, thinking of Gwynneth as I drifted off into an uneasy sleep.

The next morning Olga came to waken me. I yawned as she opened the windows. Then I sat up, the sleep suddenly receding.

"Good morning, miss," she said, turning her dark eyes on me.

I stared at her. "Where's Gwynneth?" For the girl

usually came to my room at this time, never the housekeeper.

"Gwynneth's not come back," she said, her eyes harboring an accusing look.

Fear rushed over me and I threw the covers from the bed. "Not come back? Since when?"

Olga flashed me a disapproving look. "Her bed's not been slept in."

"Quick," I said, throwing open the wardrobe and grabbing something to wear. "I must speak to Lord Rhyweth at once. Gwynneth may be in great danger."

But Olga did not seem moved by my agitation. "Like all the rest, if you ask me. You can't trust these young girls."

But I would not be intimidated by her attitude today. I grabbed her shoulders, shaking her until her dark eyes were very wide in surprise.

"Now listen to me," I said in the most commanding tone I could muster. "I have information that may help save the girl if it isn't too late. Find Lord Rhyweth. I don't care if you have to rouse him from bed, but do it. I must meet him downstairs in the library in a quarter of an hour."

When I let go of her she nearly lost her balance. Then I threw open the door and pushed her into the corridor.

"Go," I screamed, hysteria already creeping into my voice.

She seemed to understand some of the urgency and hastened out. I slammed the door behind her and struggled into camisole, stockings, dress, and slippers, having no time for anything that would require lacing. Leaving my hair in its braid from the night, I fled into the corridor and ran to the stairs, hurrying down them.

I beat Geoffrey to the library and wrung my

278

hands. *Hurry up, Geoffrey,* I said silently. Now was no time for him to be abed.

No sooner had I thought it than the door banged open and he strode in wearing a smoking jacket over white shirt hastily tucked into trousers. His hair was mussed and there were still circles under his eyes.

"Geoffrey," I said. "Something terrible has happened, I know it."

"What is it?"

"Gwynneth may be in great danger. She had an assignation with Elwynd last night, and she's not come back."

"Why did you not tell me this last night?"

"I did not know she was in any danger. I believe she and Elwynd are lovers. But this morning Olga said Gwynneth had not slept in her bed. I'm afraid she's met with the same fate as the others. We must do something."

"Let us hope it is not too late. I will have a search party start immediately. And when we find Elwynd I will have a great many questions for him."

He strode to the door, and I followed, but he stopped me. "Stay in the castle." Then realizing that I would not be content to sit on my hands he said, "Take my spyglass from the study and watch from the south tower. You may be able to spot things from there that we cannot see from the ground."

"I—" But he was off, his boots echoing on the stone floor.

I was sick to my stomach that I had not spoken up last night, and yet what could I have said? But I realized now that that course might have been the wiser. Evidently Geoffrey had been doing his own investigating and if I had told him I'd seen Gwynneth sneaking off, he might have been able to prevent some villainous crime.

I went to get the spyglass, then I proceeded to the kitchens to find Rufus. With Gwynneth gone, he might not have been fed, and I sought his company for solace.

I found him pacing about the kitchen, ignored by Cook and the scullery maids who were churning butter.

"Poor Rufus," I said, reaching down to give him a hug. "Gwynneth's missing. Whatever are we going to do?"

He gave an answering whine. Since Gwynneth never came back last night, she never brought Rufus to my room. He had remained in the kitchen.

"Gwynneth," I said to the dog, looking into his alert brown eyes. "Where is Gwynneth?"

He cocked his head. I glanced up and saw Gwynneth's apron hanging from a peg and pulled it down. I held it out for Rufus to sniff, then I said again, "Gwynneth. Find Gwynneth."

He jerked away from me toward the door. I followed him and let him out into the courtyard. There he continued his pacing toward the gatehouse and then back to me, cocking his head and lifting his ears with a whine.

"Rufus, what is it? Do you know where Gwynneth went?"

He wanted me to follow him, and as I did so, he barked and leapt toward the gatehouse. I quickened my steps, and Rufus led me across the bridge and down the road that led toward town. This was the way I saw Gwynneth take last night.

"Good boy," I said. "Find Gwynneth."

I was still carrying the spyglass and had followed Rufus to the Cliff Road before I remembered Geoffrey's order for me to stay in the castle. But I gave it no heed. The dog had picked up her scent, and there was no time to be lost. Below me on the beach I saw riders searching among the treacherous rocks where my ship had broken up. And I could hear the shouts of men combing the forest to the left of me as well.

I thought Rufus would lead me all the way to the village and hastened after him, but suddenly he stopped, sniffed the ground, looked up and seemed to lose the scent.

"What is it Rufus? What's happened?"

I looked around to see if any path verged off, but I could see none. Then suddenly he lunged into the brush and down a steep incline doubling back along the way we had come. I looked after him, thinking at first he had gotten off onto the trail of some animal. But he looked back at me as if to say, This is the way.

I hoisted my skirts and stepped into the brush. Then I could see where branches had been broken, evidence that someone had passed this way. I followed, stopping several times to pull the material of my dress which had caught. At last we came to a path which wound along the cliffs, passing between the rocks, and coming out on the beach north of the castle. I looked at the strip of sand being washed by the gentle waves.

We stood in a small, but protected cove. It struck me that the body of the girl who had been found dead had been discovered in the field just above this cove. The thought made me shiver, but I forced myself to concentrate on the coincidence. I need to use rational deduction now and not let my emotions muddle my thinking.

I remembered the ship I saw sail away that night. This cove looked deep enough for a ship to anchor. And there were no treacherous rocks here as there were in the cove that had sunk my ship. This must have been where the ships put in to load their goods in the days of smuggling. If it was deep and there was no current, it would be the perfect place to moor, unlike the shore where my unlucky ship had been lured. But here a ship could be moored to take on goods being smuggled out of the castle. The cut in the rocks I had passed allowed passage to the rocky cove and from there, the walkway had been carved up to the castle. That was the way we had taken the night I was rescued.

There was no ship here now, only a small dinghy, pulled high on the beach, its oars in the bottom.

I went to investigate the dinghy, wondering if it had been recently used. It seemed likely. There was a little water in the bottom, and the oars were wet. I looked high and low around me, but saw nothing else. Two men approached on horseback and I recognized Andrew from the stables. They reined up when they came near me.

"What would you be doing here, miss?" asked the groom.

"My dog led me here," I answered. "He picked up the missing girl's scent and we came here."

We all gazed at the emptiness around us. Andrew shrugged. "Ain't nothing here now. Best you be returning to the castle."

"Yes, I will."

He pointed to the path that led between the rocks whence I had come. "That there will get you up."

I nodded. "Yes, I know. I'll go that way. Thank you."

His partner remained silent, and they went on their way.

I trudged back, taking Rufus with me, feeling discouraged that we had found nothing. Still the fact that Rufus had led me to the cove might mean something.

Back at the castle, I sought Geoffrey out as soon as I could find him and told him about Rufus leading me there. He listened carefully, but then glowered at me. "I told you to stay within."

I bristled, but defended myself. "I thought it a good idea to follow Rufus. He knows Gwynneth's scent well. What if she went to the cove last night? Could not someone have carried her away from there?"

"The very reason I did not want you to venture there alone."

"But it was broad daylight." Still I was touched by his concern.

"There is something else," I said. "The night the poor girl was killed, I saw a ship head out to sea. It could have come from that cove. I should have told you about that too then, I suppose. Only I did not think there was any connection at the time."

I bit my lip, afraid he would scold me for this oversight as well, but instead, he nodded, the brooding expression still with him.

"I too have thought of this. And you are right. I suspect these incidents are related."

His statement alarmed me, and a horrible thought came to mind. "What you are saying then, is that these incidents are connected and that young women are being abducted aboard ships."

I saw the corner of his mouth jerk, but he nodded reluctantly. "I am afraid so."

The thought appalled me. "But where are they being taken?"

"I did not want you to be alarmed. I am sorry. It is not a pleasant subject."

My mind was slow to understand to what he was alluding, but when I put it together, my skin crawled, and my terror was no less than when I had feared that something unearthly was stalking the young women of the country.

"I . . . I think I understand what you are saying."

He went on, his expression grim. "It is possible that someone is abducting young women for the awful enterprise of white slave trade. I have no proof yet, but if I am right, the despicable characters will certainly be caught and I will see to it that they suffer, be it with my own hands."

The wrath in his tone gave me no doubt that he was serious. I was still contemplating the awful fate of the girls who had been used thusly. I had heard about white slave trading, and knew that it meant that young women were held against their will to be used in horrible ways by men who paid to have their way with them.

"How awful," I said

The prospect seemed truly frightening. I stepped to the window to gaze out, thanking my lucky stars that I had not met with such a fate. That I was safe within these castle walls.

Of course there were those who would say that I was not safe. That Geoffrey was the one responsible for the missing girls' whereabouts. But I shook my head. Someone had wanted me to believe that I was in danger from Geoffrey, but I could not believe it.

Someone had tried to distract me from the true danger by trying to make me think that Geoffrey was vampiric. Vampires could not stand the sight of crosses, it was said. And yet Geoffrey had fingered my small silver cross before kissing me. Vampires did not like the sun, but today he had strode about the estate in broad daylight. Just because he played music at night did not mean anything. And though it was true he came to me in his dreams, that was a result of my own desires.

Still I shivered, for though the threat to the young women might be worldly rather than unworldly, it was hardly less hideous.

Chapter 21

Geoffrey came to my room that night. I rose from my chair as he entered. I could see from the lines in his brow that he was greatly concerned about events.

"I've come to tell you that danger is afoot tonight," he said. "I want you to stay inside, no matter what happens."

I trembled at the word *danger*, but I was so anxious to see things through to their end that I felt impatient.

"Why?" I said. "What is going to happen?"

"I'm not sure," he answered, taking a few steps toward the windows and looking out. "But I am prepared for trouble."

I went to him and grasped his arm. "Geoffrey, what is it? Will you yourself be in danger?"

His look softened as he turned and laid a finger on my cheek. "Best for you not to worry."

The enormity of the situation seized me. "Oh, Geoffrey," I said, suddenly afraid for him.

Then I was in his arms. He responded by pulling me toward him, my head nestled against his shoulder. "Do not worry, my pet. Soon this will be all over, and then . . ."

"And then what, Geoffrey?"

How I longed for words that would console me and give me hope. But he only said, "We shall then see."

I pressed my lips together, not wanting to make a scene. Finally he relaxed his grasp on me and I looked up at him.

"Now," he said. "You will behave and remain here."

His tone had that of a stern schoolmaster, and it might have amused me under other circumstances.

"I would not like to displease you," I returned in a contrite tone, although sidestepping a direct answer.

He lifted his eyebrows and met me with a look that said he was beginning to know me all too well. But then he only exhaled a breath.

"I must go," he said.

I threw my arms around his neck once more. "Take care, Geoffrey."

And then he was gone. The door closed, and to my surprise, I heard the tumble of the lock. Curiously I approached the heavy oak door with its wrought-iron fittings. I had not noticed it before, but there was no latch on this side. I pulled on the door handle. It was locked.

Locked! He had locked me in. Horror and anger washed over me. I could not believe it. He had not trusted my word, and so he had imprisoned me. I frowned, rattling the handle to no avail. I had never noticed that this door could not be unlocked by a latch on this side. Instead a gaping black keyhole mocked me.

"Oh Rufus," I said. "We are stuck here."

He whined and cocked his head.

The knowledge that one could be locked up in this room did not set my mind at ease. Why had this room been designed for incarceration? For what purpose had it previously been used?

I whirled and went to sit on the bed, rubbing my arms with my hands. I crossed and uncrossed my feet, then I rose and paced about. Having nothing else to do, I went to stand by the window, looking over the gloomy courtyard that I had gazed at so many times before.

Like the night when the body of the poor girl had been found, a fog was creeping over the ramparts and had begun to drift along the ground. The other image from that night came to mind, and I looked out to sea where I had seen a ship slip out of the darkness before. I peered into the gloom, but saw no such ship appear now.

I sighed and shook my head. I heard horses' hooves on the cobbles coming up from the stables. Then I glanced down. A cloaked figure dodged into the shadows as the group of horsemen rode in, Geoffrey in the lead. He wheeled his mount, issued some orders, and then the group clattered across the courtyard and over the bridge.

When the horsemen had gone, the figure hurried along the walls. Suddenly a gust of wind blew the hood of the cloak back and I gave a gasp as I caught a glimpse of the face. It was Hannelore Treleaven. I rushed toward the door, then remembered it was locked.

"Olga," I shouted. "Someone. Let me out."

I was afraid my screams would be to no avail, for most likely Geoffrey had given orders I was to be kept in, but I was determined.

"Help, help," I yelled until I was hoarse. At long last I heard footsteps coming down the corridor.

"What is it, miss?" I heard a muffled voice that sounded like Olga's.

"I must get out. Unlock this room at once."

I heard the key in the lock and heaved a sigh of relief. The door opened and Olga stood in front of me, her face impassive.

"Thank you, Olga," I said, taking deep breaths. "As you can see, I was locked in. I must go out."

I started to move past her, but she blocked my way.

"I cannot imagine how it came to be locked," she said. "No one told me."

"Oh?" I paused in surprise. "Well, no matter. I have something to attend to."

"Of course, miss. Will you be returning this evening?"

"Yes, yes, I suppose."

Then I hurried past her and down the corridor, Rufus following me. I took the stairs in a rush and flew outside to the courtyard.

Hannelore was gone, but I spied a small pouch that she must have dropped in her haste. I bent to pick it up, sniffing it. A pouch full of herbs. I did not know the scent, but it was strong. Rufus would not have difficulty following it.

"Here, boy," I said, holding it out to him.

He raised his nose and sniffed, then gave a sneeze.

"Find," I commanded, holding the pouch out again.

He shook his head, lowered it, then brushed a paw over his nose.

"Rufus," I said sternly. "You may not like it, but it's important. Here." I held out the pouch. "Find."

Finally he obeyed me. He took a quick sniff and then dipped his head.

"That's right," I said. "Find Hannelore."

He put his nose to the ground, then headed toward the gatehouse and I followed. I thought we would take the main road, but as soon as we were past the bridge, Rufus paused, circling and whining. Then he struck off on a path that led up the hill.

"Is this the way?" I said, more to myself than to the dog.

But though he wandered from side to side of the path, he seemed certain that this was the way. I kept my eyes open wide for any sign of Hannelore, but saw nothing. The fog was creeping around the trees, but I tried not to let that frighten me. There was too much at stake.

The path twisted and turned and I climbed it as silently as I could. Ahead, the trees parted and there was enough of a moon that I could see what looked like an old shed of some sort. Could that be where Hannelore had been headed?

"Rufus," I called in a whisper. "Come."

He came to me and I laid a finger to my lips, taking his collar. "Quiet now."

Half crouched, holding onto Rufus' collar, we continued toward the shed. There was no light that I could see, and I wondered if Hannelore had heard me and was hiding inside.

Suddenly an arm reached out from nowhere and grabbed me around the neck, pulling me back towards the trees. I tried to scream, but it came out a croak, my breath cut off by the arm as I was dragged toward the shed. Rufus barked and leapt at the figure clutching me, but a swift kick turned Rufus' growl into a cry of pain.

As we struggled, I clutched at a man's shirt and tore the front of it. He pulled me through the door of the shed where all was darkness. But still I twisted and kicked blindly, angry and terrified.

Then suddenly my captor came off balance, and I fell away. I landed on the floor, my hand banging against a metal tool. Seeing my opportunity, I seized what I discovered was a spade and raised it. I did not hesitate when the figure came at me again, and

I swung with all my strength.

I heard a crack of metal against bone and then with a groan, the figure slumped to the floor, stunned, the head lolling to the side. I heard a scrabble of claws, and Rufus limped in.

"Rufus," I said. "Poor boy, did he hurt you?" I made a quick examination of my dog with my fingers and felt sticky blood above his eyes. Fury tore through me, although Rufus seemed all right except for the surface wound.

Still clutching the spade, I crept nearer to my attacker. I could see that my pursuer was a man, and my first instinct was to run. But I had to know who had tried to catch me, and so throwing caution aside, I tiptoed nearer until I could see the face.

Blond hair glinted in the moonlight. It was Elwynd who lay there. I feared I had killed him.

Spade still tightly clutched in hand, I crept nearer. Rufus crouched, growling a low, mean growl. I looked closely at Elwynd to try to ascertain if he was still breathing. I needed some light, so I felt around to see if there was a lantern. Feeling above me, I found one swinging from a beam overhead. I unhooked it and lowered it to the ground. I despaired of a light, but common sense told me there must be some matches if a lantern was there. Feeling along a shelf I found some, and in a moment I had light.

I was about to reach out to touch Elwynd's throat to see if I could feel a pulse, when I gasped and drew my hand back.

There on the side of his neck at the base of his throat were two distinct moles, identical to the birth marks on my own throat. I stared unbelievingly as my hand strayed to the place where I carried the same birthmarks. It could not be coincidence. There was no mirror here to look in, but I was sure the marks were the same. It was the birthmark my grandmother carried in the same place on the throat.

I heard the scrape of a foot and gave a start. My hand drew back, and I clutched the spade, my only weapon. Rufus crouched, ready to leap, and then Hannelore appeared in the door. For a moment we merely stared at each other.

I stood up, ready to defend myself, but Hannelore ignored me. She got to her knees and reached in her pocket for something which she held under Elwynd's nose. Then she bent over Elwynd, a weird keening coming from her throat.

Then outside I heard the earth reverberate with hoofbeats, and my heartbeat echoed the clamor. Geoffrey burst through the door, his billowing black cloak making him seem larger than life. The rage on his face told me that if he had gotten there a moment sooner, Elwynd would be dead.

Geoffrey flew to me and clutched my shoulders, searching my face. "Are you all right?"

I nodded weakly as he gently removed the spade from my hands. Then a curse escaped his lips.

"I won't speculate on who let you out. I might have known you would disobey my orders to stay within the castle."

"Geoffrey, look."

I led him to Elwynd, of whom I was no longer afraid. I pointed out the marks on his neck and stared at Geoffrey, who frowned and then seemed to understand.

"Damn. I should have seen this before. The same birth mark as you have on your throat. I thought when I first saw it on you that it looked familiar, but I could not remember where I had noticed it before. It was a very long time ago, and we were boys, roughhousing."

He turned to me. "Who else in your family has this mark?"

"My grandmother. I remember touching it when I was small. I thought something had bitten her. The birthmark disappeared in the succeeding generation, and showed up again on me."

"And on Elwynd."

"Yes," I said, realization dizzying me. "Winifred's son."

"And my father's," said Geoffrey. "It is what you were trying to tell me before."

"Then Elwynd and I are cousins," I said.

"And, we are half brothers," said Geoffrey. He shook his head.

Elwynd was coming around. He groaned and moved his head from side to side, Hannelore muttering to him. As his vision cleared, he stared up at us. For a moment, I shrank back at his look of vengeance. But then pain assailed him, and he murmured, "My head hurts and my ankle, I think it's twisted."

"Just as well," said Geoffrey. "Since you cannot go anywhere. Perhaps you will answer a few questions for us."

Pain and resentment filled his eyes, but Geoffrey interrogated him while Hannelore furtively ministered to his wounds.

"It's no use, Elwynd," said Geoffrey. "I've suspected you were up to no good for some time. Will you now enlighten us as to your despicable activities? It's white slaves, isn't it? Fine business for a man like yourself to be in."

I remembered feeling sorry for Elwynd and how I had extended my friendship to him. I could still only feel sorry for him, for he must be a very bitter man.

His cheek jerked as he said, "Everything would've been all right, only she came." He glared at me. "You had to go. I figured your father told you what he'd guessed of the white slave trade. I figured you'd come here to expose us. Disapproving your righteous father was, when he learned what our little smuggling game had led to."

"My father knew?"

"He thought he knew. Tipped off he was."

"By whom?" asked Geoffrey.

He glowered at Geoffrey. "Your father, most likely."

"My father knew of this?"

"Oh, he had no proof, no one had proof. You'll never catch us, you know."

"But my father guessed at it?" said Geoffrey.

"Told me he thought he knew what I was up to. That for my own good I should stop. Easy enough for him to say. High and mighty lord he was."

Geoffrey shook his head, his look bitter. "He tried to help you by setting you up in business with Rhionna's father, and this is how you repaid him. You must have broken his heart."

I slipped my arm around Geoffrey's waist, for I thought I knew some of what he was feeling, my own anger boiling over.

"Then that is why my father was in danger," I said. "You had someone cause my father's accident. You've been behind everything."

He did not deny it, but thrust his chin up. I felt at that moment that I stared evil in the face. I went on, the pieces now falling into place.

"You knew I was coming to Cornwall. I wouldn't doubt that you lured that ship onto the rocks. You would risk all those lives just to be rid of me. It's true, isn't it?"

He averted his head, but I knew I had hit on the truth. Wrecks were a way of life, and it was not beyond many a Cornishman to lure a ship upon the rocks. It was an ironic twist that he had pulled me out of the water instead of sending me to my death. And if Geoffrey had not intervened, he might have seen that I met with an accident that night, once he discovered my identity. I could see now that it had been Elwynd who had been behind everything else that had threatened me since I'd been there.

"Before that you had me followed in New York." My voice rose with a shout of mild hysteria, but I wanted to lay the blame where it ought to be.

"You had me drugged when I got to the castle, didn't you?"

"That was easy," said Elwynd spitefully. "It was the henbane I got from Hannelore."

My eyes widened as I stared at Hannelore, who was crouched in a corner. "You."

"I didn't know he'd taken it. Stolen it he must have from my cottage without my knowing."

"It was the henbane, not some curing herb, as you told Gwynneth, that caused the dizziness and stupor. I suppose you told Gwynneth that the herb had been sent from Hannelore, so Gwynneth innocently put it in the hot drink she prepared me, not realizing she was drugging me. If I had continued taking the mixture Gwynneth had prepared . . ." I looked at Hannelore for confirmation.

She nodded slowly. "Convulsions and death."

I turned away. Luckily, I had refrained from taking more of it. We were silent for a moment. Then Geoffrey disengaged himself from me and paced about, rubbing his neck with the back of his hand.

"I always knew of my father's sympathy with poverty-stricken Cornishmen. I might have known he did not consider smuggling beneath him. It was no doubt his way of getting back at the atrocious economic disregard the rest of England always had for our people, what he considered the gross social and economic selfishness of the flourishing English central government that continued to ignore the Duchy of Cornwall."

Hannelore spoke then, in mincing tones. "Arthur could never acknowledge Elwynd. He could leave him none of his lands. They must all go to you, since your older brother died. But Arthur could leave Elwynd the smuggling trade, which he did. It was all he could do."

"But Elwynd took it one step further," said Geoffrey.

"That I did," Elwynd said, ugly pride coming into his voice. "Made contacts in the East where white flesh was highly prized. Oh, your high and mighty father knew nothing of that at first. I'm not sure how Leslie learned of it, but Lord Rhyweth guessed at the matter in his final days and wrote to his old smuggling friend."

"That is exactly what happened," I put in. "It was the letter alluding to the evil deeds that I found in my father's study."

"You can't blame me now, can you?" said Elwynd, shifting to a more comfortable position. "He wrote me that if my newfound activities did not stop he would see to it that it was exposed. He begged me to cease the slave trading, for he no more wanted to put his bastard nephew in jail than he wanted to cut off one arm, but he would do just that if I didn't stop."

Madness shone in Elwynd's eyes as he spoke out at last.

"There was one way to keep Leslie quiet. My contacts were wider now than they had been in the old smuggling days. I told him if he knew what was best for him and his lovely daughter he would think no more of this matter."

"You tried to blackmail him," I said, and Geoffrey had to hold me back as I made a lunge for Elwynd, who was sitting straighter now.

"I knew there was something troubling my father in the last months before the accident. Now I realize how worried he must have been for my own safety and why he told me not to come to Cornwall. You were trying to blackmail him. Poor father, he should have told me."

Elwynd sneered. "Geoffrey got the castle and all the lands but at least I have a thriving business in the slave trade."

I turned to Hannelore. "And what did you know of this?"

She worked her mouth together, then she said. "I always knew of the smuggling. Who didn't? But I kept my silence. I didn't know of the other."

"There'll be need for silence no longer," Geoffrey said.

"And the dead girl on the moor," I said quickly. "You must have killed her! She didn't go quietly like the rest, did she? You're a murderer, too."

Elwynd averted his gaze.

I heard shouts in the distance, coming from the road. A strange light came into Elwynd's eyes. I realized the authorities must be on their way.

Suddenly, Elwynd lunged at Geoffrey. We were all off guard, thinking Elwynd's ankle was truly hurt. Geoffrey stumbled, and Elwynd used the element of surprise to rush out of the shed. But we were quick to respond. Geoffrey dashed out the door and I followed him. Elwynd had a head start on us, but he seemed headed for the beach, and we ran after him, Rufus barking as he passed us and gained on Elwynd. And the horsemen caught up to us.

"That way," Geoffrey shouted.

I stumbled once, but picked myself up and hastened on. We came to the main road and crossed it, tearing through the brush where the path led around the bottom of the castle and through the rocks to Penhallow Cove.

The tide was high and I could hear the waves splashing. Elwynd got to the cove ahead of us and made for the dinghy, shoving it out and into the water. We all followed, but stopped, breathless, at the waters' edge.

The mounted soldiers splashed into the waves, riding out as far as they dared, but the dinghy had a headstart.

"He'll never make it," Geoffrey shouted.

"I know," Hannelore answered, "the tide."

Even as they spoke, the dinghy started to whirl out of control. Then one swelling incoming wave lifted the dinghy as if it were made of matchwood and smashed it against some rocks.

I turned in horror against Geoffrey's shoulder.

"It's better this way," I heard him say. "He couldn't last out there."

Just then we heard a shout. A rider galloped toward us along the beach.

"Ship's been sighted, sir," the man said who rode up to Geoffrey. "She's moored at the inlet above Pendeen woods. The authorities are getting ready to board her."

"Thank you," said Geoffrey. "We'll come at once."

Geoffrey grasped my hand, and we climbed back up to the path. Andrew had disengaged himself from the other riders and gave Geoffrey his horse. Geoffrey gave me a leg up then mounted behind me.

"It'll be over soon," he said, then as I nestled against him we were off, flying along the track that soon joined the Cliff Road. Turf flew up under the horse's hooves as we passed the high cliffs, then circled the village, Geoffrey's men now following us.

The road bent into the trees. We finally came to the edge of the woods above an inlet where the river flowed into the sea. A three-masted schooner was moored below us. Soldiers had gathered on the banks, rifles at the ready.

Then I saw the gangplank lowered, and the troops went aboard. Geoffrey got down, but when I started to dismount, he said, "No, stay here. We're not out of danger yet. Not until the crew has been taken into custody." He strode off to the ship, but I held my mount, waiting nervously where I was.

After what seemed an interminable amount of time, the crew of the ship was led off, handcuffed. Then I saw Geoffrey come on deck and behind him a very familiar figure.

"Gidap," I commanded, digging my heels into the horse. I made my way down the hill to the gangplank where I dismounted, then went running to meet Gwynneth, who met me halfway.

"Gwynneth." I exclaimed, grasping her in a hug. "Are you all right?"

"Oh, miss. Thank goodness, you've come. I thought we was done for."

She rubbed chafed wrists, which I imagined had only recently been untied. I put an arm around her and led her onto solid ground. She turned mournful eyes on me.

"Oh, miss, it was awful. It was Elwynd did this. I was a fool to have trusted him."

"I'm sorry, Gwynneth. We know all about it now."

Her lip trembled, but she did not give in to tears. "I'll not feel sorry for myself," she said. "We're just lucky to be found."

Several other girls were now being led off, and Gwynneth turned and took hold of a thin girl with long stringy hair, who she brought over to me.

"This is my friend, Nan Goosmoor, miss."

I held out my hand, which the girl took, the fear still in her large eyes. She gave an awkward curtsy.

"Thank you for rescuing us," she murmured.

"You're welcome, I'm sure, but it was the soldiers who rescued you," I said.

"The soldiers and Lord Rhyweth," said Gwynneth. "He's the one who called 'em out to find us, they say."

"Yes," I said, still quite overcome by the turn of events.

Geoffrey spoke to the captain of the soldiers and then strode off the gangplank. Moving quickly across the ground toward us in the dark, his cloak still about his shoulders, I was reminded of the first time I saw him on the beach, not so very long ago.

"Come," he said, when he reached me. "The soldiers will take care of the rest. I've instructed them to bring the girls to the castle where Dr. Pearce can examine them before they go home."

He placed his arm around my shoulders and we walked to where one of the soldiers held his horse. I mounted first, then Geoffrey behind me. Then he wrapped his cloak around us both and picked up the reins.

"Let us go home now," he said. "Everything will be well."

300

Chapter 22

A month had passed since the trouble was resolved. Spring had advanced and wild flowering anchusa covered the moorland. With the blooms that lined roadways and adorned hedgerows came a new feeling of serenity.

I did not attend the public trials held in St. Ives, but I knew that the white slavers had come to their well-deserved end. The village was relieved that at least two of the girls had escaped unscathed. And the authorities were at work locating the rest in the countries to which they had been sent.

What gave me the most peace of mind was the fact that the malicious rumors Elwynd had spawned about the Wyckes had been put to rest. The people were once again grateful for Geoffrey's hand in solving the crimes. He was no more a mysterious figure to be feared, but their lord and benefactor.

I finally came to realize that the strange stares at the Easter ball were not caused by the ruby, but by my birthmarks, the two small moles on my throat spaced just far enough apart to look like teeth marks from a distance.

The rumors that vampire blood ran in the Wycke family had caused the gentry's imaginations to run away with them that night. Those who believed that

301

such things were possible had seen the marks on my neck and suspected that I had been a victim.

A week ago Hannelore Treleaven died in her own bed, though I doubted it could have been a peaceful death.

Geoffrey finally returned to me the two pages of his father's letter. He had kept them since the night Olga had brought him the satchel she had taken off of me. He had, of course, recognized the handwriting as his father's and by keeping the pages from the letter, he had been trying to protect me and entrap Elwynd, whom he was beginning to suspect.

This evening Winifred had joined Geoffrey, Morwenna, and myself in the west parlor after dinner so that we could watch the sun set. I watched Winifred's face as she looked out at the brilliant colors that were slowly fading with the evening. We all had had much time to think about what had happened. And Winifred voiced my thoughts. She turned a sad smile on me.

"You watch me with great concern, child. You must not do so."

"It is only that I care about you, Aunt."

She smiled softly. "It is true that I have had to face the truth about my only son, but in time I will learn to live with it. I suspected the truth long ago, and I am at least relieved that all has been brought to light. No good comes of dark secrets and lies," she said. "I know that now. No matter how painful it may be to view them."

She reached over to squeeze my hand. "I am glad for you, my child," she said.

I glanced down at the diamond that glittered on my finger, my heart swelling at a love I could at last freely acknowledge.

"I heartily bless this union," Winifred said. "It was

302

meant to be, perhaps."

I did not say it, but she must have been thinking that Geoffrey and I would have a chance to live out our love, something that Arthur and Winifred never were able to do.

"Yes," I said. "I am only sorry that Gwynneth will not be here for the occasion. I will miss her." So would Rufus.

"It is best for her though," said Morwenna, who sat in a plush chair on Winifred's left. "Her uncle in Scotland will be glad to have her."

Though I was sad to see the perky little maid go, I could understand why she wished to start life over in a new place.

I glanced at Morwenna, whose face registered more calm than when I first knew her. I saw less and less of the fiery Magdalena in her since Lord Stratton had made his intentions known. Even Lady Stratton had been brought around to approve of the match, deciding at last that a wife was what her son needed in order to make him settle down, now that the crimes of the past months had been solved. Enys and Morwenna would live in Devon after their marriage, but I was sure we would exchange visits often.

Geoffrey came to stand behind me and squeezed my shoulder while Godreven entered the room and handed round the coffee laced with liqueur.

"We have many things to celebrate this night," said Geoffrey, taking his cup. "Most of all the many myths that have been put to rest." Humor tinged the irony in his voice as he took a sip of coffee.

"But," he cautioned, "if the peasants can find nothing mysterious about Rhyweth castle anymore, leave it to them to look elsewhere for legends to speak of over turf fires on chilly evenings."

"Do you think they will?" I asked.

"Undoubtedly," he said, winking at me. "The Cornish will forever be amused by such superstitious tales, my dear. You must learn to live with that fact. It's in the blood, you see."